Spoonful Chronicles

By Elen Ghulam

For information visit:
http://www.ihath.com

Cover Design by Christa of Paper & Sage.

Ghulam, Elen, 1969-, author
        Spoonful chronicles / Elen Ghulam.

ISBN 978-0-9781872-4-8 (softcover)

        I. Title.

PS8613.H74S66 2017   C813'.6   C2017-900346-1

For Yarra Hassan

Get the Recipes

To receive recipes related to this novel, subscribe to the Spoonful Recipes mailing list here:

http://ihath.com/MailingList/?p=subscribe&id=5

Would that you could live on the fragrance of the earth, and like an air plant be sustained by the light. But since you must kill to eat, and rob the newly born of its mother's milk to quench your thirst, let it then be an act of worship.

- Kahil Gibran, The Prophet

Egg

MY MOTHER IS A LOUSY COOK. The most optimistic thing I can say about her culinary skills is that she followed Health Canada Safe Food Handling tips religiously, even before we moved to Canada.

Some say the secret ingredient of recipe perfection is love. Those people never had to dine at my mother's table. While growing up in the Middle East we had servants. The kitchen responsibilities could have easily been relegated to less loving but more capable hands. Alas, my mother grew up in Czechoslovakia, a communist country unaccustomed to exploiting cheap labour. Much to the disapproval of her Arab friends, she insisted that child rearing and cooking was her responsibility alone. No hired help was allowed within the stratosphere of her declared domain. I am grateful that, unlike my childhood friends, I wasn't brought up by a nanny. On the flip side of this shiny coin, I grew up eating variations of bland on bland. Shades upon shades of overcooked, tasteless and colorless meals presented lovingly for breakfast, lunch, snacks and dinner.

I was thrust into the world, on the cusp of womanhood, blind to the rainbow of dance movements possible upon my taste buds. My tongue—a virgin territory, innocent of partaking in delight. As a new bride, I suddenly had free access to a kitchen for the first time. With no barriers, no servants and most importantly no guides. I entered the world of cooking the same way I entered my sex life. Tragically unprepared, but feverishly curious.

Coffee

"HERE'S A SLOGAN FOR THE Iraqi Ministry of Tourism," said my sister Layal in her raspy voice on the eve of our government's invasion of Kuwait. "Come visit Iraq, before Iraq visits you!" We all laughed with heavy hearts at the dark humor, then felt pangs of embarrassment and fell silent. In our Vancouver apartment, obsessively watching the news, my dad shifted in his seat, wriggling the discomfort away. My mother rested her cheek on the palm of her hand and sighed. I stared at my hands upon my thighs, paralyzed with defeat. Layal didn't move, not even a twitch. She didn't blink. That is my older sister. Steadfast. Always steadfast. A candle might flicker in the absence of wind, but Layal is unwavering in the face of end of the world scenarios. If the zombie apocalypse is ever to descend upon us, you want to be standing right behind her straight black hair, following in her footsteps. She might not survive, but I can assure you she will not panic.

If Layal is a mountain, then I am the debris getting tossed from side to side in the wind tunnel.

If Layal is a river, then I am the green algae dancing to the whims of her flow.

If Layal is the center dish of whole roasted lamb stuffed with saffron infused rice, I am bread crumbs under the table.

It came to me gradually. In spatters and smudges. Like a Jackson Pollock painting. Splash here. Drip there. Seems accidental. You stand back and look. The horror of the furtive activity attacks you. My name should be Sabbah. Nobody ever said this within my earshot. It was a little niggling suspicion. A faint whisper in my head. It grew and multiplied. Now it is a scream. I know it in my toes. I feel it in the frazzled ends of my hair. I never dared ask directly. It is as obvious as the sun in the sky. I should be sitting here, declaring to you proudly that my name means morning in Arabic. A name that implies light, brightness, the first call to prayer of the day and the cock-a-doodle-doo of a proud rooster breaking dawn. Since my sister's name means night in our language, I have surmised my parents worried about the negative connotation that would be assigned to her in relation to me. Imagine my parents introducing us to their friends:

And here are our daughters: Night and Day.

They are as different as light and darkness.

People might have sniggered at the too matchy matchy extremes.

"Oh you called your daughters Night and Morning," those with comedic aspirations would have continued. "If you have a third daughter you should call her Noon."

Instead I have this nothing name. It reeks relativity without embodying substance. My name is Thaniya.

My name means second. I was number two after Layal. My parents couldn't agree on a name. My father wanted to call me Natheera, but my mother hated that name. She in turn wished for me to carry the name Alberta. My father jokes that we were predestined to end up in Canada. For three months I didn't have a name and so everybody called me daughter number two. In the end, both parents gave up on finding something to call me that they both could love. My birth order became my designation.

What is truly curious about my name is that in Arabic *Thaniya* means both the numbering order and a unit of time that is equal to one-60th of a minute. In English, the word *second* has the same dual meaning. I am Second in both senses of the word. I frequently wonder if there is a secret message that destiny wished to convey through my name. Am I supposed to be fast, achieving things in a fraction of the time it takes other people? Or am I destined to find myself on the less-desired step of the Olympic podium of life? Maybe I am meant to be divisive, or divided, always splitting the world and myself into two. Who knows?

Getting tossed to and fro between clashing extremes without holding on to a grain of either locale is my destiny. It is the repeated cycle of the clock of eternity. From the day of my conception until today it has been an experience of unplanned black and white without possibility for shades of gray.

According to a yearly study that ranks all the major cities of the world for livability, Vancouver is the best city in the whole entire world to live in. The same study ranked Baghdad to be the worst city on that scale. An impressive achievement if you consider that Harare, Zimbabwe and Addis Ababa, Ethiopia are on that list. I come from the most extreme bottom of that list and somehow through crazy luck ended up at the number one on top. Contemplating this fact makes my head go dizzy. Not a day goes by where I don't consider the mysterious hands of fate that have tossed me to the furthest corner of the world atlas. Had I gone any further I would actually have been getting closer to home.

Let's do a fun exercise together:

Open Google Earth.

Click on the ruler tool.

Left click on Baghdad.

Drag the ruler around the world heading west.

Left click again on Vancouver, B.C.

Note down the distance.

From the heart of the oldest civilization in human history to the furthest outpost of the New World.

This is the measurement of me.

This is the trajectory of my life.

You are looking at Thaniya's biography.

Dash dot dash dot dash dot dash dot dash

I don't care if you mispronounce my name. It is not my real name anyway. That one is a secret known only to me. One day I will divulge this truth to another soul and then my Google Earth reality will make sense to somebody other than just me.

Every morning, no matter how hectic my schedule, I wake up early to prepare a pot of coffee. I pour the black liquid into a see-through glass cup. Then I add milk one drop at a time. I watch milk drops lazily swirl around in my cup. I never mix my coffee with a spoon. I just sit there and watch two extremes doing a gentle dance together. A blob of white rises to the top, then it is elegantly pushed into halves. The blackness of the coffee caresses and sways. Whiteness pushes blackness away and then takes hold of it wanting to conquer it. "You are mine," whispers whiteness. "You can never conquer the idea of me," responds blackness.

Slow.

Playful.

Passionate.

I finally take a sip. My coffee is smooth. It flows over my tongue like honey. It gives me hope. Opposites don't have to come with jagged edges and sharp sudden starts. One day, I will learn to dance like milk in a cup of coffee. Without a stir. No violent mixing shall occur. Flavours mixing at will, giving of their sweetness gently.

Milk unmixed in coffee is at least a possibility.

Kiwi

"DO YOU WORK FOR THE CIA?" asked Juhaina. Along the crackles and static of the long distance call, there was no "hello," no "how are you?" She had started with the burning accusation foremost in her mind.

I let out a long sigh of relief. I had been worried about Juhaina for months. "It is so good to hear your voice! How are you? Where are you?" I asked questions without pausing to hear an answer. If I continued to talk, I wouldn't lose my friend again.

"We will talk about all that later, but first answer my question. Do you work for the CIA?"

"No, of course not!"

"How did you know it was time to leave Kuwait?"

"I didn't. I got lucky."

"But you were so sure, so absolutely clear you had to leave. You have no idea what hell you have spared yourself. Or perhaps you knew exactly the type of hell you were sparing yourself."

Juhaina was one of three friends I told about my plans to emigrate from Kuwait to Canada. Juhaina, originally from Yemen, the genius in our group. Nada, a Kuwaiti who, like me, also dreamed of becoming a doctor. And gregarious Lamees from Palestine. My father instructed me to keep my plans a secret for fear that the Iraqi embassy would interfere and withdraw my passport to prevent me from leaving Kuwait. I told most people that I was going to Canada for a three-week holiday. I simply didn't include the part about not coming back. It weighed heavily on me to not say goodbye to all that I loved and cared about. My father insisted that I could always write letters after I was safely installed in Canada, far away from the reach of the Iraqi government. One week before my trip, I broke down in tears. My father relented, giving me permission to inform my three best friends with strict instructions that they were not to tell anybody. And so I invited Juhaina, Nada and Lamees for a small tea party. My mother served petits fours and éclairs from the French bakery and then left us to work it out on our own.

The barrage was fast and furious.

"Why? Why? Why?"

"But you have a great life here!"

"They speak a foreign language over there and have strange habits!"

"You don't know anybody over there, you will be lonely!"

I gave them explanations that included words such as "better future," "stability," "long term plan." The more I explained the less certain I felt. The truth is I didn't know why I was leaving. It was something like a gut feeling. Only in my case it was a nose feeling. Every city in world has a unique smell. You smell it on arrival, but once you live there for a month you get accustomed to the scent and stop noticing it. Kuwait always smelled of sand and things baked in the sun. Then one day there was a new scent floating in the air. It was faint at the beginning. Then it got stronger over time. It smelled yellow and rotten. Sulfuric. Like a chemistry experiment. It hung in the air and travelled in wafts. I simply knew. It was time to move. "Find a different country," my nose instructed me. I followed its instructions.

Since I had last spoken to Juhaina, Kuwait had been invaded by Iraq and then liberated again by the US. One year later, I was speaking to her on the phone with no clue what had happened to her. Everybody living there during that time had a story of torment that could fill a whole book. I got to observe it all from the comfort of the shared TV room in my student dormitory, with Canadian students who learned of the news by studying my facial expressions.

Upon reflection, I realize that I have been unbelievably lucky throughout my life. The type of crazy good fortune that has showered upon my head is hard to account for. I was an Iraqi citizen living in Kuwait. All Iraqis living in Kuwait found themselves stuck in an impossible conundrum. The Iraqi government enacted a law that all Iraqi citizens living in Kuwait had to stay put. It meant that an Iraqi was not allowed to leave Kuwait, not even to visit Iraq. Violating the law was punishable by execution. Later when liberation happened, there was the predictable backlash against Iraqis. Iraqis were getting beaten and even murdered for revenge. But me? No, I got out like a hair out of dough. Clean. Unaffected. Innocent.

Twelve years after my call from Juhaina, back in Vancouver once more after a stint in Jerusalem, I received a similar accusatory phone call.

"Do you work for the CIA?" Jamal laughed as he asked me the question. He was mostly laughing at himself, for he was the one who had argued the hardest to convince me to stay in Jerusalem. Samih and I had left Vancouver to live in the Holy Lands for four years and then returned to Vancouver.

Jerusalem smells like an antique shop. Old stained books. Acidic furniture decaying under cobwebs. One morning, I woke up and there was a new red scent in the air. It smelled of fresh meat in the butcher shop. The iron tinge of spilled blood. I knew it was time to leave again. I started packing in panic.

Jamal and his wife Manal, my American neighbour Sarah and my daughter's daycare owner, Liat, all tried to convince me that I was making a bad move when I told them I was leaving.

"You are living at the forefront of the most exciting time in the Middle East. In Canada you will become just a number."

"There are a few hiccups in the peace process, but ultimately things will work out."

"You and your husband are exactly the type of people that this country needs. Peace requires peace makers such as yourselves."

"You are giving up on front row seats to the most inspirational historical moment in human history!"

I couldn't tell them about my nose and the red smell. How do I tell them that my nose has saved my life before, and like last time, I know I'd better heed its call. Instead I gave them logical excuses, peppering words in my sentences such as "stability," "racism," "apartheid," "self-loathing" and the most dreadful of excuses: "I want to give my children a better future." Oh yes! I am not above stooping to that level.

Jamal, Manal and Sarah were so angry with me they even refused to say goodbye. Liat cried, giving me a passionate hug when we saw each other for the last time. Eight weeks after I arrived in Canada, the Israeli prime minister Ariel Sharon walked into the Dome of the Rock, sparking the second Intifada. Once again, from the safety of my television screen, I watched riots, bombings and explosions happening in streets that I had walked a mere few weeks earlier. Once again, I had dodged a bullet. Perhaps literally.

Two years ago, I was on my lunch break. I decided to go for a little walk around the hospital that employs me to clear my head.

Two blocks away from Memorial is a fruit and vegetable stand where I sometimes pick up groceries. The kiwi fruits looked particularly attractive that afternoon. One particular kiwi sparkled in the sun. It beckoned to me. Take me. Eat Me. Taste me. And so I bought five or six kiwis including the irregularly plump one that was going out of its way to catch my attention. Later that day during a lull in my work schedule I decided to eat a single kiwi to refresh myself. I peeled the brown feathery skin, revealing lush juicy fruit. I cut it in half and there it was. Embedded right in the middle of the kiwi—a solitaire diamond ring. The type handsome men buy to propose marriage in Hollywood rom-coms. I felt like Houdini slicing a woman in half and reassembling her whole a few minutes later. As if nature, god or whatever power in charge of this universe was proposing to me.

"Will you be my bride?" Asked the Universe.

"Yes!"

"Yes."

"Yes."

A thousand yesses.

I never take that ring off.

I love that ring more than the one my husband gave me.

I have this kiwi fruit luck. The type of luck that rescues me from death. I never win in lotteries or raffles. My career has been a huge bust. Nothing I have done has been noteworthy. I don't think anybody who knows me would think of me as anything more interesting than white toast. Yet I have this unbelievable luck. The type of luck that makes people across continents suspect that I am 007 material. Only this Jamsia Bonditta doesn't go after the hidden diamond. It comes to her in a kiwi. It's a fuzzy green luck. The type that hands me what I need, never what I want. Perhaps I am lucky that I don't get the things that I want. Perhaps the things that I want would lead me to disaster. Perhaps I should be grateful for failing at things. But why me?

Why does the universe single out useless-breadcrumb me with this neon green, outrageous fortune?

Forget *To be or not to be?*—I have a better question:

A humble kiwi puzzles the brain, and doth confound the sense,

how to bear these evils we possess?

To be spared the whips and scorns of time.

And sit upon a stage witnessing others grunt under the weight of a weary life.

I tremble in dread with thoughts of purpose before death.

To search for omens in obscure signs.

Manufacture in reason merits of unworthy takes.

O creator of the whole universe, sitting upon your throne.

Unfathomable is your native hue of indication.

Why curse us with a nobler mind questioning?

When resolutions have shuffled off this mortal coil.

Salt

I WANT TO TELL YOU A SECRET.

Something I have never told anybody.

Do you know how, in mid conversation, people will show you a picture of their baby? With a look of satisfied bliss? They will pull out their wallet from a back pocket or a purse. Softly and gingerly, your eyes are tackled by an image of a smiling child demanding to be admired. And you are expected to be like "Oooooooooo! He is so cute!" Declarations of adorability must follow. "So beautiful. He takes after his father," or "He takes after his mother." "You must be so proud." "I am so happy for you." Any time I am in this situation, I find myself struggling with the perverse desire to say: "Yuck! He is so ugly. One day he will grow up and be even uglier than you."

Before you jump in to judge me as an evil person, I want to assure you that I have never acted on this secret desire. Like you, I think that all the children of the world are beautiful. It is the scripted nature of the encounter that I object to. My lack of free choice produces dark urges that terrify me. I suspect you don't have any children, which is why I feel comfortable telling you this. A parenting vibe would have scared me off. Maybe I have a hard time relating to other parents. I don't carry pictures of my children in my wallet. And I keep the oooing and aaaaahing at other people's progeny photographs to a minimum so as to discourage this act of saccharine sentimentality. It's like we all feel compelled to be happy and optimistic around each other. The way children's books all have happy endings. I have read so many of those now. I feel pressured to assume that sweet persona. I force a smile onto my face and state happy endings till eternity. The effect is multiplied around families. It's fake. This phoniness is assaulting.

Now it's your turn to tell me a secret.

Something nobody knows about you.

Now there is a bond between us. Intimacy. Something real.

When I was eight, I went through three weeks of existential contemplation. I was attempting to imagine the type of person I would become. I ran through all the scenarios of types of human behavior that my child brain was aware of.

A girl wearing ribbons in her hair falls in the mud.

Grown ups. Two men and two women are smoking and drinking. They are whispering something I don't understand.

The girl sitting next to me at school is cheating during the final exam.

My father turns off the TV when I enter the living room.

My mother is crying.

During this time, I spent my free time locked in my room daydreaming. Layal complained that I wasn't playing with her. When I explained I was doing serious thinking about life, Layal wanted to know the details. I promised to reveal all after the solitary thinking period was over. When life went back to a natural rhythm, Layal demanded that I own up.

"I was thinking about what I want to become when I grow up," I said.

"And what did you decide in the end?" Layal's eyes widened in anticipation.

"I decided to be a good person."

"You spent three weeks locked up in your room to come up with that?" She laughed.

Layal probably thought I was hatching a plan for world domination in my pink furnished bedroom. Or maybe she feared I was building a rocket that would fly me to the moon and leave her behind to be a single child. Immediately I felt silly.

Here's some advice: confide your secrets to strangers and let your close relations be what they want to be.

Which leads me to my second rule of eating: Recipes are like magic tricks—revealing the secrets ruins the effect.

I don't want any semblance of magic to take place in my life. Magicians are professional deceivers. I strive to reveal all my kitchen's secrets; if I am not fooling others, I am less likely to fool myself.

For the 20 years that followed I endeavored to seek goodness as my secret heart's desire. It was my hidden goal. Inside the depth of my yearning, I fantasized about being a good wife, good mother, good daughter, good friend, good employee, good citizen and above all else a good human being. Please don't be impressed. My pursuit was a failure. I have no claim over the geometric dimensions of the universal quality of goodness. In truth, I am as rotten as the next person. I can honestly say that I tried really, really hard to be good for two decades. And then I secretly proclaimed defeat.

On my 28th year living on this earth I could sense another bout of contemplative questioning coming. This time I knew that hiding in a room wasn't enough. I had to find a hiding country. Away from familiar sights or sounds. Undetected by loving eyes. I told my family that I felt a sudden urge to visit a real life castle and booked a three-week holiday to Edinburgh, Scotland on my own. I roamed the streets savoring my anonymity. There was nobody to notice that I wasn't doing much sightseeing. I spent hours lying in my tiny hotel room. In the evening, I would haunt the streets of the city and find a place to eat dinner before I headed back to my hotel. I stared at the ceiling and ran through a film of all possible human interactions.

Two men shaking hands.

A girl skipping rope.

A balding middle aged white male screaming: "You're fired!"

A woman turning heads by entering a room.

An eight year old boy throwing rocks.

A belly dancer moving her hips in figure eights.

A deli worker making a sandwich.

An Egyptian construction worker wearing a long grey jalabiya climbing on top of a scaffolding and about to fall down to his death due to heat stroke.

A woman taking a night run around Stanley park, but unbeknownst to her she is about to be raped.

African child soldiers slaughtering each other.

I seethed with rage. Disgust at all the hypocrisy. My stomach churned. I wanted to throw up.

Towards the end of my stay in Edinburgh, I stumbled across a bakery. The smell drew me in. In the display I saw salted caramel cookies. They looked like puffed and overflowing golden chunks of sticky goodness. White translucent salt sat on top, defiantly refusing to lose its essence and dissolve into the whole. I pointed at the glass display and asked for a caramel cookie. The young woman at the other end of the counter snapped, "It's a biscuit, not a cookie!" She stood still, refusing to oblige me until I corrected my mistake. The hard-to-get routine is usually annoying, but in this case it increased my desire. I apologized, blaming my linguistic delinquency on my residency in an English speaking country across the Atlantic Ocean. She rewarded my act of contrition with a golden nugget of baked gooey goop on a paper napkin. Caramel and salt is a mixture devised in heaven. There is no taste like it. As flakes of salt melted on my tongue, the word dropped into my brain:

Authentic.

It was the word that I had been searching for in the streets of this ancient city. I was done with failing at being good. My new objective in life was authenticity.

Doable.

Realistic.

Grownup.

The crumbs of the cookie on my napkins filled me with a sense of calm. Happiness would be the wrong word to use here. It was more a sense of quiet satisfaction. Not a *Eureka!* moment, but a *Here I am!* moment.

Fully.

Abundantly.

Unapologetically.

By the time I arrived back in Vancouver my state of bliss was replaced with panic. Goodness is a movie that plays easily in my mind's projector. Authenticity, on the other hand, has no script. We are socialized from a young age to supress our dark side. For our own good. For society's good. Once you open the lid on your psyche's basement, there is no knowing what you will find there.

What if I dive deep into my dark side and discover that I harbor a secret desire to hurt others? Or that everything in my life is a lie? Or that I am a nymphomaniac disguised as a faithful wife? Or that I don't give a toss about social responsibility? Most frightful of all, what if among the old junk of my dark thoughts I discover that I am a dull person? That I contain nothing worth supressing?

Milquetoast and donuts.

Now I am afraid to reach 48. Perhaps a new bout of contemplation will seize me. Who knows what word will find me then? Will it be more painful than reaching for genuineness? Luckily I have many more years before I reach that point. So I won't worry about it just yet.

Blood

My job is to walk around a hospital pushing a cart collecting blood samples from patients. Officially, my title is phlebotomist. I secretly call myself a vampire. My duties require me to suck people's blood. I don't sink my teeth into their jugulars. A hypodermic needle is my weapon of choice. The end result is the same. If vampires were real they would all work as phlebotomists like me. It is the only socially acceptable way to have discreet access to human blood. No patient would be suspicious if you took an extra tube or two. Nobody checks the requisition forms anyway. All day long I draw blood, label tubes and send them to the laboratory for analysis. My job is enjoyable because I get to chat with lots of people on a daily basis. I carry each of their stories in the cart of my memory. Stories from patients past get dispensed to future patients. My own form of gentle remedy. Vulnerability is the common experience of a hospital stay. In small or tragic ways people have a brush with the eventuality of their death. Most want to deposit a story to a willing recipient. Doctors and nurses are too busy performing medical duties. A blood sucker with her cart is the perfect target for a verbal bleeding.

Just yesterday, I had to take a sample from a 44 year-old woman who had silky straight chestnut brown hair and clever eyes. She spoke in a gentle manner that conveyed education and sophistication. When I asked her how she was feeling, she confided that she was feeling depressed. Her 22 year-old daughter was experiencing a passionate love affair with a hunky handsome fellow student at Berkeley. Her mother, at age 77, had found the love of her life after being widowed for a year in Romania. "Here I am," she stated matter-of-factly. "I am in this hospital all on my own with nobody to love me."

"Your mother found love at age 77? That's amazing!" I automatically gravitated to the shiniest part of the story.

"I loved my father dearly, but he wasn't a great husband. My mother had to put up with his gruff behavior. She worked the farm, accepted his drinking, there was occasional physical abuse. I don't think she ever heard a single kind word from him. Then one year after his death, she hooked up with a widower from the same village who always had a crush on her but never confided his feeling for fear of impropriety. Each time I talk to her she sounds happier and happier. The sex is the best she ever experienced in her life. They are planning a trip together to Egypt because both of them think it is the most romantic place on earth. Here's the clincher: He makes her laugh. I don't think I ever saw my mother laugh when I was growing up. Now she giggles like a schoolgirl It's like she a different woman."

"That story is inspirational. If your mother can find love, then there is hope for all the single people in the world!" I said, throwing up my hands into the air as if worshiping a pagan god.

"I know. So what's wrong with me? Why can't I find love like that?" She spoke in an academic measured tone, yet I knew that inside she was wavering like a candle in the wind.

I didn't know what to say, since she obviously couldn't see that her story contained within it its own antidote. It is a bad example of my hospital story exchange mechanism. Normally, each story deposit is rewarded with a story withdrawal. I tell them a story from another patient, and it usually makes them feel better. It works most of the time. But every medicine encounters those that are resistant to it. My secret method is no different than the Methotrexate Dr. Mizrahi is fond of prescribing.

The breakfast buffet in Edinburgh, Scotland featured an item I had never heard of before. Blood pudding. I asked my wafer-thin waitress if it was actually made with blood or if it was just an odd naming choice, the way hotdogs are not actually made out of dogs. The young woman replied that it was a Scottish delicacy, and yes it was made out of actual blood. Sausage meat is cooked in blood and it turns into a black-as-ink goop. Given my profession, I wanted to try it. I was certain I would hate it. I worried that I might throw up. To my surprise I liked it. A subtle savory taste with a creamy texture and no aftertaste. I learned that blood doesn't taste sweet. Saltiness is the predominant flavor in this unique delicacy. Turns out blood is thicker than water.

Just in case you are worried, no, this is not a confession about how I came back to Vancouver and started experimenting with human blood in my kitchen. So relax. Although it would make for a more interesting story, I am not so crazy as to give up decency for the sake of having a riveting story to tell you.

A busy hive of activity is what a hospital is. Doctors, nurses, aids, specialists, management, sales people, interns, janitors, building caretakers, human caretakers, lab-techs, paramedics, patients and those who come to visit them. A rainbow of bees. There are days when I am on my feet all shift long, going from room to room. And then there are other days, when I sit in the nursing lounge next to my cart, waiting to receive a stack of requisition forms. On slow days, I sit on my favorite chair; I look out the window and daydream:

The vampire apocalypse unfolds swiftly. It catches us all by surprise. It is twilight as I am readying to begin my shift, and a wall of unpleasant murmurs comes from behind the door of the nursing station. Soft gasps turn to shrieks, turn to a flood of screams. I open the door just enough to take in a glimpse of the horror unfolding in the ward. Men and women dressed in black leather are attacking staff and patients alike. One vampire grabs Maria (a fellow phlebotomist) and sinks sharp teeth into her veins. Terrified, I take a step back, quietly closing the door. I can hear my boss Charlotte screaming like a hyena on the other side of the closed door. I could simply barricade the door and wait. I hesitate for an agonizing minute over my decision. When I hear Dr. Nikmailean whimpering like a lamb about to be slaughtered, a mysterious heroic impulse takes hold of me. I grab the legs of the broken chair in the room, turning them into spears. I lunge into the ward, screaming "Allahu Akbar!" with a maniacal zeal that would make Mel Gibson in Braveheart feel sheepish. All the vampires stop feasting and stare at me. I plunge a wooden stake into the nearest pale-faced monster on my right. Without skipping a beat I double-bill the action on a bloody-toothed sucker on my left. All the vampires stand up and shake in fear. They recognize a slayer's heart when they see one. My lack of fear makes them uneasy. A needle vampire is far more dangerous than a toothed one. They all float in the air, escaping from doors and windows as quickly as they appeared. The two dead vampires burn, leaving behind a stinky black puddle. My coworkers cheer with delight. Leigh, another phlebotomist who was hiding in the washroom the whole time, is the loudest. The patients clap. When the police arrive to investigate, nobody believes the vampire story. They suspect mass hallucination. Building engineers are called in to examine the ventilation system. The black puddle near the nursing station is blamed for the shared hysteria. The police suspect foul play but can't prove anything. Despite the odd explanations of the events of the day, all my co-workers treat me like a hero from that day on. Especially Dr. Mizrahi. I get looks of adoration from him that hide meanings within meanings.

Mango

"I CAME TO CANADA HOPING TO create a better life for myself." That statement sounds so good, even I say it. "I immigrated to Canada to build a better future for my children." Who can argue with that? People will nod their heads in approval, as if you are uttering a universal truth. As if you were saying "Love is better than hate." Or "Murder is wrong." So true that it is meaningless. However beautiful a sentiment, at least in my case, it is a lie. Immigration for me had nothing to do with looking forwards towards anything. On the day I arrived in this country, 14 years ago, had you asked me "How do you visualize your life in this place 5 years from now?" I would have answered: "I see a grandiose void." My life had been a page filled with poetic words dancing in anticipation. A prose so beautiful as to make your heart shudder.

But when I emigrated, all the letters scurried away. The meaning dissolved the way scratches in the sand are washed away by the waves of the sea. It became a whole notebook filled with ink-resistant white sheets of paper. I saw nothing. The secret truth is that immigration was an experience of defeat. A loss of hope. Every dream, every fantasy took place in Arabic. Surrounded by a foreign language, I lost faith in meaning. My permanent relocation from the east to the west had nothing to do with looking forward and all to do with running away. I outran a nightmare, losing all facility for dreaming along the way.

Inderjit works in accounting at Memorial. For a mysterious reason, he has taken a shine to me and decided to educate me on everything that has to do with Punjab—his place of origin. A sympathetic, confident man in his mid-thirties with an immaculate beard, he shows up to work with a tightly wound turban in bright colors. Although he wears conservative long sleeve cotton shirts and pants that never exit the color spectrum between dark blue and black, his turban shines like a lighthouse of creativity on top of his head. Lilac, red, hot pink and fiery orange are but a sample of his wide head gear wardrobe. "I like your turban!" I wish I could say each time I see him. I am worried that he might mistake my compliments for teasing or mocking and so I contain myself by saying nothing. I keep hoping that one day he will show up to work in a yellow polka-dotted purple turban. If that ever happens, I will jump out of my seat, shake my hands sideways like a frightened chicken and cheer.

One day when I was sitting at the cafeteria during lunch hour, Inderjit seated himself across from me and started talking. He didn't introduce himself. He didn't ask me my name. He poked his fork into his fried rice and started telling me about the weather in Punjab. "Today the humidity in Jalandhar is 81%, that is not uncommon. In fact people feel lucky when it isn't 100% this time of the year." He was wearing a baby blue turban that day. The color was rich and soothing. Instead of feeling startled by his sudden appearance, I felt strangely happy listening to him. And so started our work camaraderie. We always meet in the same spot. With each meeting, Inderjit tells me something about Punjab. So far we have covered the weather all year around, geography, Punjabi language, poetry and notable songs. I don't know why I have been elected for this task. Perhaps it helps him feel less homesick. Perhaps I am a good listener. Perhaps there is something in my aura that requires an education on this particular subject or perhaps there is no reason at all. I have noticed he never mentions Punjab when talking with others. I am his only pupil.

Four days ago I was visiting Layal at her apartment. I left the girls playing soccer with their dad in the backyard. I sat on Layal's black leather sofa as she went to the kitchen to make us some vanilla rooibos tea. I reclined on my right side and let out a long sigh.

"Did you know that the Sikh religion is partially based on Islam?"

"Ooooohoooooo! Thaniya!" Layal exploded in my face. "Not another informational session on Punjab!"

"What do you mean?" I held my tea mug tightly with both hands, inhaling pleasant aromas through my nostrils.

"For the last two months, all you do is talk about that place. If I wanted to have tea with Wikipedia, I would be sitting here with my laptop." Layal placed her mug on a coaster on the coffee table.

"Do you remember Avani, our servant in Kuwait?" I took a tentative sip from my tea, producing an unintentional loud slurp. It was too hot.

"Of course I do! She made the killer biryani that one time our mother was at the hospital." Layal shrugged her shoulders, staring squarely at me.

"She lived with us for 10 years, yet we know nothing about her, about her life, where she came from. She was from Punjab." I blew into my tea. My tongue was tingling from the burn.

"Ya Allah! I swear, Thaniya, that sometimes you are the second most boring person I know right now."

"Who is the most boring person you know, then?" I forced a smile on my face.

"Carl from work."

"How is he boring?" I placed my right palm open on my knee pretending to grab an invisible ball.

"He will spend a whole hour explaining to me the difference between types of sourdough bread," Layal said, rolling her eyes.

Carl sounds like a foodie, a type of person I find interesting. But my thoughts about Carl remained hidden inside my head like a pearl shielded within an oyster. I invited Layal to initiate a topic of discussion to go along with our tea. Her offering was to discuss office hookup culture in the modern day corporate environment.

Two days ago, my topic of education with Interjit was the unique properties of Punjabi food. In his soothing caramel voice, he was describing how spices are freshly roasted for each dish, when a mysterious force possessed me to interrupt him for the first time ever:

"In Iraq we have a unique condiment called amba." I used my index finger to draw an invisible horizontal line on the table between us. "This pickled mango with spices is eaten with sandwiches and served alongside of main dishes," I said, drawing another line, creating a plus sign. "I always thought that amba was a particularly Iraqi thing, since it featured in no other Arab country's cuisine. Israelis, however, got introduced to amba from Iraqi Jews who immigrated over in the fifties, and they have had a love-hate relationship with it ever since." Inderjit observed my right hand as I drew three invisible plus signs.

I went on, telling him all about amba, how it had made inroads in Israeli cuisine where it failed to create a dent in Arab cuisine.

When I lived in Israel, I had heard plenty of amba jibes.

"This looks like poo!"

"Only an Iraqi would invent something so perverse."

"This tastes disgusting, but I can't stop myself from eating it."

"Forget anthrax, Saddam will kill us by shipping over an extra potent cargo of amba."

One Israeli told me that amba makes him sweat profusely and his sweat smells like amba, yet he can't stop himself from eating it.

Despite all the derisive comments, Israelis seem to love the orange-brown stuff. They eat it with shawarma, barbequed meats, as a dip, as a condiment and other plethora of uses I would never associate amba with. I keep waiting for an Israeli to invent an amba slushy.

It was only after moving to Vancouver that I learned that amba is nothing other than Indian chutney. I was having dinner with Gillian and her friend Anika at a Tandoori restaurant, and I dipped my fork in a small condiment plate. Immediately I recognized the distinct sharp burning taste and thought: "Oh no! Indians have discovered Iraqi amba. There will be no end of trouble now." I called the waitress over and asked her to identify what was in the condiment platter. She pointed a delicate finger. "Mango chutney, tomato chutney and cucumber chutney," she said.

"What's chutney?" I asked.

"It is the oldest of Indian foods, thousands of years old," she said, wobbling her head sideways as she spoke. That is how I discovered that the most unique Iraqi food is nothing more than common Indian chutney. For some reason in Iraq we only use mango; the other kinds didn't catch on. I fell in love with Vancouver in that moment. In that tandoori joint, I belonged like nobody else did. There is a long history of trade between Iraq and India in which spices and food recipes have been exchanged; but I suspect that the introduction of amba is a more recent development. In the forties, while Britain was colonizing Iraq, they attempted to import a loyal middle class from India. This Indianization of third world countries served the British well in western Africa and they thought that it would work again in the Middle East. But because Iraq had its own vibrant middle class, the effort failed in this particular case.

I could feel myself sweating. I remembered the amba-sweating Israeli. In my head a sensible voice was saying: "Shut up! Shut up! Shut up!" Yet I couldn't stop myself. I kept on talking. Amba had invaded my spirit, possessing me to spill. Words kept perspiring out of my mouth uncontrollably.

At this point, I had drawn multiple squares, shapes and all manner of variations on the plus sign. Paul Klee would have been impressed with my efforts. Inderjit had rested his left cheek on his left hand. His eyebrows gathered close towards each other.

"All Indian nationals who immigrated integrated into Iraqi society. So think what path the humble mango has taken!" I placed my right hand under the table. "To most people, mango is a juicy fruit that makes them think of vacations, messy eating experiences and sweetness. Right?" I lifted my nose up in the air and then lowered it in a nod. Inderjit straightened up in his seat. "It's turned into a sour spicy condiment by ancient hands in one country. Becomes earnestly enjoyed as an emblem of national identity in another. Finally makes its way into a new country where it is eaten ironically. Enjoyed but ridiculed at the same time! Only in Canada can you realize the full atlas of what it all means. How all these things are connected. Isn't that amazing?"

There was a long silence. Inderjit looked straight into my eyes. His gaze was intense but not unkind. I was worried I had offended him. Perhaps I had broken the unspoken rule between us—he talks, I listen. Perhaps he would never speak to me again. Perhaps he was processing what I just told him. He was seeing me more fully than before. He was looking with anticipating eyes, something was unfolding right in front of him. As if I was transmogrifying, growing testicles out of my head and shifting across time. I looked straight into his black eyes. I dived in. For a moment, we saw each other. Not as two nationalities having a cultural exchange. Not as male and female. But as two spirits standing on an infinite plane. What passed between us can't be described with words.

After several minutes, Inderjit regained his composure and broke his silence.

"Do you know what is Sanskrit for mango?"

"No!" I shook my head.

"Amba."

Tomato

YOU KNOW WHAT SHAKSHUKA IS, RIGHT?

It's a favorite among students, bachelors and those that don't know how to cook and those who can't be bothered to cook. In short, shakshuka is the Middle East's version of Kraft Dinner. Unlike mac and cheese out of a box, it is a dish you will continue to crave years past your student days and many clicks after the honeymoon of your marriage turns into mustard-sun.

The shakshuka wars started in my household on the fifth week of my marriage and have spanned ten years, traveled to two continents and have yet to reach a peaceful resolution.

It all started when, after returning from our honeymoon, Samih decided to make shakshuka for dinner one night.

I took one bite and screwed up my face. "This shakshuka is all wrong!" A rather arrogant proclamation from somebody who didn't know how to boil an egg.

"Wrong how?" Samih smiled, bemused, the way you would be entertained with a cute three year old saying a four-letter word that they didn't understand. I hate it when Samih treats me in a patronizing way.

"It's too oniony," I said in the same tone I might have used to say "Smoking causes cancer."

"You just don't know what shakshuka is supposed to taste like, that's all." Samih tore a piece of pita bread. Folded it to create a scoop. Drenched the bread in the tomato massacre on his plate. Placed the dripping bundle into his mouth. "I bet the taste of tomato with the eggs seems unfamiliar, you're probably used to scrambled eggs instead," Samih said with a full mouth. Bits of masticated poached egg stained red flashed behind his teeth with each chew.

"I know the difference between shakshuka and scrambled eggs. I know how it's supposed to taste and this tastes wrong!" I placed my fork down and pushed my plate away.

"I am certain your mother never made shakshuka." You know an argument is going sideways when your mother gets mentioned. "I grew up eating this," said Samih. He pushed my plate back towards me and placed the fork in my hand. "Plus, it was one of two dishes I knew how to make at first year in university, which means I ate it every second day and developed a vast experience in preparing it. My taste buds and my hands are far more knowledgeable than yours are in this particular instance."

I picked up my plate and placed it next to the sink. I crossed my hands over my chest and stood towering over Samih.

Samih shook his head sideways and ignored me as he continued eating his dinner.

That night was the first time in our marriage that we fell asleep without embracing each other. I slept on my side of the bed and he slept on his. I could hear my father's voice in my head:

"Argument is the spice of married life. Without it, a union would be tasteless." My father would always say that to Layal and me immediately after he and my mother argued. She would storm to the bedroom, slamming the door. My dad would smile and try to assure us that everything was normal. The world was not melting around us. That this story wouldn't have a tragic ending. The chicken would be fully cooked by the time dinner was served.

What I felt inside the night I argued with Samih was less like spice and more like a scrubbing sponge. I felt like an organic potato receiving a harsh scouring before getting chopped into pieces. I would revise my father's saying: "Argument is like the scrubbing sponge of married life: it cleans without the need to peel your life. Harsh but useful."

Later I learned to cook, and I made sure to prepare my shakshuka with garlic instead of onion. Each time I prepared shakshuka, Samih complained that it was wrong as sin. Each time he prepared it I made sure to register my disapproval by comparing his creation to a surgical procedure gone wrong. This argument travelled with us to Jerusalem and back to Vancouver. We would spend hours going over the ideal ratio of acidity to sweetness in tomato sauce, the creaminess of eggs, the consistency that is disrupted by the presence of onions, the virtues of garlic. Then Zakiya and Shatha arrived into our life. We couldn't wait for our two beautiful daughters to start eating solids. I would make my version and Samih would make his and we let the girls act as judges. Our friends were all involved in our "which shakshuka tastes better" battle. We had a shakshuka notebook in which we kept score on how many voted for mine and how many voted for his.

Then one day when Zakiya was 8, she yelled, "I'm sick and tired of this!" She held her head as if it was about to burst. We were forbidden from making shakshuka or mentioning our favorite dish ever again. Zakiya declared that the mere mention of the dish made her feel nauseous. That was the end of ten years of shakshuka wars. Thus started a new age—a bland, peaceful shakshukaless existence.

I guess Zakiya will grow up to be a fine supporter of the mythical two-state solution. I am allowed to make eggs but only without the presence of tomato in the vicinity. The truth is I miss the arguments. Samih is a very mild-mannered person. It is hard to start an argument with him. His way of dealing with any difficulty is to sit down, analyse the situation, think of pros and cons and come up with the most logical solution. Picking a fight with him is nearly impossible. Shakshuka was my easy go-to method of getting him worked up. I would make shakshuka, and boom! Ten minutes later he was yelling, waving his hands and cursing god. I secretly adore the wild in him. I love the fact that I hold the secret key that pushes his buttons, nobody else does. I need to come up with a new way of pushing that button that doesn't involve eggs and tomato, and this time I will make sure the girls can't spoil it for me.

Which brings me to my sixth rule of eating: "Never ask a cook what is in a dish. The answers might turn you off an otherwise enjoyable meal. Shut up and eat without extra philosophy."

The shakshuka wars have run parallel to another long-simmering debate we have been having for 13 years. This is the question of who is worse off in the world, an Iraqi or a Palestinian? The circumstances of both nationalities have changed radically over time, yet our argument has stayed true to its course.

I believe that being an Iraqi sucks the big one. In fact, I don't believe you could possibly choose a worse nationality for yourself if you tried. Good thing that nobody chooses their nationality, because nobody would choose to be an Iraqi and a subversive part of me is glad that such a monstrosity does exist despite it all.

On my fourth date with Samih, he told me about how hard it was to grow up Palestinian inside Israel. He began to list all the discrimination he had faced since childhood. I could hear the violin playing inside my head and I knew I had to stop his "poor little me" monologue before it became a part of our relationship. The minute he paused to take a breath after he told me he was imprisoned for participating in a peaceful demonstration, I seized the moment:

"Ha! That's nothing!

Cry me a river and I shall pollute it!

You think you got a raw deal in life? Thank your lucky stars you were not born Iraqi. If I tell you my story, it will raise the hair on your hairy back."

I secretly believe it was in that moment that Samih developed an interest in me. I understood the nature of his humiliation. Stared it squarely in the eyes and refused to feel sorry for him.

Even back then, being an Iraqi was worse off. Today, more so than before. Our debate on which nationality suffered more began and has sizzled on a low simmer setting ever since.

Samih's go-to statement to end the debate was this: "No matter what, there will always be a country called Iraq that belongs to Iraqis. The same can't be said about Palestine."

Sadly, he has stopped using that argument in the last year.

What do I usually say in reply? This is what I would say: "At least you have an enemy that you can blame for your misfortunes. We don't have that luxury. Our worst enemy is ourselves. We are so efficient at killing each other that we need no external forces, they only get in the way."

Arguing about fried tomato is so much easier.

This is gut wrenching, isn't it?

Turn the page.

Marjoram

DAMN HIM!

Damn Zaev.

Dr. Zaev Mizrahi, I should say.

He is the handsomest man my eyes ever beheld. He could put Brad Pitt and George Clooney in his back pocket without exerting an effort. These two would look like clowns next to him. He could easily be a fashion model or a Hollywood star, but instead he is a surgeon at Memorial. As if his devastating good looks are not bad enough, he is smart, has a reputation for being a great doctor and to make matters worse, he's really a pretty nice guy. If he was at least an asshole like Dr. Nikmailean, then I could handle it. But working in his sphere is unbearable. This guy doesn't have a single flaw that I can fixate on. Oh, I forgot to mention: he is married with two daughters.

This is hell.

H. E. Double hockey sticks.

I know that eternal burning damnation is well deserved for what is passing in my thoughts right now. But I can't help myself. Glancing at this man is a sin. For it sets the heart dancing, the thoughts wandering and unleashes tingly feelings to feast upon forbidden fruits. It is an all-too-disgusting state to be in. For a married woman especially.

One of the advantages of living in Canada is that it is good for maintaining married life. It's a far cry from being the land of loose morals and poor family values that is rumored in the Middle East. I find that living in Canada has promoted virtue in my life.

I know what I will say next will seem racist. Okay, it is racist. I don't care. It is how my plumbing works. I can't help it. I simply don't find Canadian men attractive. Only dark men get the engine revved up. Over here I am Snow White living among the seven dwarfs. They are cute and entertaining. None of the dwarfs set Snow White's heart pounding. In my eyes, Samih is a dark prince. Next to him most men in Vancouver seem milquetoast. Whenever I travel to the Middle East, I am reminded how temptation-free my life is in beautiful British Columbia. Among glorious mountains and pristine lakes, my heart has swelled in purity. Whenever I see a tall dark Arab man with shiny black hair and that certain swagger, my eyes begin swaying. I have to close them and tell myself: *You are married, you are married, you are married. Don't look.* I repeat this like a prayer and the feeling passes. I believe in purity of intention. It is not enough that your actions conform to your beliefs. I think it's important that in your heart, your most secret impulse dances to the same tempo, as well. I believe that a married person acts married, thinks married and feels married. Conforming to this ideal has been a cake-walk in my life. Until recently.

Now that this Zaev has entered my life, I need to evaluate my strategy with regards to lust. He has a thin pointy nose—ready to give directions. Concave cheeks that my fingers itch to caress. He is tall, has dark eyes and wavy hair. A prickly day-old stubble is always there, making me wish I could press my chin against his. He is so unbearably handsome, I avoid looking at him at all costs. Whenever he talks to me I pretend that I am looking out the window admiring the trees that line the street outside the hospital. In the hallway, whenever he approaches me, I pick up one of the patient charts and study it as if final exams will be based on the gibberish in it, just to avoid his gaze. He probably thinks that I don't like him because he is Israeli and I am an Arab. He exaggerates niceties towards me. It is his way of trying to prove that Israelis and Arabs can be friends. His own private peace process. If he had been any other Israeli I would have happily proven him right on his first attempt. Instead I avoid him as if he was an Ebola-carrying corpse.

He greets me cheerfully: "Hello Thaniya, how are you feeling today?" To which I answer a curt: "Fine." In the nursing lounge he always attempts to strike up a conversation. "Hey Thaniya, do you like movies?" "Thaniya, Maria told me that you have two daughters, I have two daughters about the same age as yours. I think all the best people have two daughters. Don't you agree?" "Thaniya, what type of music do you like?" Each time he talks to me, my body seizes up, my breathing becomes constricted and I stare at whatever distraction I can find nearby as if I was drowning in the ocean and have spotted a life raft in the not-too-far distance. I despise his niceness.

I sometimes fantasize that I grab his hand as he is walking by the supply room. I push him inside violently. "Thaniya, what are you doing?" he says, alarmed. I rip off his clothes. "Shhhh! Just shut up and fuck me."

Such shameful thoughts. It burns. Being around him burns like a scorched steak. Not good burning, like a banana flambé. The dreadful burning. When you set the toaster too high and your morning bread comes out black and smelling of the vestiges of damnation.

I used to feel judgmental towards men. The way the most intelligent man would act idiotically the minute a curvy blonde entered the room. It puzzled me why anybody would allow himself to be led by lust in such a ridiculous manner. This experience with Zaev is a giant humble pie feast. I realize now that lust can invade your body without permission and play a game of snakes and ladders with your imagination, one where you are constantly swallowed by snakes and never get a chance to climb a ladder. I suddenly feel sympathy towards the men who have to be in the grip of this torment all their adult lives. Poor fellows! How do they cope? No wonder they hate us. All the misogyny of the world is starting to make sense.

Is this a test? Why test me like this?

Why now?

There is no doubt in my mind that the devil himself placed Zaev in my path. I am not saying that the good doctor harbors any sinister intentions. As far as I can see he is an altogether nice person. But I am certain that an immeasurable evil has possessed me.

Heal me of this. Let it pass. Let me be me. Let this insane fantasy pass through me the way asparagus passes through urine. Expel these hideous thoughts.

I have a fantastic husband who is loving, gentle and with whom I mothered two beautiful daughters. He is handsome and sexy. I love him with all my heart. I am lucky to have this beautiful family. It would be insane to risk it all for a cheap thrill.

I resolved to have as much sex with Samih as possible. My beautiful husband never says no to sex. Throughout my marriage, it was Samih's job to initiate. I played the coy shy damsel who requires seduction. These days, no sooner are the girls down for bedtime, I am grabbing at Samih's shirt. Unbuttoning. I place my hand on his penis to massage a hurried erection. Then I jump on top of him, arranging his body parts to maximize my pleasure.

Samih has never commented on the change in my behavior, although it is hard to believe that he hasn't noticed. And so one evening after sex I asked him:

"Do you think I am being too slutty?" I said while caressing his left hand.

"No," he said with a snort.

"Well, do you like the sexually aggressive Thaniya?" I held my breath. I was afraid of his answer.

"I liked the shy Thaniya at the beginning, but now I like the more confident one." Samih turned towards me.

"Do you ever wonder why I changed?" I exhaled slowly and stared at the ceiling.

"You got older, you gave birth to two. Your body changed. You feel more comfortable with me because I was always attentive to your needs. You feel safe to express yourself." Samih leaned over and kissed my navel.

I normally find it annoying how Samih assumes he knows everything about me, but in this case it was comforting. I would rather he didn't suspect the hideous snake slithering in my head.

My lust-busting plan has two parts.

1- Sex my brains out with Samih.

2-Marjoram.

My mother owns an antique book that contains ancient Czech herbal remedies. Brown with age and falling apart, it has been her companion since childhood. Whenever one of us became ill, my mother would get a wise look on her face and put on her reading glasses with a slow, mysterious hand movement. Diving into the artifact transported her into a different world. She would emerge out of her trance proclaiming to have found a solution.

Layal was the first to follow me to Vancouver after I moved. Being an only child was too difficult. A few months later, my parents followed her. We all live within a 10-minute drive of one another. I couldn't just ask my mother to look for a lust remedy because then I would have to reveal my embarrassing predicament. Instead I went over to my parents' house asking my mother if I could see her remedy book. She looked suspicious.

"What are you looking for?" My mother leaned forward, ready to hear my secret.

"Nothing," I said, avoiding her gaze. "I just want to feel it in my hands."

"Books are living, breathing things; they can sense the hand that is caressing them. Sometimes they give, other times they withhold." My mother touched my right knee with her left index finger to grab my attention.

"It's no big deal, really. I'm just curious." I shrugged my shoulders.

I could sense my mother's unease as she handed me her prized possession. Her muscles were tense, her breath was shallow. She watched me like a lifeguard ready to jump in to rescue a drowning child. To get her off my back, I asked her to make me some Turkish coffee. That way I could have a few private moments with the book.

It stated that marjoram is natural libido suppressant. The anti-Viagra. And so I resolved to use as much of that herb as possible. I perfected a great spinach pie in phyllo pastry that is irresistibly yummy and is loaded with my lust-busting ingredient. Once a week I bring a fresh batch to work and leave it in the nursing lounge, hoping that Dr. Mizrahi with his ready peace in the Middle East initiative would be my compliant victim. If I can lower his libido as well, this will lower his attractiveness in my eyes. Sooner or later I will conquer this challenge. If not, then I have no choice but to change jobs.

Correction.

My lust-busting plan has three parts.

3- fasting

Islam prescribes this spiritual practice particularly to single men as a remedy to avoid sinning. Fasting means no food or drink from dawn till dusk. The idea being that by weakening the body, the spirit has a chance to soar. It allows for contemplation. Which might help me reach the root cause of my predicament.

So here I have it. A plan that has combined elements from the Middle East, Europe and North America. All the ancient wisdom of Europe combined with the pop psychology of the new country sprinkled with the divinely inspired tradition of Islam should conquer this evil that had invaded my mental geography.

"Failure is inconceivable." I imagine Vizzini saying from the movie *The Princess Bride*.

Horseradish

Gillian Is My Best Friend in the whole wide world. We met one
time at a party at DeeDee's place. I mentioned that *Tampopo* is the
most romantic movie ever made. Gillian objected, declaring that the
1985 Japanese movie about a woman on a quest to perfect the
making of ramen noodles is nothing more but the misogynist
fantasy of a man. We started analyzing each scene in the movie and
the next thing we knew an hour had gone by. Our discussions are
like a game of wireless toy boats crossing each other in a pond. I say
something, she says something opposite and then we sit and watch
the fun erupt into unpredictable patterns. I always feel like both of
us are sitting outside of ourselves calmly observing the heated
discussion at the same time we are having it. Our friendship has a
self-awareness. It exists as a sentient being. Gillian and I enjoy being

at the opposite ends of an argument. The sparring keeps both of us intellectually fit.

Gillian believes in the power of positive thinking. But I operate on the conviction that desiring something doesn't make it materialize. Gillian thinks that we are the result of our childhood conditioning. I assert that I am in charge of my destiny. Rhythmic music and international movies make her happy. I love books and exploring new restaurants.

"Never trust a person who doesn't love chocolate," used to be my third rule of eating.

That rule had to be scrapped from my book once I met Gillian. She hates chocolate, refuses to even try it, and yet she is the most trustworthy person I know. My third rule of eating has remained empty, waiting to be replaced by the wisdom of aging. A higher truth shall befall me from the sky. One day, when I perfect my ten rules of eating, I will sell them as a poster. It will appeal to the millions of foodies worldwide. I will distill my experienced delights and revulsions across the globe into unifying commandments. I will have it framed in a golden frame and hang it in my living room for all to see. It will announce to the world that I have found my place. I know how to conduct myself based on these simple guiding principles. I have arrived. All that is missing is #3. Releasing a poster with just 9 rules seems wrong, like a half-baked soufflé–runny with disappointment.

You would never suspect it, but Gillian is a prison guard at a maximum-security facility for women. Despite her soft and feminine appearance, she earns her living by keeping murderesses and gangstresses in check. Off work, Gillian wears floral patterned dresses. She styles her honey brown hair into soft curly locks. I can't imagine her in a prison guard uniform. Not even after she showed me her taser gun. I asked her once if she is afraid of the inmates. She waved her hand dismissively. "Nah! They are all deeply hurt children acting out."

Gillian claims that she has perfected a technique for earning the prisoners' respect: "All I need to do with each prisoner is listen deeply to their story. All of them just want somebody to acknowledge them; once I know their story they turn into putty. I have them all eating out of my hand like tame little lambs. Doling out attention and approval to the best behaved. They are all good little girls eager to please their mama."

I admire Gillian's strength. I wouldn't have the nerve to walk into a prison issuing commands to hardened criminals. I find it hard enough walking up to patients telling them I am about to prick them with a needle. When Mark left Gillian, I went over to her apartment, I held her hand and wept big fat hot tears. Gillian wiped away my tears with a paper napkin, smoothed away my hair and told me to pull myself together. She assured me that she could handle getting over a husband.

Gillian is a horseradish type woman. Powerful, delicious and ready to clear your sinuses. Why cry? Just eat a mouthful of shredded, pungent root. Let the liquids storm away of their own volition.

If Samih left me because he wanted to have sex with other women, I would be a total mess. I would fall apart and stay scattered for years. It would take a surgical miracle to place my aching organs back into their hollowed bleeding cavities. With the grace of a swan, Gillian went back into the business of living without a husband like it was a natural act. I suggested to Gillian she should move apartments, to keep a distance from the memories. "But I love this apartment!" she said. "Why should I leave it?" As if all those years of loving, shouting and caressing could be drowned by the rush of the present moment.

Astounding.

Twelve years of marriage. She pressed a button. Beep! It was gone.

How does she do that?

How can I get a piece of what she has?

I placed her on a pedestal after that.

I secretly hope that some of her zest will rub off on me through close association. Sharp tasting, without spiciness. Like a punch in the face.

One Saturday, at 7 am, I was still in bed when I heard loud giggles coming from downstairs. Samih was on a long distance phone call with his sister Kamila. Curiosity grabbed me by the flannel pajamas and dragged me downstairs. Samih was still laughing after hanging up. "You will never believe what happened in Lazzazza today!" Samih was shaking his head as he held his belly.

Lazzaza, a small village of 10,000 souls, is Samih's home town.

Abbas, who you don't know, was forced by his father to marry Salwa at age 18. Many years and three children later, Abbas decided to rebel against his aging father. He divorced Salwa, giving her the house and securing her with both child support and spousal support. Abbas moved on to a new life guilt-free and got engaged to a young woman from a nearby village. Salwa was demolished by the savagery of her heartbreak. Her love for Abbas was not an arrangement to keep society at bay. What she held for him in a secret compartment inside her chest was an epic flood that she had hoped would one day pull him towards her in an undercurrent of familiarity. The dam of unspoken yearnings cracked. Out poured a lava deluge. She went to visit her ex-husband's fiancé at her residence. The two women sat in the living room. One young, the other cracked by experience. Between them a gulf of misunderstanding. The discussion boiled over into a shouting match. Neither one listened to the other's point of view. Salwa's right arm turned into a wrecking ball whose purpose in life was to meet its destiny on the young woman's left eye. This punch to the face was followed by savage hair pulling. The younger woman, unaccustomed to hand-to-hand combat, found herself knocked on the ground with the dark silhouette of a banshee clawing at her flesh. She screamed for help. Her brothers came to her aid, grabbed Salwa by the hands and legs and threw her outside. Out on the concrete pavement, Salwa got up, undeterred, like the

Bride from *Kill Bill*, dusted herself off and made her way to a bus stop where she began planning her next attack.

When Abbas heard that Salwa, who had always fit the mold of the dutiful wife, had publicly disrespected him, he was shocked. "Who knew that sweet-natured Salwa was capable of such tenacity?" He arrived at his former residence. His hands grew into octopus tentacles with a life of their own. The appendages slapped Salwa's face, once, twice and thrice. Each movement produced a shrill sound that filled the house with dread. Salwa didn't cry. Not a single tear was shed. How quickly is love turned to rage? Salwa's three brothers heard about what transpired during the day. The anger multiplied, intensified and electrified. Three young strong men ambushed Abbas on his way to work the next day and beat Allah's mercy out of him. "Don't you ever lay a hand on our sister!" they yelled at him as Abbas lay on the ground. "Next time you feel the need to prove that you are a man, come to us. We will be happy to straighten you out." And they left him there.

Abbas was stunned; he had been friends with Salwa's brothers his entire life. "What is happening in this world?" he wondered to himself. Not to be outdone, he gathered all his brothers and cousins and a few relatives scheming to get revenge. In a small village nothing stays secret for long. Whispers in the night have a way of escaping through the air, reaching unintended ears. Salwa's brothers heard about the forces being gathered against them, and they did the same. They gathered all their cousins, relatives, friends and supporters. The two gangs met in the town center to duke it out. Punches got thrown. Vulgar words floated in the air like menacing dragons. Within 15 minutes, two Israeli police cars with four officers arrived, whirling through the village, sirens blaring. Men, women and children of Lazzazza saw the blue ribbon cars with flashing lights and automatically each grabbed a stone to throw in the invaders' direction. The police felt overwhelmed by the crowd, abandoned their vehicles and ran out of Lazzazza with the speed of the Road Runner fleeing Wile E. Coyote. There was not even time to go "Beep! Beep!" The raging mob descended upon the two cars decorated with authority figure insignia and proceeded to smash them to smithereens. Thirty minutes into the incident the Israeli army arrived with jeeps and armored vehicles. They stormed into Lazzazza, shooting into the air. Playing cowboys and Indians in a black and white western movie. Everybody dispersed, running home for cover.

Kamila described the curfew imposed on the whole town to Samih: "The army jeep is driving up and down the main road with a soldier shouting into the speakers: 'Anybody outside his house will be shot on sight.' The kids can't go to school. None of the grownups can go to work."

"Now that is a proper Arab woman!" I said. I was now laughing my head off, unable to contain myself. "When she feels heartbroken, she causes an international incident and makes the whole town share her pain."

Samih and I sat next to each other, fuelling each other's laughing fits. After 20 minutes there was a pause. Samih sighed. "You know, Thaniya, I feel sad for Salwa. If somebody doesn't want you, there is absolutely nothing you can do about it."

I sighed too. "Yeah, you're right! Poor Salwa. Abbas doesn't love her."

Contrast Gillian's inner strength with the outer force of Salwa. In the Middle East, we say that foreigners are emotionally cold.

That they have no feelings. We, on the other hand, we are hysterical with them. I used to think this way also, until I became Gillian's friend. Salwa's reaction appeals to my heart. Gillian's is clearly the logical way, which I need to embrace.

Boiling water versus block of ice.

Choose!

Choose!

And then, one year ago, Gillian fell in love with a parole officer named Hovan. Gillian is convinced that Hovan is her soul mate. Sparks fly when they are in the same room together. They finish each other's sentences. They communicate through simple glances, they don't even need to play verbal ping-pong to deliver meaning. But Hoven is married with two teenage sons. Gillian thinks it would be unethical to date somebody who is hitched. However, she is convinced that they are meant to end up together, and so she has resolved to wait for him to get unhitched so they can be together body and soul without moral barriers.

I tried to convince Gillian to date other men while she was waiting for Hovan to become available.

"What for? In my spirit I know that we will end up together. Anything else until then would be a waste of time."

She takes my breath away. I feel lucky to be her friend. Her sense of certainty lends her power. Constant hesitation is where I stand. I haven't told Gillian about my affliction with Zaev. I don't want to contaminate her pure spirit with my shame. In this idyllic pool, I wish to pour only beauty and drink only inspiration.

Hummus

AN EARTHQUAKE OF GUILT RUMBLES through my spine sending shockwaves down my neurotransmitters each time I make hummus. Memories of eating it at Abu Shunshi's in the old city of Jerusalem tremor forth. I see a reflection of middle-aged men sweating on top of shallow circular plastic buckets filled with chickpeas. The legume is about to be mashed by hand in lemon juice, olive oil and tahini sauce with a vigor to rival any seismic activity.

A black and white framed picture of the family's patriarch is yellowing under the strain of exposure to kitchen steam. That must be Mr. Abu Shunshi himself. He stares down on his descendants, looking assured —the family recipe is handed down father to son without the corrupting influence of innovation. At Abu Shunshi's, only men are allowed to make hummus. The Shunshi women contribute by chopping hot chilli peppers and onions—presented as an appetizer. Hairy Palestinian men making beige mush by application of physical force without the aid of modern technology. All together very sexy. It is said that prostitution is the oldest trade in human history. If you are lucky enough to taste Abu Shunshi's hummus you will forget facts and swear upon your honor that hummus-making is the older yet.

In my kitchen in Vancouver, hummus erupts out of a food processor, lacking the advantage of heritage. No ancient spirit guides my hand as I press the pulse button.

It began four years ago. Samih and I were drinking our morning coffee, exchanging a sweet nothing conversation. An easy relaxed feeling hung in the air.

"Yesterday was our annual corporate meeting," said Samih. "During the lunch break, Derek, our corporate sales rep to the Middle East, said that he had travelled all over the Arab world sampling every fine food and delicacy the region has to offer, but the best hummus he ever had was—"

I interrupted Samih, certain I knew the answer. "Abu Shunshi's in Jerusalem!"

"No," Samih smiled.

"I know, I know! Abu Fankooshi's in the old city." This had been Samih's favorite joint when we lived in Jerusalem.

Samih waved his hand and shook his head.

"That dinky old place in Ramalah with Arafat's picture on the wall."

"He said the best hummus he had, ever, in his whole entire life is the one that my wife makes."

I gasped in horror. Me? My hummus?

Samih beamed, brimming with pride, like he was directly touching greatness. Like he was that naked dude painted in the Sistine chapel, eternally pointing a reluctant finger, yet admired by millions for centuries.

How could a food processor compete with history and big burly men earnestly hunched over buckets of boiled chickpeas? It seemed obscene—no, downright blasphemous. The romantic side of me wants to believe in the sacredness of a bean from the holy lands.

How ruthless is reality.

At first, I felt a smoldering happiness. This was soon replaced with panic. *Oh No! What if my only accomplishment in life is that I made hummus exceptionally well?* I thought to myself. I always hoped that my claim to fame would be a poem. Even among dishes, if I could choose a recipe to be famous for, I would choose something sophisticated, not hummus. Wild duck in fasanjoon sauce comes to mind, a recipe that combines pomegranate juice, crushed walnuts and the seductive taste of saffron. That is a dish one can spend a lifetime perfecting. After 20 years of experimentation I would present it to the round table of family and friends, chest pumped with pride and say "Tada! Here it is, my prized creation! While you eat, I shall recite a poem I wrote." The tragic taste would meld eternally with the majesty of language, we would all cry collectively with beautiful anguish right into our food. The most human moment ever experienced. Hummus doesn't lend itself to this type of drama. What romance can you squeeze from a dip? A sense of foreshadowing came over me: such a pedestrian dish. *What is to become of me?* I took a deep breath, I shrugged and offered my hands to the sky. Oh well! You can't choose what you impress people with, better hummus than nothing.

It is very Middle-Eastern of me to submit to my destiny.

Which brings me to my first and most important rule of eating: "Food is like sex. When it's good, it's really good. And when it's bad, it's better than nothing."

And thus, my hummus acclaim grew. At party after party, people asked me to bring my famous dish. Praise followed with proclamations that included words such as "best", "ever" and "divine". I wrote down the recipe on napkins and scraps of paper when besieged. "It didn't turn out," I heard afterwards. "It wasn't as good as yours," came the response. Maria, from work, had the gall to accuse me of giving her the wrong recipe on purpose. "You don't want anybody else to have your title of Queen of Hummus!" she said while munching on a chicken breast at the office's year-end party. A pulsating bolt of icky feeling churned through my stomach upon hearing this. If only she knew how I wish my hummus reputation away. I promptly invited Maria to come over on a Saturday afternoon so that she could watch me make it live—to prove there are no hidden secrets in the making of it. Afterwards, I got so many requests for a live demonstration, that I recorded a video and uploaded it to YouTube. I sent people the link to the video instead of inviting them into my kitchen. I thought that would end the curiosity. I hoped that everybody would learn to make their own version and I would be left alone. My *How to make Hummus from Scratch* video has received 50,000 views to date and has gotten comments from as far away as Japan and as close as Seattle. Still there was no peace. "How do you get the consistency to be both liquid yet fluffy at the same time?" I was asked. "What magic do you conjure into the food?"

Just yesterday a patient shrieked with delight when I entered her room: "Oh My God! I can't believe it. Hummus lady!"

I was taken aback. "Excuse me?"

"You are hummus lady, in the video. You saved my marriage." The skinny young woman looked at me with awe as if I was a deity of some sort. This understuffed scarecrow told me that she had married an Egyptian. They had been fighting for months. Finally, he told her it was over and walked away. She accidentally found my video on YouTube and decided that instead of eating a tub of ice-cream, she would make a tub of hummus. When her husband came home to pick up his things, he encountered the plate of hummus. One taste led to another. His wife found him licking the plate clean. She sat down at the table without a word. Her husband began to cry. "This tastes exactly like the hummus I used get in the public market of Alexandria," he told her. They talked things over. Cried together. And decided to fight to stay together. Experts might tell you that a marriage should be based on respect and shared values. But if you listen to Thaniya Rasid, you would forgo all that and entrust your life partnership to a flatulence-inducing legume. I suppose marriages have been based on shakier ground. This must be the mushiest. "Why don't you make more videos?" asked the woman.

I shrugged. "I'm not sure cooking is my forte."

"Oh it is, it is, there is magic in these hands!" She grabbed both my hands as if rubbing invisible lotion into her own hands.

I wanted to tell her: "Leave your husband, he's an asshole." But instead, I grabbed her chart and focused on the medical task at hand. I could hear my stomach rumbling. I have been fasting for two weeks. Now I will have to fast for two more to atone for the sins I have committed against scarecrow woman. I wish I had the courage to apologize to her. Not about the needle prick. But for the wooden stake I unwittingly wedged into her life with my stupid hummus.

My weekly spinach pie in phyllo pastry has been winning loads of approval from the hospital staff. I am worried that pretty soon I will be called spinach pie lady. Which I suppose is better than being called hummus lady, but not by much. I wake up thinking about Zaev and go to sleep thinking about Zaev. Each time I see him the hallway I sigh uncontrollably. My medicine hasn't worked. This is a remedy that requires a long course. I am steadfast. Sooner or later fasting + marjoram + unbridled sex will kick in.

After a long contemplation, I think I understand why there is so much confusion about the making of hummus. It is a question of attitude. The secret key to hummus is not a recipe—you can look that up easily enough online. The unlocking mechanism is in the name. Hummus means chickpea in Arabic. We call both the legume and the dip hummus. The dip is supposed to taste like mashed chickpeas, plain and simple. In English, it sounds exotic and so people feel tempted to overdo. But if you call it mashed chickpeas, you will do right. The point is to let the chickpea have its say. Add as little as possible of everything else so that the chickpea taste is enhanced, but not disguised. The worst thing you can do is add too much garlic. If you have no garlic discipline then start by adding none. Proceed by adding a touch of tahini sauce, an inkling of lemon juice, a faint notion of olive oil and barely any cumin. Mash a single boiled bean between your thumb and index finger and stick it in your mouth. Taste the naked chickpea. That is what you are striving for—as naked as possible without obscenity. The rest is dressing your chickpea in a bikini.

I know what you are thinking: "This is a Middle-Eastern dish, I need to go for the niqab. I will cover it from head to toe in sauce and condiment so that no sight is seen." That is where you go wrong, ya habibi. We Arabs have a nuanced sense of humor. Blink and you will miss that you are at the epicenter of grand comedy. We present piety. If you knew what goes on in the privacy of our lives, you would curse the day a non-Arab womb expelled you into the world. For we are the original party people, we just forgot to invite the rest of the world. Think about the area between your beltline and 5 inches above your knees, go for 18A not Disney: now you are hummus-ready.

The second secret of hummus greatness is not caring. The more you care the worse it comes out. Slap it together like you don't give a damn. This is not a passionate affair of the heart. This is a drive-by fling. To the point, satisfying, in a long series of indistinguishable ones just like it. Wham! Bam! Done!

Keep love out of your food processor. A chickpea can sense affection; it turns bitter at the slightest touch of tenderness. Soak, boil and mash ruthlessly, like a savage. Stun the hummus into submission. You too can be the Queen of Hummus. Make sure to rule that land heartlessly. Saddam would have been the best hummus maker in the world.

How we Iraqis waste our talents ... eh?

Eggplant

IN THE KITCHEN, I DON'T follow a recipe. I open the fridge and examine treasure among the shelves. I can imagine a red pepper roasting into a pasty amber; garlic frying up into an aroma; olive oil pregnant with history. Oh look! There is an eggplant in my fridge. Is there anything more alluring than discovering an unexpected eggplant? *Dinner will be good tonight*, I smile, as I contemplate the curve of my surprise vegetable.

"What is your recipe?" I dread the question. If you only knew how I cook you would be appalled. My recipe is that I have no recipe. It sounds philosophical or romantic. Try to keep those notions at the door. It means cut fingers, burned forearms, messes, accidents, unpredictable results. Learning the hardest way there is to learn. Do you even know what it's like to be walking around your neighborhood minding your own business only to have a cauliflower wink at you? *Take me home, undress me, boil me and pour béchamel sauce all over my naked limbs...*

Have you asked a tuna steak if it's happy in the frying pan?

I can't teach you this madness. It comes with no guidebook. Mushrooms and cream sauce go together. How do I know? Because I tried the Rubic's cube of possibilities and I know. I didn't trust the experts. I trusted my taste buds with mushrooms and boiled potato, mushrooms and red beans, mushrooms in tomato sauce, mushrooms and broccoli, mushroom and ... . This process is exhausting. There are far easier paths to success, but none of them satisfy me.

Have you ever squished a chickpea between two fingers while whispering: "This is for your own good, darling"?

Taste and smell are the obvious. There are other delights that I can't paint with words. The sensation of dough oozing between the fingers is yet to be described properly. The bitter secrets that a rice pudding revealed to me one late evening—a confidence I shall never betray. The pistachio that got away. What is that? Oh hush ... don't mention chocolate. I am already strained keeping this PG13.

Have you ever met a macaroni that wasn't yearning for a cheese sauce bath? Please do tell; I am conducting a study.

My youthful hunger is replaced with an old satisfaction with the simplest techniques. A blanched asparagus is the queen of the castle that needs no king, yet chooses of her own free will to sit quietly next to the fetching barbequed steak. Will they find a common language? The intrigue is killing me. Will she be appalled when he spills his bloody medium rare juice? Should she smother herself with melted butter? I have to dash off with great urgency. A situation is brewing.

The best way to cook is to stop cooking. Sit back and let the food cook you.

Psssssst!

You are yummy.

Onion

MY YEARS OF OBSERVING DOCTORS in training and others in the throes of their medical practice has led me to conclude that all who get the title Dr. attached to their names are nursing a loose spring or two inside their heads. A physician's mind is a finely tuned clock mechanism that must tick with robotic discipline. Human vulnerability gets squeezed out one area. The juice migrates across membrane, plasma and cell tissue to get concentrated in less disciplined spaces in the psyche. Every doctor is a walking, talking metaphor for the world refugee crisis. They are all, as a matter of necessity, smart and hardworking, yet each one is airy fairy in one way or another.

Nobody exemplifies this paradox more that my friend Don. Don is a 50-year-old surgeon who wants to become a painter when he grows up. I passed him in the corridor on my first day at Memorial. He paused, pointed a finger at me and shouted" Hey, you! What's your name?" I was startled. I paused, afraid I was about to get into trouble for an unnamed offence the nature of which I hadn't discovered yet. I grabbed hold of my official Memorial picture ID hanging off my lapel, pointed at it to indicate that I was entitled to breathe the same air as him and said:

"I am Thaniya Rasid. Phlebotomist."

"Nice to meet you." He extended his hand to shake mine. "I am Dr. Nikmailean."

Hesitantly I extended my hand towards his. Most doctors don't bother acknowledging a lowly technician like myself unless necessity forces their hand, but Don made an effort to speak to me whenever he passed me in the hallway. With the rumbling speed of thunder, I discovered the off-putting mannerisms for which he is wildly famous. Not only does he shout as if angry when he means to explain, but Don also loves to point out the flaws in each person he meets. It is as if he is possessed to push everybody's button in an endless quest to measure their thermometer for taking offence. He told Maria she was too fat, advising her to lose at least 20 pounds. He proceeded to jot down a dietary regimen on his prescription pad, tore the page out with great fanfare, and handed her the paper with a stern admonition: "All health care professionals need to role model health and vitality to our patients. This is not just a job. This is a calling." His advice is always unsolicited. It comes without warning.

Boom!

In your *Face*!

Ejected out of your delusion balloon.

You suck!

Maria cried for a whole hour after that. I sat on my favorite chair in the nursing lounge by her side, handing her one Kleenex after the other, assuring her that she looked fine. The wheels on my chair squealed each time I rolled myself towards the tissue dispenser hanging on the wall and back. It sounded like the cry of an eagle about to claim its prey.

Time for a pep talk. "People like that disparage others to make themselves feel good," I said. It was true. He had told Leigh she mumbles her speech and should get therapy for her impediment. Leigh became self-conscious about her speaking manner for a whole year. She now communicates in monosyllabic words and mimes grandiose gestures to hide behind. He is abrasive to both patients and colleagues alike. Most have learned to avoid him after a first encounter. He told me I was 10 pounds overweight. Unlike Maria, I didn't receive a prescription for my condition. When his pronouncement didn't provoke much reaction, he told me that my intellect was starved for stimulation. His newest jibe is to tell me that my marriage is teetering on the verge of collapse behind a thin veneer of happiness. I shrug my shoulders at each one of his insights. *How can he possibly know anything about my private life given how little he knows me?* I tell myself. Don claims that he can look and simply tell what is ailing a person. Not just physically, but also emotionally. "Telling truth to their face hurts them initially, but it helps them in the long run," he is fond of saying.

Don is like an onion. Abrasive. Offensive. Causes people to cry. I suspect underneath all those layers is a softy. Perhaps there is a recipe to cook this unique doctor and turn him into a civilized ingredient in the stew of society.

Perhaps it is the challenge of attempting to insult me that keeps him interested. I can't think of any other reason for his attention. A certain friendship has developed between us. Over time we have developed a habit: he talks, I listen. This is an act of submission on my part. I tried to engage in conversation with him, but every-time he would interrupt and commandeer the airwaves. So now I drop in the odd word or short sentence, but let him do all the verbalizing. That way there is nothing to criticize.

He confided in me that deep down his heart's desire is to become an artist. He pursued medicine because he got married and desired a family. He didn't think he could support two daughters using artwork. He turned his basement into an art studio. Now that his two daughters are grown, he spends his spare time in there, painting away. His wife, Janine, hates his paintings. Or rather resents the time he spends in the studio with his painting instead of her. Janine has refused to look at his artwork, instead expressing wishes to enter his studio with a blow torch.

"My wife doesn't understand me," Don said while drinking coffee with me one afternoon during a break. "You are the only person I discuss art with," he continued. "The other doctors would just scoff at me, all they understand is biology."

This made me feel special. I mattered to somebody outside of the bounds of family duties. Don is the first person I told about my poetry attempts. Don widened his eyes and said: "I knew there was something special about you, the minute I saw you." I felt flattered for five minutes. Until I realized that he didn't ask to see my creative output. I decided to take a tentative step. *Be proactive,* I told myself. I asked him if I could see some of his paintings. Don was silent for a while, which made me regret my request. He rolled his eyes to the left, then rolled his eyes to the right, as if he was a spy checking the counter-intelligence. He looked at me with a sinister smile. "I have never showed my paintings to anybody, not even my family," he whispered. "You will be my first audience."

So we agreed that I would come over to his basement at 10 o'clock on a Sunday morning. He gave me detailed instructions of how to drive to his house. "Don't ring the bell," he said in a panic. "I don't want Janine to know that I am showing my work to somebody. Park one block away, go around the south side of the house, walk into the basement without knocking. I will leave the door open for you. My wife will be in the kitchen eating breakfast and watching TV. She won't suspect a thing."

When I told Samih about my plans for Sunday morning, he was apprehensive about the idea. He insisted on coming with me. I spent nearly an hour putting his mind at ease. "Don has never showed his paintings to anybody, this is like a secret. He is already spooked about this showing. If you come with me, it will be a betrayal of trust. I need to be respectful towards his sensitivity."

But Samih kept acting the part of the jealous husband.

"There is nothing romantic going on between Don and me, he constantly tells me that I am fat, dense and clueless. I myself find him unbearable," I assured Samih.

"Then why are you friends with him?" Samih stood before me, his arms crossed.

"I don't know, I just am," I said. "I'm going there on my own, and you have to deal with it."

I suspect I enjoy playing the role of Don's unique un-insultable friend. Or perhaps I just feel special because I am the only one who knows his secret. Either way, my acquaintance with Don is of a puzzling value to me.

Samih was stewing with anger when I left home at 9:30 to drive to Don's house. He was sitting at the dining table banging into his laptop keyboard. Seeing Samih jealous made me feel happy. I realized for the first time that I had this power over him I hadn't known about.

I arrived at Don's house at exactly 10 and quietly walked through the side door into his basement as instructed. There I found him sitting on a leather chair with eyes closed, breathing deeply. His face was contorted. "Hello!" I whispered.

"Oh! You came. I hoped you would cancel at the last minute." His voice wavered as if he was playing tremolo on a violin.

I pretended to be cheerful to assure him when in truth my stomach was rumbling with anxiety.

There were about fifty paintings, all of them stacked and leaning against the wall. Each one faced inward so that you couldn't see what was painted on them. Don got up and turned one around so that I could see it.

"This one is blue," he said, as if I was color blind.

It was a close up of his face. His big nose. His wrinkles exaggerated to show him grimacing.

"This one is orange." Another close up of his face in profile, his lips curled up as if he was smelling a rotten tomato.

"Oh, and this purple one." Have mercy on me. A close-up of Don's face from below. Strands of hair dangling in his face made it look tragically romantic.

I sat down on the leather chair where Don had been sitting earlier and patiently endured the process of Don showing me each one of his creations individually.

You probably guessed it. Every single one was a close-up of his face painted in oil, displaying a different layer of emotional distress.

It was hideous, overwhelming, every bit like Don: obnoxious, loud, narcissistic, self-indulgent, overly dramatic, dreadful in all imaginable ways and unimaginable ways as well. If there is such a place as art's horror shop, I was sitting right in the middle of it. I felt like a squeezed-out lemon. All my juice was gone. Pith and bitterness were all that remained.

Silence charged the room with a high frequency electrical current. I looked at Don's face and saw panic.

I took a deep breath and lied through my teeth. "These are brilliant!" My voice was calm and measured, but my heart was racing like a crazy chicken. I remembered my visit to Scotland. That salted caramel cookie. That word that had dropped from heaven into my head. Authentic, no more. I am too ashamed to tell you what I said next. I heaped praise on his head the way a dung beetle rolls a piece of shit. Most diligently.

When I arrived at home at noon, I found Samih waiting for me in the kitchen, fidgeting. I had to confess everything to him.

Samih laughed and laughed as I described the experience. He was so happy hearing about Don's horrid paintings he failed to notice that I was shaking with distress like poked jello. I could taste Scottish blood pudding on my tongue. Oh the salty red taste of violence. Such dread.

Janine knew her husband well. She was right to refuse to indulge his creative fantasy. I, the dumb naïve younger woman, rushed into the trap instead. Next time a middle-aged man complains to you that his wife doesn't understand him, know that his wife understands him perfectly well. For she had looked into the bottomless pit of his darkness and decided to look no more. She is done with stroking his fragile male ego.

Now there are two women who wish to enter Don's basement with a blowtorch.

Cucumber

"TRUST YOUR TASTE BUDS, they always tell the truth," is the seventh rule of eating. This one comes with a whimsical little story.

I have no memory of eating a cucumber until I was 23 years of age. I do remember rejecting them; picking them out of my salad and spitting out the green shreds that accidentally wiggled their way into my mouth. "I don't eat cucumbers" was part of my identity, my uniqueness. A thing that those who knew me well could wave as a flag of familiarity. Layal always made a small salad with no cucumbers just for me. It made me feel special. Amal, my sister-in-law, would serve salad on my plate and then point her thick index finger at each piece as if marking a land mine. "I tried to avoid them," she said, "but you have one here, here and here." My mother absent-mindedly picked them off my plate and onto hers without interruption as she told the rest of the family about a shopping escapade. My father made super sure to order a special shawarma sandwich, cucumber free, just for me. The warm sandwich would arrive wrapped in paper with my name marked on the outer rim, declaring to all that my shawarma wrap was different than the rest.

Samih simply stopped using cucumbers in salads when he married me. He compensated by eating a whole cucumber every two or three days. He would fish a whole one out of the fridge, and with an elegant swoop the green torpedo would be submerged under a sprinkle of water in the sink and fly into his mouth. The crackling crunch would reverberate in our one-bedroom apartment. Crunch, crunch, CRUNCH! Samih is a loud eater. I love him for it. He is not afraid to vocalize his mastication as if making a speech. I wish I could be more like him in that regard, but my upbringing in a particular social class prevents me from materializing this secret urge. Another wife would have found this embarrassing or annoying; not me. Samih sometimes hums nonsensical songs while he eats.

Mmmmmmmmmmmmmmmm.

hum hum hum hum hummmmm.

boom bum boom bum braboom.

brim brim brim brim brimemememeeeeeee.

A soundtrack to his eating experience. I should videotape him one day and put it on YouTube—who knows, maybe it would go viral. However, this thing he does is so adorable I want to keep it to myself. I never mentioned to him how much I enjoy watching him eat because I don't want him to feel self-conscious about it. I can always tell when Samih doesn't like his food—it's when he eats quietly.

It was a sunny summer evening and I was 23. I was sitting in our Ikea-furnished dining den listening to the reverberating crunch, crunch, crunch of my husband eating a cucumber, when he surprised me with a question.

"How come you never eat cucumbers?"

Oddly enough, I had never been asked that question.

"I don't like them," I answered.

"But they are soooooooooo good. Have you ever tasted one?"

This question stumped me. I paused to think. I squeezed my brain, attempting to remember tasting a cucumber for the first time. Nothing came up. Not one single memory. A flood of experiences with the slimy green one got projected across my imagination, but not a single one of them included ingestion.

And so I told Samih the truth, like I always do.

"I don't know, I don't remember eating one, I only remember that I don't like them."

Samih broke off the tip of his half-eaten cucumber and handed me a wet wedge. "Here! Try this." He was casual in his manner. Like it was a small thing. If he only knew he was asking me to shed a layer of my identity!

This monumental step in my evolution came back to me as I was discussing gay rights in the Middle East with Shatha two days ago. My sweet dumpling felt confused because her cousin Faris in Lazzazza posted a homophobic statement on Facebook. I was driving her to a kids' birthday party. The car has proven to be the ideal setting for intimate mother-daughter talks.

"Don't judge Faris too harshly," I said. "He's surrounded with an environment where this is the normal mode of thinking. He hasn't had the chance to have his thinking challenged with alternative views."

Shatha looked unconvinced.

"Even I used to think like Faris when I was his age."

Shatha widened her eyes. "How did you change your mind, Mom?"

"A gay man saved my life when I was 16." I was taking a left turn. My focus was on the incoming traffic. I wish I had seen Shatha's expression. But being a responsible driver meant that I had to keep my eyeballs on the road. I did hear a faint inhale, however.

"Tell me the story," said Shatha.

"Oh it's a silly story." I had managed to take advantage of a gap in the traffic flow and squeaked through towards my destination. We were minutes from her friend's house.

"Come on, Mom!" Shatha insisted.

"Maybe later. You don't want to be late for the party." In truth, I was eager to return home to get started on the laundry that had been piling up.

"Please, please, please!" Shatha is an expert at making adorable faces. Saying no to her is an ordeal.

"Alright." I parked the car one block away from her friend's house.

"I was walking down Al-Mutanabi street in Baghdad with the complete volume of Garcia Lorca's works translated into Arabic held against my heart. I was looking up at the sky, marvelling at the cloud formations. The clouds seemed to be descending. I had the feeling that a particular one would land on my head and then proceed to envelop me from head to toe. I was imagining myself getting abducted by the cloud and delivered to a faraway land."

"Mom. The story. We don't have all day."

"Okay, okay. So a shoot-out erupted nearby. I was hit by a stray bullet."

"No way!" Shatha looked impressed.

I nodded. "Yes way. I heard afterwards that it was an assassination attempt against Saddam's second son, which was foiled by his bodyguards. So there I was lying on the pavement, with a crowd of people standing over me. A woman poured water over my face. People kept asking 'Are you hurt? Are you hurt?' They helped me stand back up, the thick volume was still in my left hand. There was a smoldering hole smack in the middle of my book! That book of poetry had caught the stray bullet, saving my life."

"And?" Shatha frowned. "Then what happened?"

"That's all. End of story." I shrugged my shoulders. There was nothing else to say.

"But what about the gay man that saved your life?" Shatha pointed both index fingers up in the air, an Arabic way of asking god to be your witness. I wondered where she had picked up that gesture. I hadn't seen it for ages.

"Garcia Lorca, the poet, was gay," I said. "After that I vowed to read everything he had ever written. His words challenged my perspective about many things. Including my ideas about gender roles." A sense of unease trembled in my heart. There is nothing worse than telling a story and having to explain its meaning. I had failed most miserably in my storyteller role.

"But that's a boring story," said Shatha, sighing in disappointment. I suppose she was expecting a superhero to make an appearance.

"It's the one that I have." I sighed as well, feeling a sense of disappointment of a different kind.

I had a flashback, then, to the moment when, with Samih, I had let cucumbers into my life.

I had hesitated, contemplating my cucumber-hating specialness. I was about to forgo all those kind acts of consideration. They would no longer be required If it turned out that I liked cucumbers after all. I had looked into the black suggestive eyes of Samih as he was looking back at me, casually anticipating my next move. I had taken the smallest bite and tentatively chewed. To my surprise it wasn't vile. It didn't remind me of a volcano destroying the city of Pompeii. It bore no resemblance to death, tragic ending or disease. It reminded me of a spring's breeze. Of Stravinsky's funky music. Of the way you tell a joke and begin to laugh at it before you finish telling it and me laughing at your laugh even though I don't get the joke.

I had been overcome with a bout of deep thinking to excavate the origins of my cucumber-hating ways, and realized that throughout my childhood my mother had convinced me that I disliked cucumbers. Always picking them out of my food, repeating over and over: "You don't like those, give them to me."

When I questioned my mother about it, later, she told me how when I was one year of age, tasting solids for the first time, she had placed a cucumber slice in my mouth and I had spat it out, scrunching my face in disgust. And from then on, she made sure no cucumber entered my mouth. My mother's love had gone into overdrive.

In essence, I was brainwashed to believe that I hated cucumbers by my mother. From then on, I resolved to trust my own taste buds exclusively. Emotions and sentimentality can sway a person this way or that way. Question everything. Be that annoying person who asks "Why?" Better yet, ask "Why not?" Reality is the prison of those who lack imagination.

Love is the secret ingredient best left out of any recipe.

Trifle

WHO WOULD CHOOSE TO BE AN IRAQI? I can't think of a single reason that would lead anybody to make such an ill-advised selection. It is the worst nationality in the world. There are 35 million of us in existence. Five million of us live abroad. The most dangerous place in the world for an Iraqi is inside Iraq. The second most dangerous place for an Iraqi is in the company of other Iraqis.

As a result of a long succession of wars, there is a huge hole in our population. If you meet an Iraqi man between the ages of 20 – 50, you are sighting a rare bird. You ought to feel blessed at such an unearthing. In these conditions of scarcity, an Iraqi woman's search for a husband is a high-action drama rather than a heart-warming rom-com. When you do finally meet an eligible bachelor who doesn't have an alcohol or drug problem, isn't so arrogant as to be in danger of turning you into a murderess, and isn't so traumatized by war as to render his soul uninhabitable by a joyful notion, then there are already five other women chasing after him. You need to roll up your sleeves and fight for his male attention.

Poor Iraqi men! When they are not dodging bombs, they are haunted by the spectre of an army of bridezillas. Some Iraqi women, such as myself, avoid the whole circus and marry from a different Arabic nationality. We take a chance on being called unpatriotic. "Iraqi woman always stands by her Iraqi man," I have heard said. "Only an Iraqi man can make an Iraqi woman happy," others commented when they discovered Samih's nationality. I argued that it is the heart of patriotism to seek matrimony elsewhere. "Give the poor Iraqi man a break!" I say. "He has enough intolerable burdens to deal with as is, why should he deal with the impossible task of making me happy?"

I don't understand the source of the Arab's fascination with the practice of western medicine, but at age 18 I knew that my path towards parental approval passed through the School of Medicine at the University of British Columbia. I enrolled in first year studies at the department of Biology with fantasies that involved a white coat and a stethoscope. In Vancouver, I met Uncle Abu Rafid, my father's oldest and dearest childhood friend who had immigrated to Canada in the seventies. Not-so-subtle hints were dropped within my earshot that I would do well in life if I managed to snag Rafid, Uncle Abu Rafid's eldest son, as my husband. Two old friends conspiring behind their offspring's back to become in-laws.

Abu Rafid and Um Rafid invited me over for dinner just four days after my arrival in the beautiful city of Vancouver. I went to their lavishly furnished house on top of a hill, eager to leave a positive impression on a group of people I had never met before. All I had as my guide was a collection of stories my father had told me of a shared youth with somebody he frequently argued with, but also loved. The door opened, letting the chatter of fifteen people waft into the front lawn garden. I was ferried around by Um Rafid and introduced to the bedecked and bejewelled guests. I was introduced to Um and Abu Gazi accompanied by their daughter Zaina, Um and Abu Jaafar accompanied their daughter Farah, Um Falah with her daughter Warda, and finally Um and Abu Majeed with their daughter Hiyam. It suddenly dawned on me that this was a potential bride pageant. Everybody looked stylish and sophisticated. Tongue-tied, I felt out of place. I had arrived to the competition unprepared. I had no crown acceptance speech ready. And no plans for how to create peace in the Middle East. Abu Rafid greeted me with a smile and a handshake. "I am so happy to meet you!" he said. I took an immediate liking to him. Um Rafid seated me on a plush upholstered seat in the living room, saying: "So happy to meet you at last, I have heard so much about your father."

Fayaiq, Rafid's younger brother, came downstairs to greet the guests. I had been warned by my father to stay away from him. He had a reputation for being a Porsche-crashing playboy who didn't inspire high expectations in the department of accomplishments. Fayaiq shook my hand unenthusiastically, as his brother made his way down the stairs. The room erupted with a cheer. "Oh Rafid, there you are!" Um Majeed shouted. "At last we get to see this beautiful face!" Um Jaafar exclaimed. "You are a flower, a fresh flower." There was no need to guess who the star of this family was. Um Rafid's eyes filled with pride as she observed him making his way around the living room. Fayaiq's face darkened. He sighed, as if to say: "I won't waste your time, now that he's here you won't want to talk to me anyway," but instead he pointed his finger: "That's my brother, you will get to meet him soon." I wish I had found a subtle way of saying that I would like to talk to him as well, but instead I nodded and observed the flourished fanfare Rafid displayed as he received each person. I was the very last person he greeted. As if he was deliberately avoiding me.

"Hello, pleasure to meet you." I was disappointed to hear him speak in English. I replied in Arabic: "It is a pleasure to meet you as well."

Rafid paused and then switched to Arabic. "Affirmative. It has been my forefather, who has furnished me with voluminous tales about her, which is your forefather. It is now that I see, I feel knowledge for her family even though your face I only see now." His Arabic was a code red disaster zone. He had inverted the feminine with masculine pronoun, his accent was terrible, his diction most ridiculous. In that first ten seconds of meeting him I realized that I could never share a life with somebody who spoke so poorly. If this had been a comedy show, a fifth grader would be peeing himself laughing right now. I had given him a test and he had failed in the most spectacular manner possible.

Rafid was slim, tall, clean-shaven, dark and handsome, stylishly dressed in a sky-blue cotton shirt and black slacks. Everybody in the room was clamoring to grab his attention. He sat confidently on a chair in the middle of the living room, gesturing elegantly with his index finger when he spoke. He listened attentively when spoken to, placing the fingers of his hand gently against his cheek. He was altogether the prince of any young woman's dream. Except when he addressed me; then his atrocious Arabic had turned him into a Shrek-like green ogre.

Um Rafid announced that dinner was ready. We all made our way to dining table. Again, Um Rafid directed me to be seated at a particular chair. I was directly opposite Rafid. I didn't know if this was a sign that I was the favorite in the running, or if this was a sign of sympathy since I was the only one without an accompanying parent and a recent immigrant to boot. "Fresh off the boat," as they say. The dining table was set with fine china and covered with delicacies. Roasted red snapper, rice covered with nuts, fried onions and raisins, stuffed cabbage leaves, baba ganoush, white bean tomato stew, kufta, taboula and pickles. Mercifully, Rafid switched to speaking in English exclusively. All the young people sitting around the table spoke English since they had grown up in Canada. Switching back and forth between the two languages would have been a game of tedious ping-pong. I was at a great disadvantage, however, since my English was as poor as a humble mouse in a pauper's house. But I was relieved to not have to endure hearing my beloved language butchered.

Rafid seemed impressed when I told him that I planned to become a doctor: "There are two things I can't stand in a woman," he said, putting his fork down. "A silly girl who cares about nothing except fashion and makeup, and an idealist who wants to save the world or the environment without regard to economics." I was neither, but I didn't like the implication that I was being evaluated. I wished in that moment I could declare: "There are two things I can't stand in a man: arrogance and ignorance. Especially ignorance of one's mother tongue." I smiled demurely instead, keeping my thoughts to myself.

After dinner, we moved back to the living room. Rafid raised both his hands into the air to make an announcement. "I have a surprise for everybody. I made the dessert today. I made a trifle." Praise was lavished on Rafid as everybody ate the soggy treat.

"Rafid, you are so talented!" Said Um Jaafar.

"This is so delicious!" Said Zaina.

"I need to know the recipe!" Said Um Gazi.

"Mom! Please get the recipe as well," Said Warda.

"I love this!" Said Um Falah.

"This is the best dessert I ever had!" said Hiyam.

"Rafid, where did you learn to cook?" asked Majeed

Um Rafid got fed up with my silence as I pushed dollops of goo around my plate. "Thaniya! What do you think of the trifle?" she shouted from across the room.

The question caught me by surprise. "Ha!" I snorted.

There was an awkward silence. "Oh, it's very good. God bless your hand ... Rafid."

Before I continue to tell you what happened next, please keep in mind I was only 18, naïve, immature and very stupid. So please judge me through that lens.

The next morning, I got a phone call from my father. He wanted to know what I thought of Rafid.

"He doesn't speak Arabic," I said into the phone.

"Yes he does." My father was undeterred.

"His Arabic is so mangled, he would do the world a favor by not speaking it." I was waving my hands around even though there was nobody to witness the theatrics except me.

"What do you expect? He grew up in Canada!" Then he softened his tone. "It's impressive that he tries to speak it at all."

"I can't live with somebody I can't talk with," I said.

"You can always teach him, after you get married." My poor father was trying so hard to get me to be reasonable.

"I want to live with somebody I can look up to. How can I respect somebody I am teaching how to speak?" I chuckled at the end, as if my father was proposing the most ridiculous notion. As if he was asking me to turn my skin green, embodying an iguana in the process. Or becoming an ogress myself.

"He would be teaching you how to speak English as well, you know."

"I still couldn't marry him." I breathed out the words in a whisper. Like a faintly audible prayer.

"But why not?" The question was curt.

Here I paused, trying to think of any excuse that would pop into my head. My father had arranged for me to meet the most eligible Iraqi bachelor in all of Vancouver. Rafid was finishing up a master's degree in finance and preparing to launch himself into the professional life of a banker. He was handsome, intelligent, sophisticated, from a well-off family and rooted in this foreign country with its alien customs I had yet to learn to navigate. In truth, Rafid was the prince charming of any Iraqi self-fashioned Cinderella dream. I had to come up with a powerful reason for rejecting him.

"He's gay." The words rolled off my tongue before getting checked by my brain.

"What? Of course he's not!" I could hear the shock over the phone connection.

"I'm sure he's gay," I said, trying to convince myself more than anything.

"Based on what?"

"Last night he made a trifle," I said, pronouncing each word deliberately, as if describing a crime scene.

"A man who knows how to cook. That's fantastic!" My father's voice was light and buoyant. This would turn out well!

"What sort of a man makes a trifle? He must be gay." I was hoping that if I repeated the word gay enough times it would end the discussion.

"Not all men have to be useless in the kitchen like your father. What did you expect him to make?" My father was not going to give up easily on his dream son-in-law.

"I don't know. Something manly."

"Like what?"

"Couldn't he have burned a steak or destroyed a burger instead?"

"Darling, you are being close-minded," my father said. "You're judging him based on superficial criteria." When all else fails, appeal to logic.

"I will not spend the rest of my life with a gay man who won't even appreciate Abd Al Haleem! Find me a gay husband who speaks passable Arabic at least." I was supressing a desire to laugh.

"I will be tearing my hair out because I can't believe how superficial my daughter is," my father said, his resignation coming clearly across the phone line.

So here I was, inventing my own drama to avoid the drama of hunting for an Iraqi husband.

Rafid didn't display much interest in me either. Whenever we met at his parents' house, he was polite but not enthusiastic. To him I seemed too Middle-Eastern, provincial, unaccustomed to western ways, and backwards; plus my English was a sad state of affairs. I wonder what discussions he had with his father about me.

Now that I know how to cook, I understand why he made trifle. Trifle is easy to make. It requires no culinary skills. You layer cake with syrup, fruit, custard and whipping cream. It doesn't even matter how you layer it, it all works out in the end. He had made an effort to impress a bunch of young women based on his western sensibilities. He didn't realize that a Middle-Eastern young woman who grew up in the desert doesn't dream of a whipping cream love story but rather a fire-seared steak marriage.

So that was my closest chance to live out the Iraqi version of Pride and Prejudice. Instead I chose the drama-less option. Although, truth be told, I did have to invent a bit of drama to escape it. I can look back and laugh about my own silliness the same way I was laughing internally when I introduced Gillian to Don at a party two months ago. It was an opening reception for an art exhibit for an artist Don admires. He insisted that I come to see this new and upcoming trailblazer. Samih is not into art, and so I asked Gillian to come with me. I wore a dark green dress and high heels. Gillian was wearing a black skirt with colorful embroidery spilling down her right side. I arranged to pick her up on my way over. We arrived 15 minutes late. There were only a few other people in the art gallery. Don was standing in a corner holding a Pepsi and talking to the star of the evening. I could overhear him saying: "The use of humor in your artwork makes it seem as if you are not certain of yourself." The thirty-something young man was forcing a smile and nodding his head, pretending to appreciate the unsolicited feedback. When Don caught sight of me, he excused himself and walked over. The young man looked relieved.

"Thaniya, you came!" Don looked happy to see me. I introduced him to Gillian and they both proceeded to discuss their opinion of the art displayed on the walls.

"This looks so simplistic, a child could have painted it." Gillian said.

"That shows how little you know about art!" his retort was immediate.

"What do you mean?"

"The simplicity is deceptive, said Don. "I'm willing to bet you couldn't paint this, not even with enormous effort."

"Oh please," Gillian said, sniffing. "Anybody can draw stick figures."

"True. But can you draw a stick figure that expresses the depth of human anguish?"

Gillian pointed. "Look at this painting."

Don looked. "Yes?"

"Don't tell me this is expressing depth of any sort?"

"Seriously? Clearly you don't possess the soul of an artist," said Don. "People like you should be banished from artistic venues."

"What about Thaniya?" asked Gillian. "Are you going to banish Thaniya, as well?"

"Thaniya is different! She's a poet. Poets are the most sensitive of souls."

Gillian looked at me, appraising. "Since when has Thaniya been a poet?"

"Since childhood. She has a hard drive full of her poetry."

Gillian's eyes widened. "Is that true?"

I was burning red. "Yes, I write poetry, but it's really bad poetry and so I haven't shown it to anybody."

"Well you obviously showed it to him!"

"I have a sensitive artist soul," said Don. "There's a meeting of minds between us. Something you wouldn't understand."

"I understand Thaniya better than anybody," said Gillian, her voice rising.

"You understand Thaniya the same way you understand art!" Now Don was getting riled up. "Like a blind man looking at *Playboy*!"

"Oh yeah? And what do you do professionally?" asked Gillian.

"I'm a doctor. And you?"

"I'm a prison guard."

Don snorted sarcastically. "That figures."

"What is that supposed to mean?"

"You keep people in jail cells at work, and so in your personal life you feel compelled to place everybody you meet into a pigeonhole."

Gillian looked like she was going to deck him. "You're the most unbearable person I have ever met."

"Unbearable, because I am telling you the truth! That's always painful to hear."

"I feel sorry for Thaniya who has to deal with you at work," Gillian said, looking at me. I cringed.

"I think refined, sensitive Thaniya is friends with you because she feels sympathy for your soulless state."

On our way home, Gillian fumed the whole way, insulting Don with every expletive in the dictionary and a few invented ones that have not yet been documented. Then she turned her wrath against me. She was angry at me for not telling her that I secretly wrote poetry. She insisted that I had to show her my poems or else our friendship was over.

As soon as I got home, Don called me on my cell phone to tell me what a bad choice I had made with my friend. "I can't believe that you are friends with this lifeless wooden baton that calls itself human," he said, rather poetically. "How come you have never showed me any of your poems?"

"You never asked to see them."

"Of course I want to see them! Send me your best ten by Monday. Pronto."

And that is how I gained my first audience for my creative work. Layers of syrupy art appreciation mingled with fluffy ego. But hey! I wasn't complaining. It was time to take it to the next level.

It is one of the great ironies of fate that I escaped the clutch of the arranged marriage. Yet, my strong-willed rebellious sister Layal fell victim to the caprice of family-planned matrimony.

Brain

THREE NIGHTS AGO, Samih hosted his annual departmental get-together. He is the only sales executive at his company who hosts the whole department at his house. Samih says that it creates a positive vibe in the office and increases his profile in the company. "Plus, it would be a shame to be married to such a talented cook and not show her off. I am the envy of all my colleagues." Samih looks at me with those black-ink eyes, enchanting me into a spasm of rapture. The truth is, I enjoy the challenge of the single-handed labor of preparing dinner for 40-plus people. It requires planning, skill and imagination. For a single day I raise myself to the status of an Arab Super Woman. People marvel at my ability.

"I can't believe you cooked all this yourself!"

"You must have worked for days."

"Every single thing tastes divine!"

"I have been looking forwards to this all week."

"I never felt so full my whole entire life!"

Where superwoman can lift buildings, fight crime and look sexy in spandex, I, Arab Super Woman, uplift taste buds, fight racism and islamophobia, all the while acting the gracious hostess. This year, it was even more of a feat since I was fasting. To complete the effect, I wore my red stretchy dress with white pearls. All I was missing was a blue cape and a large letter A cross-stitched on my chest to complete the picture.

Sheryl, the wife of the southeastern US sales rep, sat down on a chair across from Shatha, eyeing the breaded cauliflower on her plate. "I wonder what this is?" she finally asked.

Shatha said, with a bored look: "Fried brains."

"Fried brains?" Sheryl said carefully, trying to disguise her disgust.

"Yes it's a speciality of my mom's." This trickster side of Shatha is new to me. I have never noticed it before.

"Oh really?" Sheryl raised her eyebrows.

I waved my hand dismissively, squeezing in a fake chuckle and a severe look in Shatha's direction.

"It's just breaded cauliflower."

"Your daughter had me worried for a second," said Sheryl, with a fake smile.

"Actually, you could eat brains," I said, before thinking. "My grandmother did cook brains for us. Fried, with eggs and herbs." Usually I'm pretty good at policing my thoughts. But there are moments when the spirit of mango chutney possesses me. I hadn't eaten any amba in weeks, yet here I was. A verbal leakage problem can't be contained with a convenient sanitary pad.

"Really? I never heard of such a thing." She adopted the tone of a tourist on an exotic holiday. Constantly amazed, but secretly grateful to be going home in the near future.

I carried on. "In the old days people used every part of a slaughtered animal. Nothing went to waste. Nowadays they call it 'Nose to Tail' dining. My grandmother called it practicality."

"Interesting. What did it taste like?" Perhaps Sheryl was now falling in love with the indigenous culture of an exotic faraway land. Unaware that white-man guilt gets frequently confused with affection. Who can untangle that mess?

"It had a mild taste. Brains are kind of runny and soft. A bit more solid than eggs. It tasted good. Delicate and sweet." It was hard to find the right words to describe the unique taste. I hoped she wouldn't leave our house tonight with the impression that we were cannibals.

Sheryl braved a tentative bite of her cauliflower.

Shatha piped up. "Mom! Does eating brains make you smart?"

"I don't think so. If that was true zombies would be the smartest of fantasy creatures." I laughed, relieved to be talking about something silly.

"But maybe that's why zombies like to eat brains! They're hoping to evolve their intelligence."

"That's an interesting theory." It's my standard response when I have no idea what to say.

"Maybe that's why you're so smart. You used to eat brains when you were little." Shatha looked at me with bright, anticipating eyes.

"I'm glad you think me smart," I said, smiling. She really is such a lovely child.

"Why don't you ever make brains for us?" asked my little pet monkey.

"Both you and Zakiya refuse to eat liver, so I never felt encouraged to try brains," I answered, placing the ball squarely back into her court.

"This is very good, even though it looks like brains," said Sheryl. Now she sounded like she had returned back home, and had recovered from falling in love with the indigenous culture of the faraway exotic land. Grateful but hurting. Carrying within her unpacked luggage a niggling little feeling that there is a great universal wisdom out there she will never understand.

The next day I was bathing in the afterglow of a successful dinner party. I felt like a stage actress the day after opening night, about to read the reviews of her brilliant performance. I was sitting at the dining table inspecting the remains of the dirty dishes that needed to be washed. Samih was lazily drinking his morning coffee. A random idea popped into my head.,

"Hey! We should do a party like this for my coworkers at the hospital!"

"Why would you want to do that?" Samih asked.

"To spread good will at my workplace."

"Don't be silly, Thaniya, no matter how much goodwill you spread at the hospital you will never be promoted to doctor."

I was suddenly seized with a pang of pain that gripped my brain. I suppose you would call it a headache. It felt like the membrane of my brain was shrinking, squeezing out cells like sacrificial lambs. I was craving shakshuka for breakfast like nobody's business. All the stress of the day before came back and pressed against my chest. Plus I was fasting. Now I felt hungry.

I remember a day, not so long ago, when I was universally considered smart. I had such high expectations for myself. What had happened to me? How did I become this pathetic woman whose highest achievement is a well-planned, perfectly executed dinner party? Is this all there is to my life?

I can't shake the feeling that I am failing you.

It was bi-nationally agreed upon, in both the Czech and Iraqi strands of my family, that I was to become a doctor. My maternal grandmother who cooked brains thought I should be a brain surgeon. "I cooked this for you, one day it might help you with your studies," she would say, presenting me with scrambled egg and brain mush with an enormous self-satisfied smile. My mother wanted me to become the type of doctor that helps deliver babies. "It is the only brand of medicine that has a happy ending most of the time," she would say. My father fully expected me to find the cure for cancer. My uncle in Iraq wanted me to become a heart surgeon. I was the genius in the family with perfect marks.

Layal, on the other hand, had declared herself independent of family expectations from elementary school. Sitting on her one-piece hardwood desk-o-chair, Layal charted her own brave course, without consultation, without guidance and without seeking approval. Getting mediocre grades was her genius way of sinking under the radar. I was left behind to be consumed by the ravaging bear of family expectations. While I got mauled, Layal ran ahead of me, scot-free. In grade 10, in high school, I fainted during biology class on the day we were supposed to dissect a rabbit. That should have been my first clue that medicine was going to become a far grander challenge than I had imagined. In medical school, I fainted so many times in the morgue before dissecting a dead corpse that my colleagues called me sleeping beauty. My plan was to take a break from studying medicine. I'd get over my blood squeamishness by working as a phlebotomist. My glorious return to my chosen profession was subsequently delayed by marriage, children and relocations. Samih keeps telling me that I should quit my job and stay home. At this point, his grandiose salary makes my earnings seem like a single pixel in a wall-to-wall display. Yet a strange stubbornness, a malicious force makes me cling to my white-coat dream. A delusion, much like the daily fantasy I entertain about Dr. Mizrahi. Sweet puff pastry. Dripping with icing sugar. My austerity produces hunger, but has yet to yield healing.

Gillian is impressed with my weight loss, but not my poetry. She sat me down in her living room to let me know that my poetry is all right, considering that English is not my native tongue. "But it doesn't rhyme," was her main objection. Secretly I scoffed at her mayonnaise-bland critique. *You do know that poetry has progressed since Shakespeare's sonnets you learned in high-school?* I said in my head. *Rhyming! That's the stupidest mud you can fling.* My dismissal quickly became shock when Gillian declared that she was-going to become a poet, too. "A real poet," she said, raising her hand in the air in a grand gesture, like a dictator saluting a military march from a suitably positioned balcony.

"But you don't even read poetry!" This I did say out loud.

"I don't need to read it," she said. "I'm going to write it."

"You don't even like poetry," I said.

"It's other people's poetry I don't like. My own poetry I will love to bits." She gestured with her right hand, palm down cutting through the air as if with a knife.

"But, but, but, Gillian! Poetry is a serious undertaking. You can spend a lifetime, and never write a single worthy verse."

Nothing doing. "I have raw natural talent," she said, poking her nose into the air.

"Really? How did you discover this?" I was already giving in to the idea.

"It's my unconsummated love for Hovan!" she said, beaming. "It will spring forth untapped beauty the likes of which nobody has imagined before." She looked beautiful in that moment.

I had to see this. "Have you written something?"

"Not yet, but I just know it will be brilliant once I do," Gillian said with matter-of-fact certainty. I envied her confidence.

Don, on the other hand, told me that 40% of my poetry is brilliant and 60% is garbage. That if I get rid of the unnecessary filling, distilling it into essence, I will be the most acclaimed poet in the world. He sat me down in a coffee shop close to his house, and read my poems line by line, highlighting high impact lines, underlining the ones that needed further execution. It seems that my poetry needs to go on a fast as well. I need to stop writing new material. Instead, I should hit my existing work with a blowtorch.

When I told Gillian about the feedback I got from Don she laughed out loud. A laugh that reverberated inside her chest and echoed in her living room. "That man is clueless. He wouldn't recognize beauty if it charged at him like a hoard of thirsty hippos running towards a watering hole in Zululand."

Secretly I hoped that Don was right, although I held Gillian in higher regard: 40% poet is better than 0%.

Beef

FOR FIVE MONTHS we lived as vegetarians. Samih and I had just moved to Jerusalem. Buying meat was a hiccup that snowballed into an ordeal. We lived in a neighbourhood called French Hill, named after a British army officer named Mr. French. Sounds like the beginning of a joke whose punch line I haven't figured out yet. Like all the Palestinians in my neighbourhood, I ventured afar to buy my meat in a butcher shop in east Jerusalem. And when I say butcher, I mean butcher. I am talking a man wearing a white apron stained with red. A carcass of a lamb, still dripping blood, would be hanging in the window from a hook. Flies would be buzzing around it, congregating in little colonies of 20 or more, forming cow-shaped patches on the naked redness. Men and women paid them no attention as they yelled their desired cuts at the butcher.

I tried hard to learn how to buy meat in Jerusalem. I honestly did. I would start by psyching myself into it. *I can do this, I can do this, I can do this,* I would coax my feet to step inside the butcher shop. *If a Palestinian woman can do this, so can an Iraqi. Yes, Yes, I can buy meat.* My breathing would become rapid, my heart would strike like a bell in a church tower on Sunday. *Just yell "two kilos of extra lean ground lamb!"* It was an easy task: walk into a shop and yell a command. *Smooth as silk, smooth as silk.* Nice steady breathing. Confident measured pace. But once inside the shop, the hyperventilating would start. I would look at the dead carcass of the animal and see a blackness on the periphery of my vision threatening to close in. I worried if I stayed one more second I would collapse. The poor butcher and his customers would be forced to revive an idiotic over-spoiled failed Iraqi housewife. I ran out with the speed of the Flash, and leaned on a wall to recover my composure. Week after week, I tried hard to exact my pound of flesh. Each time I returned home empty-handed. One time, I didn't even make it into the shop; there had been a severed head of a lamb sitting in a puddle of blood on the front step. I felt weak at the knees and promptly did a U-turn and sprinted all the way back to our apartment.

I realize that this squeamishness is hypocrisy. As a meat eater, I should be able to face the source of what appears on my plate. The butcher shop, however, was too much information for my constitution. I wanted the lie. I grew up in Kuwait, where a public market did exist, but everybody I knew did their shopping at the western style supermarket. Meat that appears in plastic-wrapped styrofoam trays tells a beautiful lie. There was no suffering, no cruelty. Your food had no eyes, no head, no feelings. You can enjoy it guilt-free. Give me the illusion. Happy cows, happy chickens, happy steak, happy chicken breast, happy eater. Happy, happy, happy. We can all be happy. Nothing needs to be sacrificed. We can all get along and smile. One big happy blue planet swimming in an endless loop of cheerful darkness.

Which brings me to my tenth rule of eating: "Cooking is a beautiful lie which tastes most delicious when it reveals no truth. Good cooks are the best liars."

A dish should never resemble a great poem. It should always be a ridiculous sentimental love sonnet. One that rhymes. Luckily I only know how to write bad poetry, therefore I believe I possess the potential to become a great cook one day. Let me illustrate with an example. An original by Thaniya:

A Fool Makes Love to April

One Says to the other

You are such a trickster

April showers bring an uncanny surprise

People adore your beauty

It's your sense of humor

that will be my demise

April replies

You see me like no other

I shall designate an entire day

in your name

April's Fools will forever and ever

be dedicated to worshiping you.

If I could turn this hideous poem into a dish, it would be a type of macaroni and cheese, but with a twist. It would be really something. A thing of beauty. It would make everybody happy. An exquisite layer of cheese bathing perfectly cooked pasta. A seductive deceit.

Sigh!

Samih was patient with me for two months, before he started complaining he was missing meat in his diet. "Come on, Thaniya!" he said while sitting down for dinner one evening. Quiche was sitting on the table ready to greet our palates. "I am a man, I need my meat." Tears flowed down my cheeks as I whispered: "I'm sorry." I felt like a weakling. A failed vampire. And a total hypocrite. Samih gave me a hug followed by a slobbery kiss on the cheek to help me feel better. All those months of failed attempts overtook me in a flood of emotion. I should learn to cry more frequently because it clearly has a powerful effect on Samih. A few tears make him relinquish even the most stubborn stance. Luckily for him, I only cry about once a year. Unluckily for me I am not able to manufacture waterworks on demand.

The next day, he came home with his older brother Lateef, holding a black plastic bag. He handed me this loot, declaring: "I bought three chickens. Please clean them up and put them in the freezer."

I looked at the black bag suspiciously. "What do you mean, clean them up?"

"They came straight from the butcher." Samih had a knack for stating things without explanation. "They just need to be washed."

"Washed from what?"

"Lateef says his wife washes chicken pieces before she puts them in the freezer."

Really? Do all men think that if they compare you with another woman, it will get them what they want?

There was no point in asking any further questions. The air between us was muddy enough. I took the bag and went into the kitchen.

Samih and Lateef sat in the living room. I tentatively fished a piece of chicken out of the bag. It was covered in blood muck, but thankfully the feathers had been plucked. I sighed in relief. *This is something I can handle.* After the fifth piece was washed, I stuck my hand back into the black plastic bag and pulled out the next piece. Two beady chicken eyes were staring up at me. The chicken's comb was flopped on the side. A black tongue stuck out of the beak. I was holding severed chicken head. I screamed in shock. I dropped it into the sink and ran to my bedroom. I slammed and locked the door behind me and threw myself on the bed, sobbing. My histrionics could be heard throughout the whole apartment. Samih ran into the kitchen. Paused. Ran towards the bedroom. Then knocked on the door I was flailing behind.

"What's wrong?" Samih screamed in alarm.

"There is a chicken head in there! I held it in my hand! Yuck! Ewwww! This is the most disgusting thing that has happened to me. Ever!" I was amazed by how much I was able to verbalize given the sobs that were choking my throat.

"Don't worry, I'll clean the chicken for us." Samih sounded relieved.

I could hear Lateef from behind the door saying, "What's wrong with your wife?"

"She's not used to seeing chicken heads, I guess," Samih said.

"You have a strange wife." Sympathy flowed from Lateef's voice towards his poor brother who had had the misfortune of marrying a foreigner. I felt like an idiot. If there was any doubt that Samih had brought home the wrong match, this incident would surely seal the deal.

A half hour later, Samih knocked on the door to tell me that all the chickens were cleaned and packaged in ziplock bags, sitting in the freezer.

"What did you do with the chicken heads?" I asked in a small voice.

"I threw them in the garbage," Samih said calmly.

"Did you take out the garbage?" I really wanted a chicken head-free apartment.

"No, but I'll do that right now," he said. A minute later, I could hear him wrestling with the garbage bag.

I waited. "Okay! You can come out now," said Samih, his voice as smooth as chocolate. "The chicken heads are out of the house."

I unlocked the door. Samih smiled at me, I smiled back. I went to the living room to ask Lateef if he would rather drink tea or coffee. I can only guess what story Lateef told his wife later that day, but I am sure it led to much laughter.

It was a co-worker nurse Rachel at Hadassah hospital that ended my meatless curse in Jerusalem. When I described to her my meat-purchasing ordeal, she told me about a chef friend of hers who swore by a butcher in Bethlehem who owns refrigerators. Rachel gave me the address of the butcher. Driving there became a monthly pilgrimage. Abu Mahmood's shop was clean. All the meat was kept in the back, refrigerated. Not a single fly would be seen buzzing around. I would walk right to the counter and Abu Mahmood would greet me with a smile. I would give him my list of purchases. He, in turn, would disappear in the back and then emerge twenty minutes later with everything I asked for in bags stacked with neat plastic packages. Aaaaaaah! To find a butcher who is willing to lie to you! You will never appreciate it, until you lose it. Lie to me well. Give me a beautiful falsehood. A type of misrepresentation that unshackles me from oppressive truth. Whoever said "The truth shall set you free?" Clearly he was a masochist.

Every morning I wake up at 6:00 to hack at my poems with a cleaver. Blood spatters, guts are splayed and the stench of raw meat wafts in the air. I am the poetry butcher. My imaginary vampire slayer self feels nourished. After each cleaving session I am week at the knees. My poor poems look at me, unrecognizable versions of their former selves. They blink at me, surprised. Sheared naked. No fat. All their fluffy fur gone. Just raw, throbbing flesh. Hannibal Lecter would eat this up for breakfast.

Gillian sent me her first poem in an email whose subject line read, "Isn't this brilliant?" The poem started with "It was a dark and stormy night." Oh My Allah! Help me! I slapped my forehead a couple of times as I read her creation. Her saccharine stanzas reeked of pretention.

Forgive me!

I am not strong enough to be true.

I replied to her mail, congratulating her on her first attempt. She responded almost instantaneously.

"No no no no! Darling. Admit it. It is brilliant! Just say it! I know in my soul I was born to do this."

What choice did I have? I wrote her back to tell her exactly what she wanted to hear. She wrote back, in turn, to congratulate me on getting over my jealousy of her superior poetic abilities.

Don says that Gillian is lingering in the solitary confinement of her spiritual certainty. "Where doubt is not allowed, nuance disappears." Thus spoke Don.

Samih is perturbed with my early morning poetry-shearing sessions. He walks downstairs into the basement where I do my creative work, bringing me a cup of coffee. I thank him and try to return my focus to my laptop. Instead of getting the hint, he seats himself on the couch next to my desk to chat. After two weeks of this, I finally had to tell him that his social visits were interrupting my work.

"Samih, I wake up early to work on poetry," I said two days ago when he was handing me a mug of hot coffee. "When I am in the basement I would prefer to be on my own." It had taken me some time to work up the courage to spit this out, and I was a little nervous.

"But I am being nice to you, I am bringing you coffee. Why are you rude to me?" Samih looked hurt.

"You are being nice, I do like the coffee, but this work requires solitude." I smiled, patted his arm.

"You can tap on your laptop while we chat," Samih said, sounding a bit petulant. Then he sat himself on the couch and slurped his coffee loudly.

"This isn't like cooking, where I am happy to chat with you as I chop vegetables," I said. "This requires deep thinking."

"I'm not standing in your way. I will just sit here and be quiet." He sipped more coffee and stared at me expectantly.

"I can't focus while you're looking at me," I sighed.

Samih got up. "I didn't realize it was a crime for a man to enjoy the company of his wife," he muttered beneath his breath as he left the basement.

I felt guilty at hurting Samih's feelings, but my only other option was to give up doing the work. I had to have the same talk with Samih three more times on three subsequent mornings for him to realize that I wasn't just in a bitchy mood, I was really and truly serious about wanting to be left alone in the basement before the kids woke up and my fasting day started.

On my last "I want to be left alone" talk, Samih seemed dismayed. "Last night we made love passionately, yet now you can't stand the sight of me? Am I nothing more than a bimbo to you?" Afterwards he stomped upstairs. This was a strange turn of events. I wasn't used to seeing the needy side of my husband. Usually I was the one making obnoxious demands on his time.

Beans

LEARNING TO BUY MEAT in Jerusalem was the hardest ordeal in my grocery shopping adventure. But that doesn't mean buying the rest of my food was a piece of cake. Oh no! In the hustle and bustle of the old walled city, history and tradition mix to produce the most impenetrable barrier against a green interloper such as myself. Nestled along the edges of its cobblestone streets, merchants erect their places of business every day, seemingly out of thin air. Pedestrians old and young, men and women, crowd the space, making it impossible for passersby to walk in a coherent direction. To get to my destination, I had to bump into countless people, each time offering my apologies. I couldn't figure out why I was the only one having these flesh on flesh accidents. Everyone around me seemed to be avoiding collision through a secret system that my mind was unable to comprehend. It was as if everybody was dancing a scrambled version of the waltz without partners. Deciphering the steps to the choreography became a subject of deep contemplation.

I skipped the bootleg DVD stand, the plastics stand and looked down, facing the vegetable seller, an old woman in a traditional Palestinian hand-embroidered robe. Her face was one long continuous wrinkle. Her hands were so callused from years of manual labor that you could have grated a potato on them. I suddenly felt conscious of the smoothness of my own hands, the lifetime of comfort they betrayed. She squatted among her boxes of tomatoes, onions and green beans. I pointed at the green beans and cupped my hands together, saying "Give me a handful of those."

"That is nothing, take the whole box," she said, waving her hand dismissively at me. It felt like she might reach up to smack me in the face.

"But I only need a little," I explained.

"Listen, young lady, stop wasting my time! Send the person who actually knows how to cook to buy the vegetables." She frowned, placing her hand against her ribcage.

"I am the cook in my house," I said, pointing my right finger on my chest.

"If that was true, then you would know that a handful can't feed a family. Not even if you use it to make salad." She clicked her tongue in dismissal and then asked god to give her patience in having to deal with me.

"We are a small family." I placed both my hands on my thighs and squatted opposite her to look her straight in the eye.

"I've had a bad morning," she said, wincing in disgust. "The checkpoint was hell to get through and I have a headache, I can't stand myself, little less you, I am not in the mood to teach you the facts of life." She turned her face away from me.

"I really want to buy some green beans." I suddenly noticed my pistachio green jeans. The way both my hands were hanging there between my legs. They looked floppy.

"Then take the whole box. A handful won't even feed one person. "She packaged the whole box of green beans in a plastic bag and handed it to me, demanding 20 shekels.

I walked away with what felt like five kilograms of beans. At the time it was just Samih and I. Zakiya was only two years old. Most of those beans rotted before I was able to cook them. Most of them ended up in the garbage.

For several months, my fruit and vegetable shopping was punctuated with crying fits and wastage. Finally I was able to find a brick and mortar grocer in Ramallah who allowed me to hand pick my own produce. I walked into Mustafah's store one day and explained my predicament. I told him I wanted to hand pick my own fruits and vegetables and that I wanted to be allowed to buy as little or as much as I wanted without any commentary on what a loser wife and incompetent mother I was in the process. "Say whatever you like about my character behind my back," I said to him. "In return I will be a loyal customer and pay you whatever you ask." Mustafah smiled and said: "My store is your store." I would walk into his grocery greeting him with a hand wave. He would nod his head in acknowledgement. Then I would grab a little plastic bag and proceed nonchalantly to pick out my apples or tomatoes. His staff would look bewildered, accustomed to clients pointing a finger at the desired food, getting assistance from an expert produce bagger. Young men, barely twenty, would look at their boss, as if to say: "What should we do about this crazy customer?" Mustafa would extend a hand in front of him in a gesture of submission, ordering them in that way to leave me be. My fruits and vegetables came from Ramallah and my meat from Bethlehem. Jerusalem offered a little too much transparency in the food procurement department; I had to travel east and then west of it to find an acceptable brand of custom-made lies.

I no longer cry as I shear poems to their bare minimum size. I have sunk into a pitiless well. Tell the truth O little poem. Perform a parkour of honesty on behalf of my cowardly self. I am Luke Skywalker, my light saber striking words like the limbs of stormtroopers ... Better yet, I am the Antar of my Beni Abs fields.

Help me be a savage.

Nowadays, Samih leaves me all alone in the basement. I can hear his steps puttering in the kitchen. He makes himself coffee. I can even hear his eating noises while he chews his breakfast. He hums a musical accompaniment.

Shupidoupimoubilooooooooooooooooo. Goes along with toast.

Sumsomzomzoomblablablaaaaaaa. Is the cereal and milk song.

Tahtibahtitahtibahtimalamalaleeeeeeeeeee. Is for fried eggs in olive oil.

I wish I could run up and join him. Apologize for my rude shunning of him. Be a happy wife instead of the tortured poet. My words blink at me through the faint moon like the light of a laptop monitor. Over here my cruelty is needed. Up there, my love and understanding. What devilish force keeps me sitting on this chair from 6 to 8 every morning?

I have been telling Don that he should exhibit his paintings in a gallery. Don believes that he has yet to produce a true masterpiece, something that looks as compelling as what he sees in his imagination. "All my paintings are disappointments," he keeps repeating. "One day I will paint something and not feel betrayed by it, only then will I unleash it onto the world."

One day I was wandering aimlessly along the streets of old Jerusalem when I realized that I hadn't bumped into anybody for over 45 minutes. I had been living there for over a year and somehow I had learned the frazzled waltz of the locals. I looked up at the sky. It was bright blue with picture-perfect fluffy white clouds. The sky looked back down upon me approvingly. The trouble with moving into a new place is that you look at everything and everywhere without filters. It takes time to tell yourself stories that prevent you from seeing that which causes you pain. I had made myself comfortable in a frantic city. It was time to see what was deliberately obfuscated by the act of practical living. The sky seemed to be telling me to explore the city further. I felt an urge to witness the sunrise at the Mount of Olives.

From then on, once a week, I would wake up at 5:30 in the morning, put walking shoes on and slip out the door. Samih and Zakiya were fast asleep in their beds. Shatha was nothing but a possibility without a physical existence. She had yet to bless my life with her toothy smile. I would walk out of our apartment complex, past the British Cemetery where presumably Mr. French was buried along with his colleagues. I would walk past Hadasa Hospital where I worked, and curve around the back of the university that sat on top of the hill. My feet would steer me through the dark towards my destination, past the burial site of Rabia Al Adawiya, the first sufi mystic in Islam. There was no other stirring in the vicinity. Sometimes I would encounter a donkey or stray goat that had escaped from a farmer in the nearby Palestinian village of Isawiya. When I reached my final destination I would sit on a rock and witness the most glorious sunrise in the world. Over the old city, thundering rays ran across the Negev desert, bathing the golden dome of the rock in shiny molten color. My breathing would stop. For a few seconds, everything was perfect. All was covered in magic. Nothing needed to be said or explained. All was plain light.

As I headed back to our apartment I would again throw a glance toward the burial site of Rabia and ponder if I should head there for a visit. Rabia grew up in Basrah, Iraq. As her awakening grew, she moved to the holy city where she lived in absolute austerity in a cave in this mountain. Reciting poetry about pure divine love, she had many followers. Her name means Fourth, for she was the fourth daughter in her family. My name means Second for I am the second daughter in my family. She rejected numerous marriage proposals, preferring instead a life of solitude devoted to a single purpose. I read in the tourist guide that many continue to come from far and wide to visit her burial site. On my weekly returns from my visit to the sun, I could sense in my heart that Rabia was turning me away. *Hey Rabia! I am an Iraqi living in Jerusalem like you. Like you I was named based on my birth order in the family. We might find something in common to talk about.* But Rabia would turn her head away, and I could hear her saying: "Go away, Thaniya!" I continued my lonely walk home.

I would find my lovelies still sleeping soundly in their beds. Still covered in light, I would sit quietly in my living room, basking in the golden residue.

Gillian had arranged a birthday party at her apartment. She spent weeks pondering if Hovan would come. It was as if the whole shindig was for him. She was visibly disappointed when he didn't show up. DeeDee came with her husband. Anika brought her favorite yoga instructor. I came on my own. There was a bright-eyed young couple she met at the swimming pool, and Danny the ex-prison guard who is now pursuing a law degree. My gift was a book of Dylan Thomas poems; I hoped it would inspire her. Gillian laughed when she unwrapped the book. "That is so sweet! Such good intentions! But I have no need for Dylan Thomas—what lives within my chest is far greater."

Then she declared to the whole party: "Thaniya here is a classic example of a lack of positive thinking at work." Everybody in the room was now looking at me. "She has a hard drive full of poetry she has never showed anybody. She spends all her spare time admiring the works of others. Writing poetry is difficult because she believes it to be so. I, on the other hand, decided to write poetry a month ago. With the power of positive thinking on my side, I will write brilliant poetry the likes of which nobody has encountered before. Poetry is easy, because I believe it to be so."

DeeDee cheered: "Bravo!"

Her husband hooted and clapped his hands.

"That's the way to do it!" added Anika, raising a fist to the sky.

The young couple clapped their hands politely.

Danny said: "I look forward to seeing your name in the newspaper soon."

I felt humiliated. Yet, to see her so confident, I was convinced she would succeed in her goal. Her sheer faith was alluring. Her face was radiant. A twinkle sparkled in her eyes. Her honey-brown hair swelled with pride, swaying softly from side to side. She was standing inside a cone of magic. I wished I could get one like it to shine on me.

Butter

I AM IN TEXAS, TEXAS (yes, there is a city in Texas called Texas!) receiving specialized phlebotomist training. Memorial has purchased high-tech blood carts and I am to learn the skills required to operate a mobile labeling machine. Upon my way to this former Mexican colony, I imagined Texas to be full of racist rednecks, on account of this being the stomping ground of George Bush and his kind. Yet everybody I have met since I arrived has been nice, considerate and pleasant to talk to. For one thing, there are many immigrants from Mexico, some of whom don't speak English. Or maybe they are not immigrants, maybe they are locals who never left. Although I don't speak a single phrase of Spanish, they all greet me politely at the hotel, smiling warmly when I say hello. My training instructor, who has blue eyes and blond hair, seems about my age, I am 32. His vowels glide melodically; the ends of his words stay open as if unfinished. His sentences float in the air like helium balloons, bumping against each other in a subtle teasing aggression. Leigh had predicted I wouldn't understand the heavy drawl, but I find I am delighted by it. He explains things methodically, step by step, constantly showering all the trainees with praise. "Well Done!" "Good Job!" and "Thank you for asking that question!" This is disturbing. I want to encounter a single mean person so that I can go back home waxing poetic about what an awful backward bunch the Texans are.

My daily training class is four hours long. The rest of the day I am free to do as I please. I spend the hours wandering around downtown Texas, poking my nose into retail stores and sitting in coffee shops and people-watching. Earlier today I came across a park where I sat on a bench and contemplated a rose bush. From a distance I noticed a police officer looking at me.

Aha! At last I will have an encounter with the racist Texas police, I thought.

The police officer looked at his watch, looked up, and then walked towards me.

Yes! Clearly he is targeting me because I am an Arab. I felt an electrical current buzzing in my chest.

Maybe I am about to get arrested! My breathing became short.

I sat on my bench, staring defiantly straight at the peach-colored roses. When the police officer's shadow appeared in my vision, I noticed that his shadow and mine were different. As if we were being lit by a different sun shining on us from a different angle. His was tall, slim and tilted towards me. Mine was short, stout and reaching towards him. My shadow head was leaning on his shadow chest as if listening to his heart beat. I looked up, ready to stand my ground.

"Sorry to bother you ma'am," he said, gentle as a breeze. "A crew is about to arrive here to build a makeshift stage. There is going to be a free public performance here later today. I have to clear this square. Can I please ask you to sit on a different bench in the park?" His gait was apologetic, his words wafted across like fluffy clouds. It was impossible to say no.

I walked away feeling disappointed. Even the police are nice in Texas! What gives? What do I have to do to meet a redneck in this city? This place is not living up to its reputation.

I wandered further afield, until I came across a bookstore. Once inside, I breathed in the familiar scent of books, an odor that is identical all around the world. My habit is to visit the poetry section first. In a back corner, among dark brown shelves, I glimpsed a volume of translated Rumi poems. For the first time, I sensed Rabia Al Adwiya inviting me to step in. It felt like a knock on a door. Only it was more like an electric doorbell that was playing the sound of a finger knocking against the muted thud of wood. It had tingy, brassy overtones that signalled modern technology, yet retained the old-fashioned warmth of something as ancient as a simple knock on a door. It wasn't an actual sound that I could hear. It was a pulse that came pressing against the wall of my heart. All the times I had walked past her burial site, I never felt her inviting me to visit. Here I am, in bloody Texas, with her dead body buried in Jerusalem—and the bitch decides to give me a sign. What is wrong with you, Rabia? All the times I needed your guidance, you never gave of yourself. I get it! Maybe you were tired. Maybe you had had enough of all the hordes that have laid their troubles at your door. The centuries and centuries of human hurt, guilt and yearnings. I would be downright zapped if I were you. So why bother me now? I have given it a rest. I have moved on. You are just toying with me at this point. You are a tease. Just to spite you, I am not going to buy this book. Instead, I will open it at a random page. Whatever it is you are trying to tell me, it better be there in plain sight. I am not going to waste any more of my time with your cat-and-mouse games. Maybe you wish to refashion yourself as Jerry. But I have no wish to play your Tom.

I pressed the book between my hands, inhaling its smell deep into my lungs. With eyes closed, I allowed my right index finger to brush against the jagged sharp ends of the pages until it rested on a notch that felt just right. The pages parted in front of my eyes. Out unfurled a gentle tornado of words. In my mind Rabia was reading them to me in a stretchy southern drawl. I didn't buy the book, so I don't have the exact words, but the story went something like this:

If I told you there is a path that will not make you rich, in fact might make you less rich, will not make you more popular, in fact might make you less popular, will not bring you enlightenment, will not give you happiness, will not solve the problems that plague your life and disturb your sleep. And definitely, for sure, without a shred of a doubt will not make you a better person.

Would you follow this path?

Why should you chase a shadow you can never catch?

No sales pitch has sounded so bleak. No self-help expert, ever, dreamed so meekly. No spiritual guide inspired so little. No intellectual claimed a discovery of less significance.

I am not a sales person, not a psychiatrist. I am not a life coach. I am not spiritual. And I do not hoist the little intellect I possess on a pole like a flag for all to salute. I am a humble storyteller. What I have to offer you is not worth much. But I offer it wholeheartedly.

The only promise I make is solace in a dark hour. A quiet satisfaction garnered from pursuing life with integrity away from the shores of delusion and sentimentality.

Listen.

Listen to what I have to say.

Place your heart in the palm of my hand. Trust me to be the pulse that dances through your chest for the next few minutes.

There once was a king who had three equally impressive sons. Each was generous, wise and fiercely brave when the need arose. They stood like vibrant burning candles before their father, ready to set out on a journey to explore the four corners of the kingdom they were meant to inherit. They wanted to witness first hand that all was being administered fairly and well.

"Go wherever the fancy takes you" said the king. "Try everything, taste everything, see everything and experience whatever you will, don't be afraid to make mistakes, you will learn from those. Dance along the way. Enjoy each morsel of delight that comes along. Nothing is forbidden when you are the king. And I mean nothing. Murder, rape, theft—those words do not apply when you are wearing a crown. I only request that you do not enter one particular castle, the one called The Fortress That Takes Away Clarity. It is a gallery that combines all the most beautiful artworks from all four corners of the earth. Da Vinci, Van Gogh and Monet would weep with pains of inadequacy had they caught but a glimpse. "This castle," here the king sighed as if feeling an old wound, "causes great difficulty for members of the royal family. Others can risk going there, but not you."

The three princes saddled their horses and set forth on their journey. They arrived at one village where they were greeted with spectacular fanfare. Banquets and celebrations were held in their honor. People danced in the streets from joy of having such esteemed visitors in their midst. Hordes approached them asking for advice. Businessmen wanted counsel on how to prosper, farmers asked for guidance on how to make their crops bountiful, married couples asked for relationship advice. The depressed, oppressed and dispossessed all came running, asking for help. To each person and to every party the three brothers gave exactly the right advice. The masses were dazzled by the wisdom of the young men. "Wow! The future of our glorious kingdom is looking friendly. We feel safe knowing these three will be at the helm one day." Everywhere they went they dispensed pearls of wisdom that would have made Confucius blush with shame. "Be patient, you must endure," they said to the impatient. "Just Do It!" they said to the reluctant. "Love is all you need," to a quarrelling couple. "Can't we all get along?" to feuding clans. Aaaaaah! Such universal truths!

And so it was in the second village, third village, fourth village and fifth. But with each stop the three princes felt less enthusiastic about helping others and more interested in talking about the Forbidden Castle.

At night before going to sleep they would sit together. Eventually one of them would ask, "I wonder what The Castle That Takes Away Clarity looks like? I wonder what kinds of artwork are displayed on its walls?" With time the three princes could talk of nothing else. Finally, the eldest brother said what the other two were already thinking: "Look at us! We are celebrated for our strength and wisdom. Our father is over-protective. I am certain that we will be able to handle whatever danger lies in the castle."

The three brothers saddled their horses and set off towards the castle together.

It had five gates facing the land and five gates facing the ocean, as the five senses take in color and perfume of happenings and the five inner senses open onto the mystery.

The great hall broke into hallways filled with thousands of pictures everywhere the eye fell upon. The eldest headed left, the middle brother headed right and the youngest brother headed straight forwards. Each one, on his own, wandered the castle for hours, amazed by the immense beauty. Each looked and looked and looked. The more each looked, the more he felt hungry for more. The experience was exhilarating, yet made each restless. Completely drunk with beauty, all three arrived at a particular portrait at the same instant: it was a woman's face.

They fell hopelessly in love. Instantly they realized their mistake, but it was too late. "This is what our father warned us of. We thought we were strong enough to resist."

They stumbled out of the castle bewildered. Outside they met an old wise man. "Who is the woman in the portrait?" they asked him.

The old man shook his head. "Oh, I feel sorry for you already." But he took pity on them and told them, "She is the princess of China. The hidden one. Her father, the king of China, concealed her as the spirit is wrapped in an embryo. No one may come to her presence. Birds are not allowed to fly over her roof. No one can figure a way in. I would advise you to give it up and this would be wise advice indeed, but I know that you are in a place where wisdom can't reach. I can see it in your eyes. So instead I will wish you luck."

The eldest said, "We've always been bold when we gave counsel to others, and look at us now! Pathetic. We used to say, 'Patience is the key.' But the rules we made for others are of no help now. All the advice we gave others, what a laugh! Where is our strength?"

In despair they set out for China, not with any hope for union with the princess, but just to be a little closer to a dream. They left everything and headed towards the hidden beloved.

In China, they weren't three celebrated princes, they were three nobodies. They left their fancy robes, royal status, family, friends, fans, heritage, language, and all that was familiar to live as refugees and vagabonds, hoping some way into the palace might reveal itself through chance.

Finally, the eldest jumped up: "I can't wait like this! I don't want to live if I have to be separated from my yearning. This woman is my soul mate. We are meant to be together. I know it in my bones. I am absolutely certain. I am going to confront the king with my desire."

His brothers tried to change his mind, but failed. He sprang
up and went staggering into the presence of the king of China, who
knew what was happening, though he kept silent. The king knew
the three brothers, but he pretended not to.

 The prince knelt at the king's feet and stayed bowed down.

"This young man is sincere in his yearning. Such love is rare,"
said the king.

The prince heard this, yet said nothing. His soul spoke
invisibly with that soul. The prince thought: "This is it. I have
arrived. Nothing could top this experience." He stayed bowed down,
enraptured. "Such intensity! I am bathing in light, swimming in
purpose, floating above reason." This joyful waiting zapped the
prince. The picture of the princess left his mind. He found union.

This part of the story can go no further. What comes next
must stay hidden. There are realities that can't be dominated by
words. Meaning that doesn't fit inside language. I can't explain. I
can only stand in awe. The divine is closer to you than the veins
delivering blood to your brain, yet he or she seems impossibly far
away.

Thus the oldest brother died, and the middle brother came to
the funeral.

"Who is this?" mused the king. "A son of the same father,"
came the answer.

The sublime kindness descended again. The courtyard
unfurled to the middle brother like a rose blossoming with
openness, all possibilities existing side by side.

The second brother had read about such revelations. He kept
asking for more and the king was happy to give it to him. Fed from

the king's nature, he felt a satisfaction he'd never felt before. Suddenly came pride.

Am I not also a king, the son of a king? Why do I allow this one to lord it over me? thought the prince.

The king thought, I feed you pure light, you regurgitate bile in return.

The middle brother realized what he had inwardly done, but it was too late. He lost the humility necessary to sustain this state. His light was dimmed. Stripped away from cosmic beauty, he was bewilderment incarnate.

He asked forgiveness, but with his repentance came the deep pain that belongs to those losing union after attaining it.

This story must be shortened. Some things must be lived. Elaborating would slay the meaning. I can't plug love out of a hungry cloud to feed the wry sun. It is natural to wish to possess with words. There is no explanation. I can only stand here in utter defeat.

When the king came out of his own self-effacement, he found one arrow missing from his quiver and the middle brother dead, shot through the throat. The king wept, both slayer and chief mourner. Yet all was well. The middle brother too had gone to the beloved through the killing eye that blasted his conceit.

It was the third brother,

who had been ill up until now.

He received the hand of the princess.

He lived the marriage of form and spirit,

and did absolutely nothing,

nothing at all,

to deserve it.

Blueberry

THIS MORNING I EMERGED OUT of the basement to find
Samih in the kitchen eating his breakfast. I sat down at the dining
table, and quietly observed him standing next to the kitchen island,
meticulously spreading blueberry jam on a piece of toast. He dipped
a butter knife into the jar to fish out a splotch of the sugary spread.
With long elegant swoops he massaged the jam onto the bread. He
was humming a soothing song to himself.

Hmmm Hmmmm Hmmmmmmm.

Hmmm Hmmmm Hmmmmmmm.

Hmmm Hmmmm Hmmmmmmm.

The morning sunrays reflected off the knife. Sparkles of light
floated above my head, landing on the wall. With each movement of
his knife, the reflections performed a dance right in front of my

eyes. Like a disco ball, only far more refined. In that moment, Samih seemed like a sexy angel piping light directly into my heart. If only I could capture a poem that elucidates how Samih spreads jam on his toast. It would be the most erotic poem ever written.

Blue is the rarest color.

In the food kingdom, it doesn't exist. Nothing edible is blue. Even blueberries are not really blue. Blue cheese bears but the faintest witness to its namesake. It's as if edibility has divorced itself from this one color and then, to spite it, turned around to marry all others in a big polygamous communal wedding.

Sobbing heaves came down the phone line last night. I barely recognized Gillian's voice. Alarmed, I frantically jumped into my walking shoes to go over to her apartment. I looked so frazzled that Samih wanted to come with me, but I prevented him. Gillian told me there had been a riot at her prison, and that she had been blamed for causing it. She had taken it upon herself to enlighten the inmates by reading her poetry to them while they ate lunch. Their murmurs were followed with complaints and finally ended with the whole prison running amok. "Cruel and unusual punishment," is what the prisoners called it. A complaint to the human rights tribunal has been filed. I squatted on the carpet next to Gillian, massaging her shoulders and caressing her hair the same way I do with Shatha or Zakiya when one of them is crying. The only difference is that I can't fit Gillian in my lap and so instead I sat next to her.

"Why didn't you tell me that my poetry was so bad?" Gillian punctuated each word with a sob.

"You made it clear to me that anything other than adoration would be betrayal." Was I being mean by telling her the truth at that moment?

"It's all your fault I started writing poetry!" The heaves were now followed with a sharp sound that punctured the air with sadness.

"Me? My fault?" I wasn't accusing, just curious. Loving, accepting, not defensive.

"It's the way Don looked at you in the art gallery when he said 'Thaniya has a poet's soul'. Like you had something eternal, grandiose that placed you on another plane. I imagined Hovan would look at me that way one day. He would read my poetry, realize how deeply I loved him, and leave his hideous wife who doesn't understand him. He would run to me. He would kneel before me, begging me to accept him. I thought the prisoners would love my poetry and some of them would talk about it to their parole officers once they were out. Eventually my declaration of love would reach the ears of Hovan." Her breathing was slowing down as she spoke. "That was my plan to capture his heart. I was already visualizing myself spending an eternity gazing into his blue eyes. Now everything is ruined. I am the laughing stock of the whole penal system." Her crying gradually reduced to soundless waterworks.

To comfort Gillian I sang to her *Volare*, originally called 'Nel blu dipinto di blu', which I had once heard on a recording by the famous Italian singer Domenico Modugno. It tells the story of a man who is so deeply in love that being with his lover catapults him into raptures of happiness. It's as if he has painted himself blue, and miraculously finds himself flying, at one with the sky. The songwriter was waiting in a coffee shop for Domenico Modugno to go sailing on a boat. Tired of waiting, he got drunk while staring at a reproduction of a Chagall painting depicting a blue-faced man floating in the air. When he woke up the words to the song dropped into his head the way bird poop drops from the sky.

This blue-drenched-in-blue song gave me one of the most sublime moments of accidental pleasure of my life.

When I was 13, I fantasized that I would grow up to become a greatly admired medicine queen—a mix between Queen Victoria and Doctor Bethune. Adored not only for my beauty, but also for my intelligence and integrity. Men would fall at my feet hoping to grab a glance of my attention. Women would clamour around me hoping a speckle of my glamour would rub off on them. I would gracefully move around healing people, dispensing medicine as well as sage advice.

Two years ago, Samih had a business trip to Italy. He was selling ambulances to a hospital in Rome. He suggested I accompany him on the trip. We left Zakiya and Shatha with my parents for a week so that I could play tourist in the grand Italian city for five days. On our fourth night, there was a business dinner in a beautiful restaurant. Since others brought spouses, Samih assured me that it would be all right if I joined in as well. Luckily I had brought an elegant embroidered black dress and black pumps, just in case such an occasion should arise. "You look sexy," Samih said, looking at me with a naked desire that made me feel tingles in my crotch. It was so unusual for him to notice what I looked like. It was almost a shame that we had to leave the hotel room and go to the dinner, but we did.

Among the doctors, hospital administrators and their elegant spouses, I didn't look out of place. Nobody wanted to sit at the head of the table and so I sat there. To my right was Armando, a top executive at the hospital. Mario, a head surgeon, was sitting to my left. We were all looking through our menus when Samih asked Armando, "What is Carpaccio?" Before Armando had the chance to utter a single word, I interjected: "It is paper thin sliced raw meat, usually beef."

Armando widened his eyes with surprised pleasure. "Brava, brava! You have only been here for few days, yet you are familiar with Italian food."

"Italian food is popular world-wide," I said, hoping to flatter the famous Italian nationalistic zeal I had read about.

"Isn't it the best cuisine in the world?" asked Mario.

"Oh it is, it is," I assured him. I added a dollop to the pile: "I feel sympathy for any Italian who has to live abroad. After growing up with the best food in the world, how can you adjust?" I was spreading the flattery as thick as deep dish pizza.

"Ah," snorted Armando. "I lived in England for three years. It was pure suffering."

"That had to have been painful," I said.

"It was torture! The worst part was that nobody else understood the depth of my suffering."

"Nobody who hasn't lived in Italy would be able to relate to what you had sacrificed. Honestly, if I was Italian I would never leave Italy for longer than three weeks." I wriggled my fingers in a fan shape. "I have been here for only four days, already I am dreading what I will eat once I am away."

"Samih," said Armando, "Where did you find this jewel of a wife?"

Samih smiled. "Yes, I am a very lucky man."

"Not only are you lucky, you're extremely intelligent in your choice. Your wife has been here for a few days and has penetrated into the soul of Italy. Some people live here for years without gaining this understanding." Armando, ever the Italian, waved his hands up and down to emphasize what he was saying.

I was pleased to be reflecting positively on Samih. After that I listened attentively as both Armando and Mario took turns telling me about their favorite dishes. Mario told me about his adventures hiking a mountain to find truffles that he took home and cooked into a risotto. Armando elucidated the regional nature of Italian cheese.

When I was half way through eating my steak, Mario asked: "How is your food?"

"My stomach is so happy right now, I want to sing!" And then I sang the refrain to *Volare*.

Mario opened his mouth wide in surprise: "You know Domenico Modugno? That's amazing!"

"You are the most cultured person I have ever met in my life!" said Armando. "I can't believe it."

Armando jumped out of his seat, demanding everybody's attention: "We are all lucky tonight to be sitting in the presence of a most amazing, most cultured woman. Allow me to propose a toast in Thaniya's honor."

Everybody picked up their wine glasses while looking at me. "To the exceptional beauty and intelligence of women," he declared. Everybody repeated after him. I picked up my glass of juice, raised it towards everyone sitting around the table, nodding my head in acknowledgement.

Afterwards he sat down and began singing *Volare*. Mario added his voice, and then the rest of the party joined in. Samih didn't know the song but he hummed along as if he did.

I felt the same way Cinderella must have felt the minute her eyes caught sight of the glass slipper. The fantasies of my 13-year-old self were coming true. I didn't have the heart to tell them the only reason I knew *Volare* was because the Gypsy Kings sang a rendition of it. I had been curious as to why they were singing something in Italian and ended up discovering Modugno in this way—by accident. *Let them think I am this amazing cultured and intelligent person,* I thought to myself. *I might never meet them again, they won't be any the wiser.*

The minute Samih and I set foot in our hotel room that night, a rainfall of soft kisses landed all over me. My cheeks, feet, torso, neck ... all got smothered. I was duly getting worshiped.

"I should bring you with me on all my business trips, you had those guys eating out of your hand," he whispered in my ear between kisses.

Within minutes we were both naked, making love like porn stars. I fell asleep that night in Samih's arms wishing that such glamorous nights were not so few and far between. I was floating in the sky, embracing the grand blueness. Blue painted on blue. Among fat well-grazed fluffy clouds.

When I told Don about Gillian's predicament he laughed hysterically. He was bending over clutching his stomach as he laughed.

"Who knew that criminals were poetry snobs?" Don stood in the nursing lounge, filling every corner with his cackle.

"Oh stop it, Don, Gillian is genuinely hurt by all this. Who wouldn't be?" I was sitting at the table eyeing his sad-looking tuna sandwich.

"Those inmates, they probably eat slop, they give up their personal lives, their privacy in prison. But when it comes to bad poetry? That's where they draw the line. Those women are my heroes. I love each and every one of them for fighting mediocrity where it matters the most." Don had his fists clenched in a punching victory sign.

"Stop Don, Stop." I sighed with irritation.

"You stop pretending this isn't funny!" he pointed a finger right at my nose.

"Okay, it is funny, just a little." I relaxed into a smile.

"It's the most hilarious and fantastic thing in the whole wide world and you know it."

I found myself laughing in the end, with occasional spasms of guilt. It's sadistic to feel pleasure at somebody else's pain.

Pizza Pocket

TODAY I WAS TOO LAZY TO MAKE dinner, so I stuck a frozen pizza pocket into the microwave. Instead of pressing 2:30, I pressed 23:00. When I returned I found pizza guts exploded all over the microwave and my only dinner option was to scrape the cheesy mess together to reconstitute a pizza patty of dubious origins. Who knows? Perhaps I will invent some new food in the process. Well! Today, I feel like those pizza pocket guts smeared on the innards of my microwave. I am not sure I want to pull myself together. Perhaps I should leave myself splattered to rot and call it a work of art. My solo art show would be called *Disgusting but still edible.*

Ever since Gillian shared with me her fantasy of Hovan running to her after hearing her poetry, I keep having a similar fantasy. Until now, I have been only fantasizing about sex with Zaev. Now we have whole conversations in my head. He gives me his opinion of every single poem. "This one is brilliant!" he says with eyes wide open, bathing me with adoration. After he tells me how reading the poem has changed his life—made him into a better person—we jump all over each other. Who knew that Gillian's Hovan disease was infectious? It is rather ironic that I am doing my best work in my most degraded state. Then again, perhaps it only seems to me that I am doing good work because I have the Hovan/Zaev affliction.

Please help me. I am helpless in curing this disease.
I would rather be whole than become a poet.

I have been contemplating the story of the three princes that fell in love with the portrait of the princess. Clearly in that story I am meant to be the youngest brother. The one that succeeds where the two others failed. But succeed at what exactly? I'm not in love with a picture of a princess. And who are the two that are meant to fail before me so that I can accelerate past them? If I had two older sisters, then the metaphor would be clear. Unfortunately, I only have one sister. So it is not about family. I need to identify two people who are my metaphorical brothers/sisters in a common pursuit. Then sit back and let them fail while I forge ahead in victory. Thinking about this leaves me restless. My destiny is hidden within the folds of that story. A visitation from Rabia is not a thing to be taken lightly. It must be an important life lesson, the correct interpretation of which will bring about the realization of my deepest desires.

Perhaps my companions are my two coworkers at the hospital, Maria and Leigh. One day, our manager will retire and I will be promoted to her position. It would give me such pleasure to watch Maria's face when the news is announced that I am about to become her boss. Her expression will scrunch up like she was forced to eat a whole lemon. I will come up with ridiculous rules at work just to annoy her. I will ask her to fill out spreadsheets with what she did every 30 minutes during the day to keep track of her productivity. Then I will force her to print them all out and keep them ordered in folders in the central office. Once a month I will go through this unique reporting system and find a flaw in it, and Maria shall proceed to receive a severe dressing down for failing the hospital system. Imagining myself giving Maria a speech on work responsibility and teamwork fills me with satisfaction.

"There is no 'I' in team."

"How can I trust you with patient safety when I can't trust you with the timesheet folders?"

"You are proving to me that you are not a team player."

"Your conduct is unprofessional."

"By failing me, you are failing yourself."

All this will wipe Maria's smug attitude off the map of her existence. It will be good for her personality. In fact, I think I would make a great boss.

So if Maria is clearly the middle brother whose pride gets in the way, Leigh must be the eldest brother. That means Leigh is the overzealous one in the group who fails because she tries too hard. She doesn't seem that way. It must be a hidden trait in her personality that has not yet been demonstrated in her actions. I expect her to start working super hard any day now. If this interpretation of the story is correct, it means that Charlotte (my boss) is on her way out. She isn't retirement age. Destiny must have something else in store. An accident? Illness? Family tragedy? Perhaps a promotion? Transfer to a different department? Career change? Who knows? The options are endless. I can imagine organizing a goodbye party for Charlotte. I will write a poetic speech about how much we will miss her leadership as I get ready to take the helm of the Phlebotomy department. That will make me the chief blood sucker. Should I warn Charlotte that destiny is about to throw her a curve ball? It seems only fair to let her know what is coming down the pipe. Yet it might come across as weird. I better leave all my insights to myself. Acting all surprised when it goes down will look better.

The new blood carts that Memorial spent 1.5 million dollars purchasing are useless in our hospital. The hi-tech wireless technology hinges on the Wi-Fi which is blocked by the way the hospital's walls are constructed. The labeling machine jams up and refuses to print out the labels for the blood vials. All the patient records get mixed up. The experts and consultants have been in here to try to fix the problem. They have been clogging our hallways for two weeks now. Hemming and hawing with no resolution in sight. In the end, management has placed the shiny new carts in storage and told us to use the old ones. So my trip to Texas was a waste of time. This makes me very angry. Very, very angry. These management types get paid millions of dollars to make decisions, yet the insane level of incompetency on display is hard to take. How could they waste so much money without testing it first? Even a moron could have told them to give it a trial run before throwing all that money away. The most stupid people bubble up to the top while the competent people do the grunt work. I don't know why I care. I get paid a salary to do what I am told. Why should I care if the president of the hospital is a dimwit? I could make half the mistakes that he makes and be happy making half the money that he does. Memorial would save a mountain of money if they placed me at the helm.

Thinking about this makes me edgy. As if something that is rightfully mine was taken away from me. Some great injustice has been committed. An affront to humanity. I feel annoyed at the whole world. Incompetence at work. Corruption in our political systems. Stupid people on TV. Pizza pockets that explode in microwaves. Everything is the opposite of what it should be.

Pork

There are no more forbidden topics left.

Let nothing remain unsaid.

Discuss the flow rate of body fluid exchange.

Ridicule prophets.

Raise naked tourists up on holy mountains.

Bring God down to earth.

Wish poetry dead.

Flip a sentimental family value for breakfast.

Come on! Don't be a gent.

There are no more secret territories left. Except for one.

Things are about to heat up in here. If you are squeamish, get out now.

One last forbidden topic.

I relish hearing that pop.

Mothers who cook badly—that is what I am talking about.

Before we proceed, I need to clarify.

I am not talking about myself. I just heard a rumor of such a Sasquatch sighting.

I am the privileged speaking on behalf of the less fortunate.

I myself am a good cook.

Feel free to ask anybody. Just don't ask my children.

We place food porn on a pedestal.

Like its other cousin, just like the tooth fairy, that stuff isn't real.

Soggy sandwiches for lunch.

Standardized menu with the same boring food, day in, day out.

Tasteless bland stews.

Spices and garnishes out.

Soup that tastes of soaked dirty socks.

Overcooked meat.

Lop-sided cake.

Cream-colored spinach.

Spaghetti with a crunch.

Jellified chicken.

Moldy bread loaf that has sat around too long.

A bloody, undercooked steak.

Sugar replaced by salt in carrot cake.

Icing that is a train wreck.

Home cuisine that makes airplane meals seem better than sex.

What is it that makes somebody go on and on?

Without talent. No ability. No artistic touch.

No inspiration. No music.

No dream. No song in the heart.

No veggie thumb.

No magic.

Just a burden to stomach.

Insisting, three times a day, on putting slop on a plate.

That is what I call love.

It is hard work to do that which you are poor at

above and beyond.

So eat up those vegetables before you grow up.

Only your mother is willing to cook for you badly.

That is why most of the finest chefs in world are men.

They are not motivated by duty.

Meh! They just have talent.

Falafel

YESTERDAY I HAD A HUGE SHOUTING match with Samih. I forget how it started. But I remember vividly how it ended. He told me instead of wasting time on poetry I should be ironing his shirts more promptly. I responded with a true zinger: "Ya einy! "I stood there, both hands on my hips, swerving from side to side provocatively. "You came from behind the cow. Now you want to play emir over my head."

I never saw such hurt in Samih's eyes. I swear to god he winced as if somebody had slapped him. I felt dreadful the very moment the words had come out of my mouth. Samih didn't say anything. He turned around and left the house and returned late at night. He hasn't spoken to me since. Then this morning I had a tense exchange with Charlotte at work. She accused me of doing sloppy work. I took two samples of blood instead of three and sent blood work to the wrong lab. One patient complained that I was rude to him. To be fair he was rude to me first. I left Charlotte's office promising to improve my performance.

But never mind.

I have a confession to make. This is a burden. Some things are better left unsaid. I never talked about this to anybody. Not even Samih knows. A strange feeling sizzles within my flesh with the thought of it. Disgust. It is wrong in every which way you look at it. You'd be better off not knowing. Clearly, I am reckless about your wellbeing. Otherwise, I wouldn't be talking about this. I don't know the best way to approach this, but directness is the appropriate course of action in these situations. So I will just dump the garbage at your doorstep and be done with circling around this issue like a swirl of maple syrup on a pancake.

I hate falafel.

You read that right. Can't stand the stupid darn things. Looks like kangaroo dung, to start with. Doesn't smell good either. Tastes awful. For a deep-fried food, it is considered healthy. How stupid is that? How could something that is deep-fried be healthy? But the thing that really gets me is that it tastes icky. I mean, deep-fried anything should taste fantastic. Potato. Carrot. Banana. Meat. Fish. Cheese. Dough, sweet or savory. I can't think of a single deep-fried food that doesn't taste amazing as a result of being submerged in burning fat for the right amount of time—except falafel. It's the sacrilege of culinary inventions. Whoever invented falafel should end up in a special place in hell where sinners' taste buds are plucked with tweezers one by one. Needless to say I can't talk about this with either Arab or foreigner. Every Arab's identity is enmeshed with his national cuisine. You can produce a tasteless mush, but as long as you call it traditional Arabic food, every Arab will insist that it is the best mush God ever gave permission to humans to manufacture. Making a falafel confession to that crowd would expose me to accusations of treason. As for a foreigner, somehow, the international community of eaters have all been hoodwinked into thinking that falafel is this healthy, exotic vegetarian food that comes from the fairy tale land of the Arabian Nights. Declaring my falafel stance to that set would render me an unnatural freak. A dream buster. A party pooper. A stick in the mud. A stick in the mud that has a stick up its ass.

I tried hard to like falafel. I sampled it at all the popular falafel joints in the Middle East. I even learned to make it at home, hoping that private experimentation would help me unlock the secret of my dislike of this popular food. I hoped I could make adjustments to improve the taste. I experimented by adding avocado, green peas, pureed green peppers, garlic, cabbage and even truffles. No addition or subtraction could eliminate the kangaroo dung effect. In fact, I hate my own falafel the most. Homemade falafel is the worst. This is the only the food in the universe that tastes worse when you make it at by hand using fresh wholesome ingredients. The worst part is the after-smell. It lingers in the house like cigarette smoke, clinging to hair and clothes.

When all efforts failed, I resorted to prayer.

Teach me how to like falafel.

Reveal to me what others are able to taste in this icky delicacy.

If the almighty heard me, He certainly gave no indication.

If I was to one day make an animated movie it would be inspired by *Cloudy with a Chance of Meatballs.* My version would be called *Sunny with a Certainty of Falafel.* This would be a film noir cartoon, unsuitable for children, in which a small sleepy town called QuiKan is bombed by falafel at random times with no reason given to explain the phenomenon. At first the inhabitants of QuiKan enjoy the treat. It seems like an odd blessing from the heavens. Within two weeks, the QuiKanians get tired of eating the same food every day. They realize that the Falafel showers are a punishment from above. Normally people pray for water to fall from the sky. Falafel is no substitute for life-giving rain. People repent. Vow to stay upon the path of righteousness. Sacrificial lambs are offered to the gods. Men and women give up sex, partying, music and dancing. The last thing to go is language. A communal vow of silence is declared as an emergency measure. The very last human words heard are these: "All speaking is forbidden. We will delve into silence at the end of the long beep."

Beep.

Beep.

Beep.

Beeeeeeeeeeeeeeeeeeeeep.

No matter the sacrifice, QuiKan continues to get pelted by a shower of Kangaroo-dung-like balls. The vow of silence leads to an intricate system of hand and face gestures to facilitate communication. Elders begin fearing their native tongue will be forgotten. An epidemic of voluntary chastity leads to the disappearance of children. For ten long years the beleaguered population lives like monks and nuns. No amount of repentance or holiness improved the situation. In desperation, historians dig into ancient forgotten books seeking clues for the curse. A rebellious scientist called Knah suggests the falafel showers are the ecological result of nuking the neighboring state of ShmoTan fifty years earlier. All citizens of QuiKan temporary suspend their piety to enter a communal rage session against Knah.

"Traitor!

Infidel!

Insane!

Delusional."

All human language sounds beautiful after such a lengthy deprivation. Some QuiKanians curse Knah just to enjoy the simple pleasure of speaking. Knah is called every insulting designation in the dictionary. Everybody knows the nuking of ShmoTan was an unavoidable pre-emptive strike. For their leader NeHoj had been pure evil. His people were all brainwashed. Knah refuses to relent. He insists falafel showers are not a punishment from the gods, but rather that they could be scientifically explained by chemical reactions in the chickpea fields outside of ShmoTan following the nuclear bombardment, combined with the particular weather patterns in the valley where both states are located. Once Knah is safely installed in a dungeon, everybody returns to their ordained repentances. Solemn order rules QuiKan.

The movie will be 90 minutes of mostly silent sacrifice, with no rainbow in sight at the end. It will be a truly Slavic story. Everybody dies after prolonged turmoil. Quality suffering. Death by Falafel. Sunny every day.

The idea for *Sunny with a Certainty of Falafel* came to me while watching the news one evening with my father, during the second American-led war on Iraq. The clever reporter's coiffed hair enveloped her head like a helmet. In her tailored beige suit, she was interviewing an Iraqi-American family. They were discussing how the war in the old country was affecting them. In a lavish house the father, mother and two sons were seated on an expensive-looking sofa. A mahogany coffee table was placed on top of a silk Persian carpet. Lace curtains framed the background. Clearly, this was a well-off Iraqi family.

"I am worried sick about my family," said the mother, holding back tears.

"I feel helpless, I don't know what to do," stated the father, his face grim with seriousness.

"When I watch the news, I think that could have been me getting bombed on the ground," chimed in son number one.

My father and I weren't paying attention to the predictable heart-wrenching sentiments, though. Our attention was glued to the life-size camel statue placed right next to the fine custom-made sofa. You could say it was the proverbial elephant in the room. Nobody had mentioned the monstrosity.

"Ya Allah! Is that a camel in their living room?" I asked.

"Imagine. With all the money they have, that is what they decided to buy to impress with," my father responded.

"Impress? It must be a joke!"

"No, I think they feel very sophisticated having that thing. Very Middle-Eastern."

"Perhaps they have other camels in other rooms." I laughed.

"Perhaps each family member has their own camel." Dad's voice began to crack.

"A camel in the kitchen for mama, a camel in the bedroom for son number one," I said, counting off on my fingers.

"A camel in the master bedroom for papa," Dad joined me, sticking his fingers next to mine.

"A camel in the washroom for son number two." We each had four fingers raised side by side.

"The living room camel is for house guests!" Five fingers, we each had to add the other hand.

"A whole camel herd." I was now flashing fingers on both hands.

"Do you think they ride the camels?" Dad said, chuckling.

"Yes, at night they each ride their own camel." I began to mime camel riding with my hands and torso.

"Helps them feel better about the situation." Dad joined me in my imaginary camel-riding expedition.

"Makes them feel connected to home." I nodded my head, acknowledging a fellow traveller.

"Keeps them bonded to the old country." Dad waved his hand at me as if I was at a great distance.

"The family that rides together, stays together." I was pretend shouting and waving back.

"Could they think of anything more ridiculous to place in their living room?" Dad gave up on his imaginary camel and collapsed in his chair, laughing.

"It would be a like a Chinese family playing an oriental riff each time a visitor comes to their home." I said, tears streaming down my face.

"Or a French family speaking with an exaggerated French accent whenever they welcome an American."

"Or a Mexican family showing up to a party in sombreros and fake mustaches."

"Or a black family wearing blackface makeup."

We exploded into a laughing fit so hard that both of us were wiping away tears. At some point I started to roll on the ground grabbing my stomach with both hands, afraid I would rip down the middle from the force of my laughter.

There is nothing more tiresome that when a Canadian friend, at a party, offers me her homemade falafel. Just the other day, Leigh from work invited me to a Christmas party at her house. There were all sorts of goodies laid out on the table, buffet style. Roasted vegetables, artichoke dip, tapenade, an assortment of cheeses and crackers, freshly sliced pineapples and cold cuts. It all looked tastegasmic. All except the homemade falafel, that is. It was like a skyscraper blocking the perfectly serene mountain view. Leigh noticed me eyeing the food spread. Before I had a chance to wince, she'd said: "Finally an expert who can tell me if my falafel is authentic or not!"

With eager eyes she watched me take a bite out of the dry brown balls. "Mmmmmmmmmmm! Tastes just like back home," I lied, forcing a smile. In my mind I whispered to myself: *Tastes just like back home, like vomit, that is.* Leigh's face opened up with relief. "I have been making this recipe for years! I was worried that tonight I would discover that I was making it wrong. You are the first Arab to taste my falafel. You don't know how nerve-wracking that is."

I didn't have the heart to explain to her that until 50 years ago, falafel wasn't a popular food in the Middle East. It was a rarely-eaten dish, a poor people's food. Most Canadians are shocked when Samih tells them his mother never made falafel at home. Or that he rarely ate the cursed sandwich growing up. How do I tell well-meaning Leigh that falafel became trendy in the Middle East only after it reached superstar status in the west? *"You white people latched onto the very bottom of our cuisine,"* I would say. *"So now we are forced to cook to the lowest common denominator. I am compelled to walk around like a tourist brochure, pretending to savor the dregs of the Arab kitchen. Let me cook you a proper Arabic meal, darling. No hummus or falafel allowed within a whiff of any present nostril."* I am having a hard time imagining what I would cook for innocent Leigh. For certain there will be saffron rice and a salad of some sort. Beyond that, I'm not sure.

How can I seduce Leigh's taste buds when my imagination is under occupation?

Cauliflower

I WOKE UP TODAY, SCREAMING "Is something burning!?" I
peeled myself out of bed like a spoon out of molasses. It was 6 am,
my head was pounding and my nostrils were assaulted by an
alarming smell. I had gone to bed at 3 am. Charlotte had assigned
me the night shift, which is harsh on my family life. I suppose it is
her form of punishment. I ran downstairs into the kitchen ready to
inspect the source of the stench. Nothing was out of order. I ran up
to inspect the girls' rooms, certain Zakiya was playing with matches,
but both girls were still swimming in dreamland. I ran down again
inspecting every room in the house. Nothing. Right when I started
to question my sanity, Samih informed me of the news. One
hundred and eighty forest fires erupted all over British Columbia last

night. Wind has carried the ash and smoke into the city. Vancouver smells like an ashtray and sits covered with a gray haze. I felt relieved to discover that I wasn't imagining the smell and that my house wasn't on fire.

♦

With the self-imposed fasting, I feel all together spread too thin. I had to cancel my writing session. My darling poems will have to wait patiently until their creator has time to give them attention. I made breakfast for the family. As I was frying hash browns, my hand reached over into the spice cupboard to fish out the cumin container. A dash of spice found its way onto the sizzling potato. It is unfair to be experimenting with a recipe that I am not going to eat. I can't even have a taste. My heart was yearning to grab a whiff of cumin. The word cumin makes me think of the word "coming". With every sprinkle I imagine something coming for me. I hear a destiny roaring towards me. It is nearer. Nearer still. So close, I can almost taste it. In Arabic cumin is kamoun, which sounds like "come on!" I was moving the potatoes in my frying pan, saying,

"Come on!" to nobody and nothing in particular.

"Coming!" came the reply in my imagination.

"Come on!"

"Coming!"

"Come on!"

Once breakfast was done, I got started on lunch sandwiches. Afterwards, I supervised all the millions of bits of things that need to take place so that Zakiya and Shatha can go to school. Teeth cleaned, hair brushed, school agenda in the backpack. Each time I get the two girls to school on time I feel like doing a victory dance. I want to jump up and down declaring to the world: "Look! I am a good mother, I have my act together, I am one of those women who usually gets her daughters to school on time." Then I drove home eager to sink that spoon into the jar of molasses. I was hungry for bed.

The sky was covered, shielded with a gray haze. The sun twinkled aimlessly behind a foggy curtain. It felt ominous. This would have been the perfect setting for a tragic happening in a story. Like the middle of the novel when the main character's whole world collapses and she has to rebuild her life from scratch by scraping the bottom of the barrel. It made me think of the oil field burning in Kuwait after the Iraqi invasion, the one that I missed by a hair. I wonder if it smelled like this? Did it feel like this? I felt filthy. A whole world on fire. Is this what hell is like? You could say something was in the air that day in Vancouver. An overused literary metaphor that turned all too real. Speaking of overused literary metaphors—have you noticed how weather is frequently used to reflect a character's inner state? As if the reader is too stupid to figure out that when the wife dies, the husband might be feeling sad. If I were to write a novel one day, I would do it in opposites. I would set the most horrid part in a sunny beautiful day and give gloomy miserable weather to happy resolutions. I would do it just for fun, just to stick out my tongue at the reader. Keep them confused. Because you are supposed to use your god-given faculties to process things instead of somebody masticating the story for you. In poetry this kind of lazy writing doesn't cut the cake.

As I got home that burning morning, with sleepy drowsy eyes, I noticed a white and black bug sitting on the staircase leading to the second floor. It looked like a cockroach, only it had black and white blotches on its outer shell. It looked like Rorschach from the graphic novel Watchmen. It suddenly occurred to me that Rorschach's constantly morphing inkblot mask must have been inspired by an encounter with this insect. It was both hideous and beautiful. It was sitting behind one of the rail legs, stationary. It didn't move, not a whisker. Not a single twitch of the leg. I was certain the thing was dead. Zakiya's school essay on the Roman Empire was lying on the bottom step of the staircase. I ripped the front page of the printed essay, intending to scoop Rorschach and throw it outside my house. As soon as the paper touched the thing, it flipped upside down, wiggling thin hairy legs into the air. My initial guess was wrong. This thing was only playing dead. Five scooping attempts only managed to flip the poor thing. Legs up, legs down, legs up, legs down, legs up. Seeing it helplessly laying on its back, struggling for mobility, reminded me of Gregor from Kafka's *Metamorphosis*. It's the story of a young man who wakes up one morning to discover that he is a six-legged insect lying helplessly on his back.

Is that you, Gregor? Have you snuck into my house? Sorry, buddy. You can't stay here. I don't care how sweet-natured you are. Or how human your feelings aspire to be. Your physicality belongs squarely outside my domesticity. Don't worry, Gregor. I shall not throw apples at you. I shall not hurt you in any way. I accept you exactly as you are, precisely because I don't love you. I shall do you the favor your family didn't have the guts for. Look! I even ripped up my daughter's homework for you. I shall gently scoop you up and leave you in my garden. There, you will lead a happy insect life among grass, flowers and Samih's fourth effort to grow a fig tree. Come here, you ugly fascinating monster. This here is a flying carpet, it shall magically carry you exactly where you need to go.

I finally managed to place Gregor on top of my daughter's words, which were probably copied from Wikipedia. As I moved gingerly to the front door, Gregor flew, landing on top of a little cloth rug I had placed at the bottom of my staircase. Oh no, Gregor! This is not the time to discover that you have wings. This is the wrong moment to aspire to your highest potential. I picked up both ends of the rug to bring them snugly together. Gregor looked relaxed at the bottom of the tear shape formed by the rug. I opened my front door, stepped outside and shook the carpet, certain Gregor would have landed on the front porch, even though I couldn't see him anywhere.

Then I heard a peculiar clicking sound. It sounded like a piston that was going on and off at a regular interval. At the end of each cycle there was a click. There was a breathy nature to the sound. Like an old smoker dying of lung cancer labouring for air. Half mechanical, half living dead. I had stepped inside with the rug hanging in my left hand, when I realized the heckling was coming from the rug. Gregor was holding on with all his might, vocalizing his disapproval of his eviction. In a panic, I opened the door, threw the rug outside and stepped back in. I could see Gregor crawling on top of the tossed rug. His hissing got louder and louder. Sorry, buddy! You stay outside! You can hold on to the rug like a safety blanket for a little while if it makes you feel better. It might make the transition easier. But make no mistake about it. Transition into nonhuman abode is where you are headed. I closed and locked the door behind me. I threw Zakiya's homework into the garbage bin. Washed my hands. Ran upstairs and threw myself into my bed, eager to lose myself in a happy sleep. My mind was racing. The smell of forest fire tingled in my nose. My breathing was labored. I could hear Gregor's clicking sound in my head. Gregor is outside stomping his feet. Fuming. Dear Gregor, you are transferring your anger with your mother onto me. Heaven hath no fury like an insect-human with displaced mommy issues. Don't you see, Gregor? This situation is not my fault.

Oh Kafka! You miserable grim writer of nightmarish stories. Some tales are so visceral you can't get rid of them. You can't unread them. The only antidote for such a story is a story of a negating force. Equal but opposite. After half an hour of tossing and turning, I got out of bed. Sitting cross-legged on the carpet of my bedroom, I rewrote *Metamorphosis* with a female protagonist to silence the sound of Mr. Gregor Samsa in my head. There was no other way.

Makeover

When Elizabeth Sesame awoke early one morning from a dreamy sleep, she found herself changed into a radiant white cauliflower with sparkling florets. She lay on her bed, her head down in the lush green leaves, weighed down by an amorphous bumpy white body mass covered in plastic. Where are my feet? Which florets are my hands? Is this my torso? When the questions had run their course, Elizabeth's first cogent thought in her new state was: *Thank god! I am the food Mark Twain called 'A cabbage with a college education.' I am my favorite vegetable. This is super duper okey dokey fantastic!*

Elizabeth looked around her bedroom. The sun was sending down golden rays that peeked through the curtain. The laundry sat unfolded in a basket from the night before. An Art Nouveau style poster hung on the wall. She was particularly fond of that poster and had set it in a golden-finished frame. It depicted a woman with a flower wreath on her head. Her look was stern but content. She was decidedly not happy, not smiling. Not attempting in any fashion to please anybody nor be pleased. Elizabeth was proud of her taste in art. The way she discovered beauty in places others missed did her sense of refinement justice.

Elizabeth glanced at the alarm clock. *Oh No! 7 am already! I need to get up to make breakfast.* She wiggled her limbs, attempting to rip off the plastic covering, but that didn't work. Then she tried vigorously to toss herself off the bed, hoping that if she could stand up straight, she could go about her daily routine without interruption. But swerving forwards, backwards and sideways on her head was making her feel nauseous. Soon little Timmy would be rousing from his sleep and Frank would be expecting his morning bacon. There were school lunches to be made. James needed to be reminded to take his helmet because his class was going ice-skating in the afternoon.

People say that mothering is the most difficult job in the world. Nah! Mothers like to say that to glorify themselves. If you only knew how rewarding it is. A mother's job is simple. You anticipate needs and fill the holes before tantrums arise. It's that simple. A fun game of Whac-A-Mole. A mother stamps out obstacles so the whole enterprise runs smoothly. James was the first to walk into the master bedroom. The door was usually open. Even when it was closed, James and Tim walked in without knocking. It was only when Elizabeth and Frank intended to have sex that the door got locked with a key. It was the thing that signaled to Elizabeth that Frank was feeling amorous. He would get out of bed and close the door, lock it and then double check that it was locked by turning the handle back and forth. Elizabeth would hear the jingly jangle of the door lock and call it foreplay. This morning, thankfully, the door was wide open. James ran in enthusiastically.

Mom!

Mom!

Mama!

Mama!

Mom!

Mom!

"Fine, I will just tell you," he said. "I know you are listening anyway. Today after school I have a play date with Jason and then I want to go get pizza with a couple of friends and then I want to go to the mall to check out the newest Super Smash Bros. You have all morning to call all the other mothers to arrange who will drive us. Okay? You're not saying anything so that means you agree. Okay, thanks mom. You're the best!"

James ran out with a happy skip in his step. Fifteen minutes later, little Timmy walked into the master bedroom.

"Mom! I don't feel so well. I think I need to stay home. You don't believe me? Look! I have a runny nose."

That's when Frank walked in, instructing Tim to stop stalling and hurry up and get ready for school.

"Hey darling Liz! Are you not feeling well today? Perhaps you just need a day resting in bed. Is it that time of the month? No worries, I will take care of everything. You just focus on getting better. See you later this evening."

All along, Elizabeth had been screaming "I am a cauliflower, I am a cauliflower!" But only little mumbles were coming out. Elizabeth would have to master the art of speech anew. Being positioned head down with the rest of her body pressing on top was not helping. Her heart was racing now, like a train. She was agitated. Elizabeth told herself: *No point in getting excited. Everything in the universe happens for a reason. I shall calm down and focus on breathing, certain that even this is for the higher good although I don't understand how yet.* Elizabeth found the exercise of spending the whole day in bed surprisingly refreshing. She assigned body part functions to her new mass and began a self-assigned rehabilitation training on the spot, moving each limb to maximum capacity to increase mastery of motor skills.

Sooner or later somebody will notice that my ass is sitting on top of me, Liz consoled herself.

At precisely 6pm, Elizabeth heard Frank walk through the front door. She heard the familiar rustling sounds that he produced as he placed the mail on little side table in the living room. Afterwards, he sat down to take off his shoes. Elizabeth's heart seized with apprehension. *Oh no! No doubt Frank will seethe with anger when he discovers that no dinner is waiting for him.* Elizabeth heard his elegant footsteps moving across the living room into the kitchen. She heard him opening pot covers and closing them. She heard the creak of the oven door sliding open and then closing. Then she heard him call Tim and James. Elizabeth relaxed. There was no anger in the house. Only acceptance. An easy flow. "Hey boys, let's make dinner together. James, you find an onion. Tim, you choose some spices. Let me see what we have in the fridge." Soon there was happy clicking and clacking sounds coming from downstairs. Happy chatter, laughter punctuated by playful arguing. Shortly afterwards a smell wafted all the way through to the bedroom. Burning, pungent smells. Elizabeth felt horrified. She could tell the dish, whatever it was, had been ruined by too rapid application of heat.

At precisely 7pm, James walked in with a plate. He laid it on bed next to her. "Mom! Here's your dinner. We made it with our own hands. Your three men." Rice topped with a bean and vegetable stew. The onions were clearly burned. What disturbed Elizabeth the most was the sight of cooked vegetables. Boiled carrots, wilted zucchini, it looked like a murder scene re-enacted on a plate. The same thing that might have made her salivate was now making her wish she could scream in horror. At 8pm, Frank walked into the bedroom. He noticed her dinner hadn't been touched. "I don't blame you, darling, I know my cooking isn't anything special. The boys spent the whole dinner laughing at me. I am trying my best and that is all that matters. I see that you are still not feeling well. Perhaps you need more rest."

Frank patted her side affectionately and covered her with a blanket.

On the second day Frank made pasta salad. On the third day tuna sandwiches. On the fourth he came home carrying pizza. Tim and James rejoiced; pizza was their favorite food. Elizabeth could hear little Timmy jumping up and down, clapping his hands when his father came in. The smell of cooked dough filled the house.

Each night a plate with food was placed next to Elizabeth on her bed and was carried out untouched. On the fourth night, Frank sat next to Elizabeth after clearing away her dinner.

"What's the matter, Elizabeth? You haven't moved from your spot for four days and three nights. As far as I can tell you haven't eaten a single bite. You haven't said a single word to either me or the children. I don't know what I am supposed to do. Should I take you to see a doctor? Are you giving me the silent treatment? Are you upset at me? And what's with the plastic covering? Is it some new beauty treatment? Some stupid new fashion you heard about at the spa? Please don't say that you are on yet another fad diet? This had better not be a sexual fetish. I told you not to read those novels."

Frank became agitated. He spoke louder and louder.

"What is it, Elizabeth?

What's going on?

Just talk to me!

Tell me what you want me to do!

I've had it with this!"

Frank was possessed with an anger he had never felt before. He tossed aside the blanket that was covering Elizabeth, ripped the plastic covering off of her and flipped her downside up.

"Phew! Thank you, darling," said Elizabeth, feeling floods of relief.

"What's going on?" asked Frank.

"I am a cauliflower."

"What?"

"A cauliflower."

"Is it a new haircut?"

"No darling, it's a miracle, like the stuff that takes place in the Bible. Stuff that nobody understands and only makes sense one thousand years later when people read about it in a holy book."

"Are you saying that you are the Christ? The second coming?"

"No, no, no, this is a new world order in miracles. A new evolution. A revolution evolution. I am a plain humble cauliflower. Future generations will make sense of this, for now I am determined to simply live out my life same as before using my new state in the service of the greater good."

"Is that why you are so pale and wrinkly?"

"I am not pale and wrinkly, I am iridescent and abundant."

"Your hair is green. Kind of stiff. Maybe you should shower?"

"I know. I am the funky punky now. Makes me feel very hip."

"We need to think how to explain this to the children in a way they will understand."

The first order of business was to hold a family meeting and have a talk about the new situation. To Elizabeth's and Frank's amazement, James and Timmy didn't even raise an eyebrow when they were told that their mother was now a cauliflower. It was nothing like the horror Timmy had experienced when he had discovered that Santa Claus wasn't real. Or the heartbreak James went through when Robin died in a Batman comic. Both boys shrugged their shoulders and said "Okay!" They didn't even raise any questions.

Soon Elizabeth was able to function the same as before, gaining full human mobility in all her limbs. She performed as mother and wife—except for cooking. She did laundry, cleaned the house, drove the car. With the right amount of makeup and suitable fashion she could almost pass as a human. She even taught herself how to wear high heels again. But seeing chopped vegetables was revolting to her. Food of any kind became a forbidden zone. She nourished herself by sitting in a water bowl, exposing herself to the sun. While Frank, James and Timmy did the cooking, Liz went for a walk to avoid witnessing the carnage.

As far as the intimate part of her marriage, that bedroom door got locked every single night. Fred was happier than ever.

At first, her husband and two sons were saddened to see Elizabeth missing from the kitchen. They missed Elizabeth's cooking. But soon, all three learned to cook. The three men realized that cooking wasn't hard at all. Little Tim dreamed of becoming a chef. James planned on owning a chain of restaurants. Frank discovered that talking to a cauliflower was more fun than talking to a woman. His newly transformed wife never answered back and never contradicted him. It has been scientifically proven that cauliflowers make better companions than women do. Elizabeth herself was more self-satisfied as a cauliflower than she had ever been as a woman. For one thing, now that food was repulsive to her, there was no need for diets. Her new physique was always waxy and firm. Exercise was a thing of the past. No matter what she did, she was always fresh. Goodbye sweating. Goodbye to diet shakes. No need for unpleasant bodily functions that humans suffer from. Menstruation was a thing of the past. Only inner beauty remained. A pure essence radiating into a physical form. When you become perfectly at ease, self-improvement becomes meaningless because becoming perfect is no longer the goal.

This revolution is so subtle it won't be televised. It won't be tweeted, Facebooked or youTubed. This is just one of those things that happens that everybody notices, yet nobody talks about. Not ever. Not even to their dog.

So this brings up an interesting new philosophical question. If a tree falls in the forest and everybody and his dog hears it, yet nobody mentions it and nobody reacts, does the tree actually exist?

One afternoon, James came home from school with three friends. All three were dressed in grey and blue. The one holding a skateboard seemed to be the leader. James and the other two clearly looked up to him, imitating his behavior. James introduced his friends to his mother.

The leader noted: "What's up with your mother? She looks special."

"Oh, it's nothing," said James, nonchalant. "She identifies as cabbage."

The leader nodded his head: "Cool! I wish my mother would identify as cabbage as well."

The rest started to nod their heads as well and everybody repeated the word "cool" as if it was a mantra. They all ran up to James' room to play video games. After three hours they ran down the stairs to head to their homes, shouting, "Thank you Mrs. Sesame for letting us play with James!" as they stepped outside the door. Elizabeth watched from the window as they swaggered off and thought to herself: *Oh, the wonderful exuberance of a teenage boy.*

The years passed. James was studying business. Tim entered culinary school. He entered a cooking competition but had no idea what to prepare for it. By this point, Elizabeth had started to wilt. She knew that her end was near. (It turns out that there is a single shortcoming for living as a vegetable. Cauliflowers have shorter life spans than humans. All that intense being can't be sustained.)

Elizabeth instructed Tim to cook her for his creation. Tim resisted the idea, but his mother was persuasive.

Here's a piece of advice: Don't argue with a cauliflower, they say little, but when they do it is pungent.

He chopped Elizabeth up into thin slices, which then he blackened with spices and smoked like a salmon. Elizabeth did experience pain. But after giving birth twice, it hardly registered on her pain-O-meter. The end result was a unique blend of flavors that puzzled the taste buds of all the judges. Here was something nobody had tasted before. A vegetarian dish that had more kick than bacon. This new dish relegated bacon to the back pocket of the trash can of history. Tim called his invention *Cauli-liza*. And he became a celebrated chef worldwide.

Cauli-liza became an international sensation. Everybody in the whole entire world agreed that it was their favorite dish. In China, South Africa. In Portugal. Chile even Antarctica. Hindus, Muslims, Christian and Jews. Even Atheists agree. This food is a miracle. For the first time in history all living humans agree. Men, women and children. Leftists, environmentalists, the privileged join in. People who are happy and those who are sad. Mentally challenged and those who just mad. Freewheelers and those who live in a box. Luddites, Scientologists and Star Trek fans—all united. Even those who love to disagree, the ones who contradict everything just for the pleasure of it. Even those people can't resist enjoying this special treat. All join the party. Not a single person is left out. A new dawn descends on Earth. For if we can synchronize our stomachs, then think! What else could we accomplish?

A new age of possibility. All the great thinkers, philosophers, authors, poets, composers, economists, scientists and theologians.

They all turn to their mothers for new ideas. Each one seeking his holy grail. His own cauli-liza. Tim Sesame, the miracle chef. A role model for thousands of years to come. Forget heroes. Forget sacrifice. Forget Nelson Mandela, Martin Luther King, Ghandi. Forget Batman and Superman. Forget struggle, armed or peaceful. Forget social justice. There is no such thing as freedom. A beautiful illusion. Find a dark little corner in your heart. Get creative instead.

Elizabeth died a happy and satisfied death, shedding only a single tear during her butchering. She had been of a greater service to her family and humanity as a cauliflower than as a woman. *Praise be to God, who created me with a vagina so that I could give birth to my beautiful two sons and then turned me into a magnificent cauliflower so that I could offer optimal companionship and sustenance to them. If only all women were as lucky as I have been!* A shard of cauli-liza thought to itself as it was about to turn into poop.

Now Frank was happily remarried. In place of bacon he ate cauli-liza daily. After breakfast, he would take a private moment or two. He would tsk tsk and sigh. *Young women these days. They are okay. But my first wife, Elizabeth Sesame? Now that was a real woman!*

Yogurt

GAZPATCHO COLD IS HOW I WOULD describe things between Samih and me. He says hello when he walks home and I say hello back in a forced polite hushed tone. Then we don't say anything to each other until after supper, then Samih will thank me for cooking dinner as I clear away the plates. You know a marriage is falling apart like a three-tiered cake hit by a bazooka when the husband is pretending not to take his wife for granted. The sex component in my self-prescribed three-part remedy is out the window. We continue to sleep in the same bed. Each one says a polite "good night" and then keeps to his side of the mattress. Magically, Shatha and Zakiya have not noticed the jumbo-sized chill front passing between their parents. How I wish we could make shakshuka and dish this out in style. It would give us relief. Deprived of our means of warring, we each suffer in silence.

For the past three weeks since our argument, I have noticed that when Samih arrives home from work he places his black leather briefcase on the floor right by the front door. He then kneels by it and opens up the side pocket by parting the two velcro flaps. He grabs a piece of paper out. Reads it. Nods his head. Then places the piece of paper back into the folds of his briefcase. Curiosity is eating away at me like mold on blue cheese to discover what is on that piece of paper. Pride prevents me from asking directly. That would show interest and warmth. I feel tempted to just have a peek into his briefcase when he is distracted, but I know that would be wrong. So I am left to this niggling puzzlement.

Three nights ago the hospital had its year-end party. We are not allowed to call it a Christmas party anymore because it might offend non-Christians such as myself. I don't know whose idea it was that calling Christmas 'Christmas' would offend. I guess white man's guilt acts up in silly ways because the effectual ways would cost too much. The party was held in a ballroom hall in a fancy hotel with a view of the cityscape. A buffet style dinner was laid out while a live band played insipid jazz music. Samih and I were among the first to arrive. People with young children are always the first to leave a party and therefore it makes sense that they should arrive early as well.

Samih looked devastatingly handsome in his dark blue suit and paint-splatter-patterned silk tie. Each table had a decorated centerpiece of flowers and balloons. Maria arrived 45 minutes after us and sat herself in the empty chair to my right. She was wearing a stretchy blue dress with blue suede golden-rimmed shoes. Her eye makeup was unusual, a dark blue line drawn across the upper eyelid, outlined with a thinner white line above it. The total effect made her eyes look bigger and shinier. Her forearm was garnished with cheap plastic bangles, one blue and one white. Her long straight black hair was raised into a swirl in the back. A blue flower was carefully placed to the left side of the back of her head. She looked too matchy matchy. Like somebody who was trying too hard to grab attention, but all together stunning. Maria—like I have never seen her before.

She reached her arm across me and extended her hand to Samih. "My, my," she whispered into my ear. "You never told me your husband was so yummy." I winced but didn't say anything in reply. To be honest, I wanted to punch her in the face. *Keep your salivating desperate single woman paws away from my husband, bitch!* I thought. After dinner, the seat to my right stayed mostly empty since Maria was getting asked to dance by every bachelor and divorcee in the room. One of the disadvantages of being married is that nobody asks you to dance. Not even your husband. Maria was living the blueberry chapter of her story. I, on the other hand, was having a tofu chapter type evening. So tasteless and boring it is not even worth including in the novel. Zaev was sitting at the other end of the room. His wife is a knockout—every bit as beautiful as he is. She was wearing a strapless number in red and black.

I was just feeling a rock-heavy agitation coming on when Don sat down next to me, yelling into my ear, "Hey! Is that the man himself? Thaniya's husband?" His sudden appearance startled me, and I nearly fell out of my chair. Samih rescued the situation by extending his hand to shake Don's hand.

"Pleasure to meet you at last!" yelled Don. "You must be a special man to deserve the special wife that you have." Samih looked confused. He didn't know how to respond, but Don just carried on. "So I hear you are from Nazareth! That's a part of the world I have always dreamed of visiting." Samih and Don plunged into a trippy conversation comparing their childhoods. Both were shouting over me, and it was giving me a headache. I excused myself, allowing the two men to be consumed by boyhood memories. I walked over to Leigh's table hoping some socialization would improve my mood.

Take a deep breath.
Inhale.
Hold.
Hold.
Exhale.

I don't remember where I learned this trick. It does come in handy when I feel overwhelmed with emotion. When thoughts race through my mind like scurrying mice or the bile of anger rises from my stomach into my chest, or when a yellow wind of resentment sweeps through, creating a dust storm, I hit the pause button. Place the jinni back into the lamp where it shall lie dormant for thousands and thousands of nights. Many wish to rub the magical vessel for three magical fulfilled wishes. My only desire is to keep it all contained. I scour and perfect my bottling technique.

There are blotches in my practice. Tiny air bubbles ferment from the bottom of the container. A break from the white sour consistency always catches me by surprise. Goes poof in my face. It happened once with my sister.

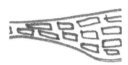

Layal always towered over me, not just with her height but with her attitude as well. She selectively exercised the role of older sister. She would shower me with pontificating lectures when the whimsy swayed in one direction. Then the pendulum would tilt in the other direction, and I would shrink and become invisible. At school, Layal, was constantly getting into trouble. Fist fights, talking back to teachers, playing hooky, breaking the uniform regulations and even getting caught smoking cigarettes. A never-ending stream of visits to the principal's office. It was Layal's good fortune that our principal Abla Smeera had a crush on our father.

"Ya Abu Layal, I don't understand. Two daughters as different as night and day. One we never hear a peep from. The other, a flood of complaints from all her teachers."

"Oh dear respected educator Sameera, you hold high esteem in our household. I don't need to explain to you the unfathomable nature of human impulses."

My father would shine his warm smile in the general direction of our headmistress. Layers of sternness would peel away like a melfe cake losing its puff pastry. Nothing but custard would remain. She would turn to mush. Abu Layal always promised that Layal's punishment was best portioned out at home. Her many trespasses never got her expelled or suspended, not even once. The heartfelt smiles and double entendre were swept away. True to his word, my father doled out punishment the minute we arrived home. Layal was spanked, grounded, her allowance withheld, her TV taken away from her room, she received angry lectures about responsibility and was told to be ashamed of herself because her younger sister was her role model instead of the other way around.

The truth is I envied Layal's rebellious nature. She didn't care what anybody thought. Not our parents, teachers or any grown up. Yet a part of me also craved the self-righteousness of being a good girl. The approving looks I received from my teachers. How I made my parents happy.

Look at Layal today. A divorced forensic accountant. She drives a Jaguar. Travels around the world to uncover crime in bookkeeping irregularities. Her apartment is a temple. I love sitting on her couch. So quiet. So tranquil. Every object is exactly in the same spot month to month. Family photos and mementos from Latin America and Africa sit unperturbed in their designated spots. The most beautiful site is inside her fridge. I open her fridge to marvel at the empty spaces in there. Like a tourist on a train in Switzerland drinking in the bucolic pastures and vineyards passing by from a window. Makes me want to yodel with delight. My fridge, in comparison, is a densely populated urban center. Tupperware is stacked in high-rise formations to maximize space vertically and horizontally. I suspect Layal doesn't even know what Tupperware is.

When I was 13, Layal took a blouse from my closet without asking, getting ready to go out with her friends to the shopping mall. I demanded that she take it off on the spot. She looked back defiantly with those coffee eyes and laughed at me. I yelled louder. She laughed some more. "What are you going to do about it? Ha!"

I forgot to breathe.

A break in my character. A crack.

I went to the kitchen to retrieve an unopened tub of plain yogurt. I tore off the lid and threw it on the floor. Then I peeled away the tinfoil cover in one forceful swoop. I ran towards Layal like a panther on a mission. With the absolute determination of a comic book superhero, I plunked the whole 500 grams of sour white goop on top of Layal's head. I stepped back to marvel at my creation. Yogurt dripped from Layal's hair onto her shoulders and chest. The white on black contrast was beautiful. It was nearly artistic. The look of shock on her face was worth a million dinars. I only had a second to enjoy this rare break with my personality. I had to run towards my room on the second click of the stopwatch. For Layal was coming at me with her fists up in the air. The only thing that spared me the beating was the fact that I was able to make it into my room in time to lock myself in before she grabbed hold of me. I could hear her cursing and banging at my door. I confess to experiencing a wicked joy from hearing the anguish in her voice. She was forced to go change her clothing, clean up her hair and head out in a hurry, because her friends were waiting right outside our apartment building.

"You're lucky I don't have time to deal with you right now!" she screamed as she slammed the door on her way out.

Behind my door, I was seized with a giant fit of panic. I was certain my parents would mop the floor with me for my transgression. There was a gentle knock on my door.

"Thaniya, open the door, she's gone now," my mother whispered.

"No!" I yelled back through the door.

"Don't worry, you're not in trouble, just open the door."

I hesitated, but then I opened the door.

My mother walked in, laughing, and sat on the couch in my bedroom.

"You should have seen the look on her face! I've never seen her so angry in my life."

The lack of anger in my mother's face left me speechless.

"I don't think she will ever help herself to your clothes again." My mother was now holding her stomach, laughing in a fit of hysteria.

I started to laugh as well. I sat next to her. We both laughed till we cried.

After about five minutes, my mother said: "Come on, help me clean up the yogurt drips on the carpet."

When my father came home from work, he laughed as well, once my mother told him what happened. My mother mimed the yogurt oozing down Layal's hair with her hands. Then she acted out the look of shock followed by anger on Layal's face. They both laughed. There was no punishment. No lecture about good behavior. Nothing. I got off scot-free. You would think that given the lack of consequences for my bad behavior, I might have been tempted to repeat the performance. I am sitting here on Layal's couch in her lovely silent apartment while she prepares tea for both of us, and I am ashamed to report that I continued to behave like a good girl despite all the encouragement I received to do otherwise. My only retribution was that whenever Layal was punished for a trespass, she would remind my parents of the yogurt incident.

"Thaniya never gets punished, no matter what she does. Remember the day she dumped yogurt on my head and both of you did nothing about it? If I do the most tiny little thing, I immediately get punished."

I had to listen to those words for years and years. How I wish I could have grabbed the gravy accompanying the roast beef at the Christmas party and poured the whole lot on Maria's head. It would have been so satisfying.

Kubeh

THE MORNING AFTER THE CHRISTMAS party, Samih was
making buzzing sounds while eating his toast. In between bizz bizz
and buzz buzz he managed to ask me: "Explain to me, how come
you are friends with Don? That man is unbearable. I spoke to him
once and I have no desire to encounter him a second time." Samih
was throwing me an icebreaker. I must have been invaded by the
Christmas spirit, because I was happy to receive it.

"What did he say to you?" I asked, innocently enough.

"He told me I look like somebody who walks around with a
chip on his shoulder. That I married somebody more exceptional
than myself and suffer from an inferiority complex as a result."

We both laughed heartily at these remarks. "Oh, poor Don," I
said. "He is stuck painting the same portrait over and over again."

My plan for the day was to take Zakiya and Shatha to an indoor amusement park that had opened recently. Samih told me to go ahead without him, he hated those sorts of places, plus he had a presentation to go over for Monday. Zakiya and Shatha had such a good time at the place they didn't want to leave. Between jumping around in the ball pits, visiting the slides and driving the electric cars, we ended up spending over ten hours at the place. We were practically kicked out five minutes before closing time. Both girls were exhausted after their day of frantic activity. The minute I drove off, they both fell asleep. As I drove home in the dark, I pondered a dilemma. How would I carry both Zakiya and Shatha into the house without waking them up? They were too heavy to carry at the same time. I didn't feel comfortable leaving one of them in the car while I carried the other one in. Whoever woke up would get agitated, and it would take a long time to get her to fall asleep again. I tried to think of a solution the whole way home. I finally decided that I had no other option but to carry Shatha and wake Zakiya, forcing her to walk with me. I sighed with disappointment for failing to find a more ideal solution. As I approached my usual parking spot in front of our house, I saw the silhouette of a male figure standing straight with his arms crossed in front of him. As I parked my car, I saw that it was Samih standing there all alone in the dark. I jumped out of the car. "What happened?"

"I am waiting here for you."

"Why?"

"Since it was getting late, I knew that both girls would fall asleep in the car. I guessed you would need help carrying them in."

Samih opened the door and whispered, "I will grab Zakiya first, can you manage carrying Shatha?"

"Yes, yes!"

We carried our two daughters inside and placed each one in her bed. Taking off their shoes we decided to leave them in their clothes, undisturbed. Then Samih asked me if I was hungry.

"I'm starving," I replied. "The girls had burgers and fries, but you know how much I hate that garbage food. So I ate nothing the whole day."

"You're in luck, I made some maqloubeh. Here let me microwave a plate for you. Sit down. You must be tired."

There is no place like home. There is no place like home.

In Jerusalem, I met other Iraqis. Oded worked as a male nurse in Hadassah hospital. Chatty by nature, he introduced himself to me on his first day working at the hospital, proudly declaring that he was from Iraq.

"Have you been to Iraq?" I asked, eager to listen to an interesting story.

"No, my parents immigrated here in the fifties, but one day I will go back."

"So that means you grew up here, right?"

"Yes, but in my heart I am Iraqi. I am even taking Arabic classes at the university. Do you know that Iraqi colloquial Arabic is different than the Palestinian Arabic?"

"Yes, I know."

"So I learn the wrong Arabic at university and then my mother corrects it by teaching me the Iraqi version. "

I sat quietly while he told me about his adventures learning his mother tongue, not revealing that he and I had something in common. Oded was a mystery to me. I didn't understand how somebody who had never been to Iraq and whose parents left Iraq after having been persecuted, expelled sans all their belongings, would develop such a passionate sense of identification with the country. Each time I talked to him I wanted to say: "Hey! I am Iraqi too." Parts of his personality seemed familiar. Most of him was a mystery. I wanted to understand before I revealed myself to him.

Three months later, I was having lunch at the hospital cafeteria. Oded sat across from me at the table. His ready smile preceded his greetings.

"What's new in your world today?"

"I am so impressed with the food at this hospital," I said, trying to start some form of small talk. Back then I was naïve. I thought food was a safe topic for conversation. The foolish notions of youth get dissolved in the stew of experience.

"What do you mean?"

"This spinach salad," I said, pointing at my white plate, "is really good. Much better than anything I would expect to find in a hospital. It is fresh. Contains blue cheese, walnuts and dried cranberries."

"I never eat here." Oded waved his hand against the sky as if pronouncing a prophesy.

"What type of food do you like?"

"I only eat home cooked meals my mother makes."

"What about your wife?"

"She doesn't know how to cook," said Oded. "She is not Iraqi. She is trying to learn from my mother but has yet to produce a single dish that qualifies as edible."

Hearing Oded talk about his wife made me appreciate Samih. He never compared my cooking with his mother's and always ate what I prepared, even when it was horrid.

"Wait until you see what I have here, you will envy me until the end of time," Oded said, opening an aluminum thermos to reveal piping-hot kubeh hameth soup. "This soup will warm your heart and make your stomach sing with delight. This is the Ferrari of all soups. I insist that you taste it. I am certain that after one bite you will renounce all other cuisines. Palestinian, Israeli, French, Italian, Chinese .... all garbage, next to the ancient cuisine of the cradle of civilization."

My own countrymen are a mystery to me. I am more likely to understand a green alien from Mars than an Iraqi. Since the fall of the old regime I keep reading about ethnicities from Iraq I never knew about. Yazidies, Kurds, Marsh Arabs, Chaldean Christians, Armenians, Athuris. My head is dizzy with details. I guess that encounter with Oded was the first of many that taught me how little I know about my country. It is the irony of ironies that I understand Palestinians, Egyptians, and even Canadians better than I understand Iraqis. It is a blessing that my fate united me with a Palestinian husband. Had I married an Iraqi I would have been doomed to a life of the perpetual maze walker. Always lost. Always searching for the exit.

I couldn't take it anymore. My months of restraint cracked.

"I know what kubeh hamoth tastes like. I am Iraqi too."

Oded gasped with surprise. I spent the next 20 minutes answering Oded's questions about my life. With tears in his eyes, he held my forearm saying: "You are the first non-Jewish Iraqi I have ever met. This moment is the fulfilment of a lifelong dream." Oded looked at me as if I was his long-lost sister. I looked at him as if he was E.T. pointing an illuminated finger towards home. Only this E.T. was much better off exactly where he was. *You don't want to go home, E.T.! Stay on earth.*

"I always knew there was something special about you," said Oded. "It's in the way you walk. You walk with pride and confidence. Your head held high. Neither Palestinians, nor Israelis, nor North Americans have that walk. I sensed that you were my sister the first time I laid eyes on you. I finally understand the feeling."

"How can you know for certain that kubeh hameth is the best soup on earth, when you never try anything else?" I asked. "You only eat your mother's home cooked meals. You never eat in restaurants. You refuse to try the food prepared by your wife. Don't you have doubts? Perhaps Italian minestrone soup is better. How can you be certain if you never tried?"

"My heart is my atlas. Why waste time wandering when I already know my destination?" He leaned in towards me with an intensity in his eyes..."Please don't take this the wrong way. But had both of us not been married already, I would have proposed marriage to you right now on the spot."

"Wouldn't your mother object to you marrying somebody who is not Jewish?" I asked.

"Yes she would, but for an Iraqi daughter in-law she would forget her religion."

I didn't know what else to say and so instead I dipped my spoon into his kubeh soup, fished out a ball and shoved the whole thing into my mouth to keep myself silent.

You start by making a sour tomato-turnip soup. I like putting spinach leaves into mine. Something about spinach goes well with this. I can't explain it. It just feels right. Then you add semolina balls that have been stuffed with fried beef—that's the kubeh—to the soup, and simmer it to cook them. The cooked balls emerge drenched with sludgy tomato sauce. Ideally kubeh is eaten in two bites. The first bite to discover the surprise of what is inside, and the second bite to fully savor the combination of flavors. The initial surprise is gone. Pure pleasure remains. True to its Iraqi origins, this soup makes no sense. Lemon juice in tomato soup makes no sense. Turnips? Why turnips? Who thought it was a great idea to put kubeh in soup? Despite its massive weirdness, it works.

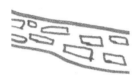

Unlike Oded's mother, my father gave up his religion a long time ago, yet God hasn't seen fit to reward him with an Iraqi son-in-law. As a form of compensation, I took my father to a traditional Iraqi restaurant when he came to visit me in Jerusalem. The Three Brothers Restaurant was famous for their kubeh hameth served by three burly, hairy Jewish-Iraqi men. We sat down at a communal wooden bench across from each other in the noisy popular joint. Among the sounds of dishes clacking and the ancient-sounding singing of Nazem Al Ghazali blaring through the speakers, we both noisily slurped our soup.

When our plates were cleared, I looked at my father with anticipating eyes: "Aren't you impressed with how authentic this experience is?"

My father scoffed. "This place has good kubeh hameth." With the mocking smile still lodged on his face he continued, "If this place was an authentic Iraqi restaurant, it would be so dirty that my shoe would be sticking to the tile right now." He lifted the cuffs of his right leg pants and pointed to the floor. "Look at these tiles. They are so shiny, I can see my own face in them from up here." I laughed. My father laughed too.

It felt good to be Iraqi for five minutes afterwards.

A rare experience.

Olive

BETWEEN GILLIAN WHO HAS FLUNG herself into acclaim with reckless abandon and Don who is circling around his anonymous wound like a buzzard, there has to be a middle ground. A sensible approach—neither masochistic nor self-indulgent. So I finally did it. I found the camcorder—the one Samih bought the day Shatha was born—and decided to record myself reading *The Digital Me*, a poem that has received multiple shearings. I felt so awkward standing in front of that lens that I had to wait until the house was empty. I didn't want to record myself with Samih, Zakiya and Shatha watching. I was certain they would laugh at me. There is something about talking to yourself in an empty room that feels crazy. *Yay! I am finally talking to myself. I've totally lost it. Should I dress up, apply makeup, do my hair? Or should I just be myself?*

Samih decided to take the girls for a walk in our neighborhood to look at the elaborate Christmas decorations some of our neighbours have put out. At night, with thousands of lights flickering off the streets, it captures a sense of magic. I said I would stay behind to tidy up. My secret agenda was to film the video I had been thinking about for weeks. In the end, I decided to appear natural. I applied a bit of lipstick and nothing else. In the first recording, I was too jittery. Then I was hesitating. The third recording felt too flamboyant. The fourth too dramatic. In the fifth I moved my arms around and looked like a flailing squid falling out of the sky. The sixth I spoke too fast and was unable to understand myself. The seventh try was the one I uploaded, but only because I was tired and didn't want to film myself again.

It is curious how easy my hummus video was in comparison to this. Behind my kitchen counter, with a food processor blocking most of my torso, I felt safe, confident, arrogant even. Here, standing with just a piece of paper in my hand, I felt metaphorically naked. I sat watching my creativity getting uploaded. I felt the same way I do when I go to the supermarket searching for a unique difficult-to-find ingredient and walk away with a generic ingredient instead. Like that time I was looking for pomegranate molasses and walked away with brown sugar. Unlike my hummus video, my poetry video received very few views. Most of the comments on *The Digital Me* video asked me to stick to making recipes. One asked for a baba ganoush video, another wanted to see me make falafel. I consoled myself knowing that at least my poem didn't cause a prison riot. But I do feel heartbroken. In my mind, I had imagined people loving it.

Don says that if I am going to upload video then I need to worry about the visual aspect. "The light, sound quality and framing is your downfall. The poem is great." Sigh! I don't know what to do. I could make people happy and just make one recipe video after the other. Or do the hard work of making poetic-looking poetry videos.

Why can't anything be easy?

I didn't tell Gillian about the video. In fact I didn't tell anyone I know in person, except for Don. A few hundred disappointed strangers desiring a cooking video plus Don are my audience.

The best way one rebels against parents is to embrace their teachings fully. By stretching their ideals to their natural conclusions, you force them to stand at the abyss of their own creation. Nothing illustrates this more eloquently than the story of my private cultural revolution.

To say that I grew up in Kuwait is to say that I am a spoiled brat with no connection to reality. Do you think that an Iraqi growing up in Iraq is the same as an Iraqi growing up in Kuwait? Do you think that a Palestinian growing up in Kuwait has similar experiences to a Palestinian growing up in a refugee camp in southern Lebanon? Pfffft! You're kidding yourself!

I grew up in a bubble of affluence, in a country where people have water faucets made out of gold. I myself never saw these fantastical creations but everybody knew somebody who had seen the house of some rich guy who had golden fixtures, so they must exist. Anything that money can buy was available in Kuwait. As a teenager I spent weekends hanging out with friends at the shopping mall. When we weren't at the ice-skating rink, that is. Yes! An Olympic size ice-skating rink in the middle of the desert. Imagine that! In the summer when my family wasn't vacationing in Europe, we were swimming at the pool in one club. The other club we visited to play squash. There was horseback riding, tennis and even golf. Like everybody else we had servants.

Against this shimmering background, I was raised by left-leaning progressive parents. I grew up being lectured on the value of social class blindness.

"The lowly beggar on the street is no different than you," my father was fond of repeating. "His circumstances are dissimilar to yours, but don't think for a minute that you are better than him."

"The school bus driver is equal to you."

"Our servant Avani is equal to you."

"The woman at the cash register is equal to you."

"The man selling cigarettes at the news stand is equal to you."

"The young man flipping burgers at the tennis club is equal to you."

I became envious of all the people who were equal to me. I wished I could be equal to me as well. I wanted a taste of raw reality like all those people who were equal to me, yet I was living a fairy-tale princess life. One bite from the forbidden apple and I would be doomed to a prolonged slumbering fate.

My ninth rule of eating is this: "Food is judged by its appearance. That is the way it is. Deal with it."

My in-laws in Lazzazza looked shocked when I told them I would be participating in the olive harvest. One week later, I was putting on old sweat pants and a torn t-shirt. I tied a scarf around my head for protection against the sun. "Ready for farming duty!" I declared to the mirror at 6 am. Jenin, Kamila, Amal and I descended into the valley at a confident pace, ignoring the mushy ground that enveloped half of each shoe with every step. Jenin set up three tarp canvases beneath a particular tree. I hesitated.

"What do we do now?" I whispered to Kamila.

"Just milk the tree branches the way you would milk a cow," Kamila said. She was already making the green olives drop to the canvas like rain. They made a "pluk,pluk,pluk" sound as they hit the tarp. Jenin and Amal followed her with elegant hand swoops that made them look as if they were hugging and caressing the tree like a long lost relative coming home from a lengthy trip abroad. My anxiety subsided. *This is easy. I don't need a special certificate, or enrollment in a training program to learn how to do this. This is awesome!* Within minutes I was performing my own tree tango dance. I was fleecing the tree of its fruit and in return it was dropping particles of dust and leaf bits on my head.

In 1966, Chairman Mao initiated a cultural revolution in China, which was marked by forcibly relocating the intellectual class from urban to rural locations. The idea was that all the smart people would sympathize with the hardworking peasants by doing their work.

I read somewhere that Andy Warhol was fed Campbell's soup every day for lunch by his mother. Have you ever tried Campbell's soup? It tastes dreadful. Both Andy Warhol and myself have Czech mothers. I am not going to tell you what I was fed for lunch nearly every day. Suffice it to say that I totally get the tomato soup painting. Like totally get it in ways I can't describe in words. What I can describe in words, though, is why I appreciate the Warhol's chairman Mao silkscreen. I like how the image both ridicules yet glorifies at the same time, in equal measure, two extremes sitting on top of each other comfortably.

I will never forget the look in my father's eyes when he came to visit us in Lazzazza that summer. His precious little daughter turned into a peasant! In that moment, while picking olives in Lazzazza, I became the Andy Warhol Chairman Mao painting in my father's eyes. Everything that he had claimed he stood for. The icing on the much-coveted cake was much more disturbing than he had bargained for. He didn't say anything, but in his eyes I read his own self-loathing. "What have I done?" He probably cursed at himself for many months afterwards.

The taste of freshly squeezed olive oil is a direct delivery from heaven. It has a peppery spiciness that crawls across and sideways on your tongue with the lightness of a ladybug and the precision force of a hypodermic needle. Better than chocolate. More pure than sex. Although I would argue that nothing is better than sex. But if you can imagine an innocent stylized form of sex, freshly squeezed olive oil would be better than it. Forget all the three-star Michelin restaurants. Forget all the family meals you ever had. Forget love. Don't even mention your grandma's secret recipe. Watch your dreams and hopes for the future wash over you. Who needs peace on earth? What utility is there in pursuing happiness? Life has no meaning. You can't bottle this, nor ship it to a supermarket. If people knew about this, they would all be flocking to give up their professional lives, titles and degrees. They would all want cultural revolution. Mao would become their un-ironically anointed idol. We would all lift up the red book to the sun and chant with religious passion in unison: "Make me an idiot!"

Please.

Freshly pressed olive oil tastes that good?

Freshly pressed olive oil tastes that good.

Mashed Potato

A COUPLE OF WEEKS AGO I was sitting in my parent's living room drinking tea, half distracted by the TV, when my father was silenced in mid-sentence. Ouch! Here it was again, the family secret that, throughout my childhood, hovered over our heads like a dark cloud. Sentences that abruptly ended in silence. Knowing looks that got exchanged between my parents at the dinner table. I sensed there was something unsaid. It felt like a heartburn that creeps up on you suddenly and you pretend you have no idea where it came from. And then you remember the hot dog stand that came running into your path. The nauseating smell of boiled fatty processed meat. Mustard. Relish.

I was determined to diagnose the source. I didn't catch what my father said, but I caught the apologetic look he was sending to my mother. The unspoken exchange hovered over all of us.

"What is it?" I asked. Enough was enough.

"Nothing?" My father looked at my mother again.

"No, it's something."

"It's the thing we don't talk about," he said.

"You don't think the time has come for us to talk about the thing we don't talk about?"

In my mind I was speculating what the family secret could be. My list contained:

1 – I am adopted.

2 – My father has a son from a previous marriage back in Iraq he never told us about.

3 – My mother is an extra-terrestrial from planet Zlungobashee.

My mother got up to grab a box of tissues, then sat back in her seat to tell me the long-hidden family secret. One year after Layal was born, my mother gave birth to a baby girl who died two weeks later. This event plunged my mother into a depression that resulted in her neglecting her mothering duties towards Layal. My father picked up the slack. The short version of the story is that my mother blames herself for Layal's rebellious nature. Layal herself doesn't remember any of this. My mother has convinced herself that this early childhood neglect marked Layal and has resulted many years later in her being a divorcee. I arrived one year later and my mother's normal state was restored. My mother was wiping tears and snot away as she told me the story in a longer form. I squeezed myself next to her on the seat to give her a hug and assure her that she was a good mother.

"It's perfectly normal to feel depressed right after losing a child," I said. In my mind I kept thinking: *I have been doubly misnamed. I am not even the second daughter.*

Gillian has stopped writing poetry to rethink her approach. She had to sign a written assurance never to recite poetry at her work place again as a condition for returning to employment. She went to see a psychic called Divine Sensor to help her figure out where she had gone wrong.

"Thaniya, you must go see this woman," she said. "It was amazing what she was able to tell me about myself."

Gillian looked disappointed when I told her that I wouldn't go see her psychic. "But you must! She will provide you with ten years of insight in one hour, things you would never see on your own." I must have looked sceptical, because she wouldn't let it go. "What are you afraid of?"

"I'm not afraid, I just don't like the idea of it," I said.

"It's your judgemental self that prevents you from taking advantage of this golden opportunity," she said. "You think that talking with somebody with unexplainable ability will undermine your intellect, but you need your intellect shaken out of its comfort zone." She paused, and then changed her tack. "Don't you believe in a world outside of the material one?"

"I do. You know I do."

"Why not accept the gifts this unseen world has to offer you then?"

"I have my way and you have yours."

"Do you think I'm crazy?"

"No," I lied.

"Then you do believe that this woman is psychic?"

"I believe that you believe it."

Gillian gave a snort. "You always know the right words to use."

"Shlimpi-Flok"

It's a thing my mother is fond of saying. A made-up expression that she uses whenever she means to say "it is what it is," or "take me as I am," or "accept things as they are." You are not allowed to say Shlimpi-Flok unless you shrug your shoulders and raise your hands up in a gesture of submission while you say it. It is mandatory that you start on a high note and dramatically descend on the second part. I have heard plenty of shlimpi-floks throughout my life.

"I don't like parsley on my rice!"

"Shlimpi-Flok."

"Why do I have to wear a sweater when I don't feel cold?"

"Shlimpi-Flok."

"I hate going to the dentist!"

"Shlimpi-Flok."

"Shlimpi-Flok."

"Shlimpi-Flok."

The shlimpi-flokness stopped the day Layal informed my parents that she was filing for divorce from Jasim, her husband of three years. My father looked as grim as if there had been a death in the family. My mother looked worse. In her usual manner, Layal had dropped the bomb and walked away. It was my job to pick up the pieces and play therapist for my parents.

"I am suffering over this the way the Christ suffered on the cross," my mother told me three months later with tears in her eyes.

"Shlimpi-Flok," I said.

"Shut up! Don't you dare shlimpi-flok me!"

"I have been shlimpi-floked all my life," I said. "I think I have earned a few shlimpi-flok points to my credit."

"Go ahead, step on me while I'm down."

Sheesh! You can never win the guilt game with your mother. All the same I tried to reason with her. "Number one, the divorce is happening to Layal and not to you. Can you empathize that this is painful for Layal as well? Nobody gets married because they hope to get divorced."

"Layal is being foolish as usual, she doesn't realize what a mistake she is making. It is a woman's job to endure."

"It's her life and we need to accept it."

"Her decision is affecting everybody in the family. What is your dad supposed to say to your uncle in Baghdad?"

"You act as if Layal was afflicted with a mental illness."

"She should be diagnosed with something." My mother blew her nose loudly into a tissue.

"How about free will?"

Nobody tells you that when you fall in love you become a prisoner. You no longer belong to yourself. Your heart betrays you. Your thoughts are no longer your own. Helpless and pathetic you will follow your beloved against the better judgement of your parents, community and even your own counsel. Love is the worst kind of humiliation. The only thing that can make it tolerable is if you are loved back. At least then you have a weapon. You can inflict pain back. It becomes like the cold war between Russia and the US. I have a nuclear weapon and you have a nuclear weapon, let's agree not to annihilate each other. Let's not leave each other as charred shadows pressed against the wall. Samih owns the warhead with my heart at its cross hairs. I, in return, am a third world country with no means of self-defence except strong rhetoric. The age of slavery will end when love is outlawed and a vaccine for it is invented.

I was a perfectly happy independent young woman, logically weighing my options as to who to choose as my life's partner. It was all very civilized. The second I encountered Samih's black eyes and his straight black hair—total devastation. I pursued him. I pretended to go for leisurely walks in his neighborhood, hoping to bump into him. I invited myself to parties merely because I heard a rumor he would be there. I placed myself in his path and prayed to god that he would pick me. Oh I prayed. I never prayed so hard in my life. I promised god every virtue. A long list of good deeds.

Just let me have this one thing and I will be in your service for a lifetime.

We had known each other for two months when I asked him to marry me. I was eating seafood shepherd's pie at a restaurant on

Granville Island in Vancouver. With the creamy taste of the sea in
my mouth I gained courage to say what was in my heart. It was all
very simple. I looked into his eyes. I said truthfully and without any
embellishments what was on my mind. "I want to spend the rest of
my life with you. Will you marry me?"

Samih paused in mid-chew. I don't think he ever met a
woman so daring. Not in the east and certainly not in the west. He
opened his mouth for five seconds and I could see the half
masticated food in his mouth. I felt I was looking into his heart.
Mangled and confused. Big lumps. After swallowing he finally
replied: "I need time to think about it."

"Fair enough," I said, then moved on to talking about the
health benefits of fasting in Ramadan. Every night I prayed. I prayed
with tears in my eyes. I got exactly what I wanted. One month after
eating seafood shepherd's pie, Samih showed up at my summer job.
I worked at a Greek deli where I spent the day slicing salami and
portioning white cheese. I told him I would be done in ten minutes
and he gestured with a single finger that he would be waiting
outside. I nodded, understanding. I rushed outside to meet him.

"Let's go for a walk," he said.

This is exactly what he said, word for word:

"I have thought about it with great detail and given it ample
consideration. I am ready to get married. I am of the right age. I
believe you would make a fine wife. I am here today to ask for your
hand in marriage."

I wanted to jump up and down with happiness. I wanted to
scream: "yes! yes! yes!" I got exactly what I prayed for every night for
the last month. But nothing gave me the courage to be transparent.

Instead of expressing what was in my heart, I just said: "I need some time to think about it."

"Fair enough," he said, and moved on to talk about how the economy expands and shrinks in patterns similar to a water pond in Winnipeg.

My life is like mashed potatoes, bland but satisfying. I feel like I should be happy with what I have. Some of the time I am happy with what I have. And then I feel guilty for being too satisfied with myself. I am lacking in ambition at those occurrences. Then I start yearning for wild mushroom saffron rice. Exotic. Expensive. Unique. Exceptional. I feel guilty for not being content with all the existing abundance of my current situation. I have plenty to be grateful for. I am healthy. I have a good husband. Two beautiful daughters. I am in possession of lime green kiwi luck.

The best part about any potato dish is that you have to start by peeling. It's a meditative task that takes both time and concentration. And then there is the swooshy peeling sound. Swoosh! One thin strip jumps off. Swoosh! Swoosh! Now I have a mountain of potato shavings building right underneath my hands. They fall in a random pattern. If I flick my wrist I can make the peel jump up into the air like a lively wiggly worm. I am always surprised the shavings stop moving the minute they fall on my kitchen counter. When I am on my own in the kitchen I succumb to the temptation to play a game with the potato peels. I arrange them side by side according to size. I stack them up into a tower. I roll them, one on top of the next, to see if I can form a gigantic circle that explodes outwards with the force of its own momentum. One peel pushing another peel in an effort to straighten itself. Finally, the peels sit on my counter, mangled and wet. The time has come to dispose of them. That is why I enjoy making mashed potatoes. Saying goodbye to the peels is not so sad because I still have the mashing action to look forward to. The peels provide just enough entertainment while I am waiting for the potatoes to boil. Out comes the masher. Squeezing lumps of pliable mush through uniform holes. I am not excessively diligent with the masher. A few lumps signal that the food is home-made. How can something that is so bland be so enjoyable to make? So satisfying. Heartbreak? Friction at work? Annoying person on the bus? I make mashed potatoes and the awful feeling fades away.

So here I am. I have escaped two wars. Been spared death numerous times. I speak four languages. My awareness of the east and west transcends knowledge and scoots into the area of instinct. And yet I am living a mashed potato life. Why would destiny place great luck down my path? Perhaps I am meant for a grander purpose. I should take all this good fortune and turn it into gold. Do good in the world. Bring about change. Positive transformation. Be the best that I can be. Live out my fullest potential.

I can't decide which is more devastating: Getting exactly what I wanted or not getting it. I always cry when I hear a song of unrequited love. Warm tears of self-satisfied anguish trickle down my cheeks. Samih is faithful, loyal and hard-working. He helps out with housework. He probably changed about 40% of all the diapers that got changed in our house. He is the definition of dependable. If there is a problem, you can be sure that Samih will be there to take care of it. If somebody is sick, you can bet your top dollar Samih will show up. Yet I find myself fantasizing about a man who says: "Thaniya, I love you, I love you, I adore you, I worship you, you are the most magnificent woman in the whole entire world." I realize this makes me a shallow person.

My ears suffer from a sugar deficiency. I told Samih that I loved him two weeks into our marriage. We were lying in bed next to each other during our honeymoon in a hotel. There was silence between us. I mashed out a simple sentence: "I love you." He looked away and asked me if I would like a cup of tea. I said nothing and he brought a cup of tea to me in bed anyway.

Gillian once told me that her psychic told her: "You need to accept love in the form it arrives, rather than seeking love in the form you imagine." I try hard to put that lesson into practice. When I ask Samih if he loves me he always replies like a politician, saying words that imply little meaning. "Why else would I be living with you?" He responds with another question. "I am here, aren't I?"

So then I resorted to writing love letters. For three years I wrote him love letters. Long and short. I would seal them in an envelope, write his name on the outside and leave them around the house for him to find. The letter would disappear from its sitting place on the dining table, pillow, underwear drawer or shaving kit. Once in a while I would mail it to him by post to his office. There was never any acknowledgment or reply.

At this point I stopped telling him that I loved him. I also stopped writing him love notes. I accepted that my marriage is propelled by the force of my love for my man. I can love for the two of us.

Samih drives me crazy with his efforts to make mashed potatoes interesting. He keeps experimenting with recipes.

Curry mashed potatoes.

Mashed potatoes with cheese.

Mustard.

Oregano.

Replace butter with olive oil.

Mashed potatoes with pesto.

Mashed potatoes with tomato sauce.

Roasted garlic mashed potatoes.

I keep telling him: "You are missing the point, the blandness is what makes it work. It's like chicken noodle soup. If it ain't broken, don't fix it." Mashed potatoes with canned tuna was his response. Samih is trying to turn comfort food into an exotic adventure.

Mashed potatoes with sriracha sauce.

He doesn't realize what he is sacrificing in the process.

Mashed potatoes with cream of mushroom sauce.

Sometimes I am a bitch to Samih. I turn mean and say hurtful things. I tell him that he is stupid, unsophisticated, a pseudo-intellectual. I imply that I had better opportunities. It is his quintessentially Arabic identity that prevents him appreciating the naked simplicity of mashed potato. I, on the other hand, am a half-breed; I have a taste for both sides. I think I secretly resent him because of how much I love him. It is like there is a future heartbreak hanging in the air between us. One day, he might decide to leave me. I will be devastated and he will not. I will fall apart and he will be whole. I envy him his freedom. His independence. Untouchable.

Mashed potatoes with boiled onions.

Which I secretly liked, but I pretended that I hated. "It tastes like uncooked potatoes," I said, when in reality it was the closest thing to the perfect plain mashed potato he has come up with.

Mashed potatoes with boiled eggs.

Eeeew!

He presents me with his creations with a twinkle in his eyes. The same look I have whenever Zakiya or Shatha come home from school to show me an art project. "Hey, Mom! Look what I made today." I find it so easy to pat each girl on the head and praise her talent. With Samih, I approach each innovation cautiously. I poke with my fork around the edges, testing the texture, anticipating the degree of my displeasure. A little lump ends up in my mouth. I chew slowly. "What do you think?" Samih asks, impatiently pushing his luck.

Mashed potatoes with red beans.

(It looked like barf.)

No need to taste that stuff.

Your eyes will tell you to stay away.

Stay.

Stay.

Stay.

Stay away.

Cinnamon

TODAY I FEEL LIKE TOMATO SAUCE that has been spiked with cinnamon. Something you can force yourself to tolerate, yet clash with every step of the way. Every bite and lick screams of the wrongness of this mixture. I have been fasting now for two months. The practice has rendered me sensitive to unexpected things. The level of noise in the hospital is one example. Beeping machines, the buzz of the air conditioning. The faint squeak of the wheels of my blood cart. The collective moaning and sighing of the patients. It is all grating on me. I can't tune it out. Sounds push themselves into my awareness like bees on a mission. An army of them. Ideally, my spiritual practice would take place in seclusion in a quiet place so that I could hear my own thoughts. It is so much harder to be spiritual when there is real life to attend to.

It's making me short with the patients as well. With each patient, my routine is to introduce myself and let them know that I need to take blood samples. Right before I am about to prick them with the needle, I usually ask them a personal question. Talking about themselves distracts people from the slight discomfort of the needle prick. I make an effort to listen to each person as long as they need with maximum compassion.

Today there was a middle-aged man whose appendix had been removed. Wearing flannel pajamas, lying on his back with eyes closed, his hands placed on his chest as if he was praying, he looked serene. I felt guilty about disturbing him. His lunch tray was still in his room and so I asked him what his favorite food was. He stared right into my eyes and told me with eerie determination: "I don't believe in God." I looked down at his hand to avoid his gaze. He insisted on being acknowledged: "I don't believe in God," he repeated. I don't know what came over me then. I never challenge patients. I figure if somebody is staying at the hospital they have enough to deal without a lab tech giving them a hard time. Despite my better judgement, I found words spilling out of my mouth the way milk seeps through a cracked jug. "So how do you find meaning in life if you don't believe in a higher power?" I asked.

"There is no meaning. There is the here and now. This is all there is. Everything else is just a fairy tale."

I became visibly irritated. My hand began shaking. The silence stretched between us like an overbaked cheese strand refusing to let a slice leave the mother ship pizza. He didn't elaborate, perhaps fearing I would leave the needle in his vein. I didn't, of course. But as I was leaving his room I turned back and said: "You're wrong."

I realize that my reaction was silly. Unprofessional. Idiotic. The poor man was probably on painkillers.

I keep thinking about the story of the three princes that fell in love with the portrait of the princess of China. I just know it holds the secret of my destiny, if only I could decipher its meaning. I am certain that the story is not about work, since I don't have any desire to replace Charlotte as the head of phlebotomy. That is such a small potato. It would hardly be worth Rabia's time. Furthermore, there is no evidence that Charlotte is about to leave her position. She has 20 years till retirement and gives off no signals that she is about to leave her post willingly.

I suspect the story is about Gillian, Don and me. Each one of us has a creative passion he or she is pursuing outside of work. Gillian's poetry, Don's painting and my poetry. Gillian is the overzealous eldest brother who wants to attain success in an instant, even though the intensity of such an encounter would kill her. Don is the arrogant middle brother who believes his paintings are so brilliant that nobody is worthy of seeing them. I shall emerge from behind both of them, the grand poetess of my generation. This theory makes sense. Rabia was a poet. The story was revealed to me through the poetry of Rumi. The signs could not be clearer. Each week, I will choose the best poem and create a youTube video. Poetry should be recited, read out loud. Proudly. YouTube is the modern public square. Over time I will gain a following and become a modern day popular poet of the masses. Like Robert Burns, whose most famous poem was written in appreciation of haggis. All over the world, aficionados hold a Burns Supper to celebrate the life and work of this most awesome poet. The evening is kicked off with a haggis carried on a silver tray behind a bagpiper. After the ceremonial cutting of the haggis, the famous poem is recited. This beautiful tribute to poetry is held each year on the birthday of Robert Burns. If I am reading the signs correctly then Robert Burns is the king. Through his inspiration I shall achieve the perfect balance of integrity in art and popularity.

Oh, this is so exciting! I can't wait to get started. Just having this thought makes me feel better. I can feel the cinnamon getting seeped out of the sauce through a miracle of osmosis.

Here is a pot of tomato sauce.

Here is spoonful of cinnamon.

They stay separate.

All will be well in the kitchen henceforth.

Ravioli

DESTINY IS DANCING IN OUR WOUNDS wearing slippers
lined with salt. Here I am going for a walk along the beach in the
windy cold with Gillian. I would rather be home drinking
chamomile tea while reading *Captain Underpants* to the girls;
instead I am listening to Gillian recount tedious details of things her
psychic, Divine Sensor, has told her.

"All the signs are aligned," she says.

Hovan is meant to be with Gillian like a super moon eclipse.
There is just one little snag in this beautiful soul mate story, and
that is that the factual reality is not lining up with the fantasy.
Gillian goes over the matching horoscopes, his body language, their
two histories, the certainty in her heart and all of Divine Sensor's
ramblings. Gillian has been visiting her on a weekly basis for the last

three months. She calls her D for short. She records everything that D tells her in a journal.

The wind is lashing our faces with coldness. The sea is turning into menacing shades of gray that match the clouds. It is going to rain any minute now. There is no doubt about it. Yet Gillian is walking straight ahead, oblivious to her surroundings, with a journal in her hands.

"I don't understand," she screams in anguish. "Eight weeks ago our souls were this far apart." She points at a drawing of two stick figures, one male and another female, in her journal. "Six weeks ago we were getting closer. Based on D's estimates we are supposed to be together based on natural progression."

I stand in front of Gillian to stop her and grab the journal out of her hand. "Do you notice that the beach is empty, there is nobody here except the two of us?"

"So? Who cares?"

"Has it occurred to you that D is a charlatan who tells you what you want to hear in order to make more money?"

Gillian grabs the journal back and walks forward, pointing out on the page the progression of the two stick figures meeting in the middle.

"I don't understand what happened!" she wails. "He was supposed to leave his wife by now."

I just walk by her side listening to her endless loop as compassionately as possible, bracing for the downpour of rain that will fall on our heads with the same certainty that she has that her hand-drawn stick figures will lovingly embrace at the end. We all suffer from a lack of objectivity. Here I am nursing my own fantasy, helpless to expel it, even with the clarity gained by fasting. I wonder what crazy delusion Don suffers from that keeps him locked in his basement night after night. Here he is, a mighty accomplished surgeon. Not afraid to open people's guts with a scalpel. Getting paid to play God. Outside the operating room he plays surgeon with his words, ruthlessly—like a serial killer maniacally wielding a chainsaw in a horror movie. He cuts people with words that make them bleed for days and sometimes months.

Who knows what lies in Hovan's heart? Who knows what lies inside any man? Men are the trick question you are certain to get wrong. They are the mystery hidden in a gift box buried under the ocean by diver-eating Jinni. I never understood men. There is no logic to anything that they do. Jamal was the first man who taught me that.

Jamal was so memorable that I don't remember how I met him. Yet he was the first who demonstrated to me how little I understood of men. It was a lesson that was to be repeated in a cyclical pattern, tattooing itself on the inner membrane of my brain. Somehow he ended up being part of my social group in my fourth year at university, in Vancouver. We called ourselves el-shila (the group). Samya from Gaza, Ma'an from Jordan, Sana from Lebanon, Khadija from Tunisia, Jamal from Egypt and myself. We were young, ambitious and on our way, or already there; professionals itching to conquer the world with our brilliant ideas. Our optimism was of the wattage that lights Christmas displays in malls. We gave each other solace by swimming the kiddie pool of Arabic in a sea of English.

True to our upper middle-class upbringing we had all our professions picked out for us since childhood. Jamal was already working as a civil engineer. Samya was doing a master's degree in computer science. Ma'an was a pharmacist. Sana was studying dentistry and Khadija was destined to be a lawyer. I felt proud of myself for I was working towards the truffle of all professions — medicine. We were the cream of the crop. We were the best Arab society had to offer. Or so we conducted ourselves. Ma'an was smitten with Samya, who lacked any word descriptor that could be attached to feminine beauty. She was tall and skinny, with a large nose, wavy short hair, droopy eyes, and dressed in a tomboyish manner. All in all, she looked like Popeye's Olive Oyl. Just like the spinach-crazed sailor, Ma'an sighed with longing each time Samya spoke, made googly eyes whenever she entered a room and complimented every single thing she expressed. Observing her cold indifference to him only intensified the humor of the Samya/Ma'an saga. Samya confided in me that Ma'an had proposed marriage to her twice. Rejection only intensified the flames of his passion for his beloved. He was a man on a mission: to keep showering Samya with affection until she agreed to marry him. Nobody dared flirt with Mr. Popeye. For you were more likely to injure him than flatter him with feminine energy that was not sourced from Samya.

So that left Khadija, Sana and myself with nobody to play the flirting game with except Jamal. Sana and Khadija competed with each other to heap flattery and smiles upon his head. Jamal enjoyed the attention the same way a plum-stuffed dumpling takes to a thorough smothering in butter, sugar and poppy seeds. Being shy at the time, I kept myself reserved. Most people laugh when I tell them I used to be shy, since my current predisposition carries not a trace of my former state. But in my early twenties I was painfully shy. I used to be the sort that would sit in a gathering for hours never uttering a single word. I could participate in a heated discussion and never betray an opinion. And then one day in my mid-twenties I decided I didn't want to be the shy person any more. Practicing non-shyness was painful but it paid off with material rewards that far outweighed the feminine pull of keeping myself mysterious. The truth is that I wished I could flirt with Jamal as well. Having attended girls-only schools, I never had an opportunity to practice this important life skill. All the young men I knew beforehand were family relations. I didn't find Jamal attractive, but he seemed like a nice enough person. Sana and Khadija were having a mountain of amusement with giggles and coquettish whispers. They both teased him affectionately.

"Hey! Jamal!" said Sana during one of our dinner gatherings. "How can we take you seriously as an engineer when you have no bald spots, don't wear glasses and look so generally fit?"

"Yes! Jamal!" Khadija sing-songed. "I am worried people at your office mistake you for a gym instructor."

Jamal cracked a smile and looked at me briefly to see if I had anything to add to this physique-admiring fiesta. My tongue tied itself into a snake-slithering knot. My cheeks blushed. I looked down demurely instead. Jamal laughed. "I compensate by wearing stern clothes and serious ties. It is amazing what a finely tailored dark blue suit will do to a man's image." It would have been a great feat of liberty to contribute: "Oh yeah! You probably look even more striking in a tailored suit that you do right now wearing jeans and a t-shirt."

I envied Sana's and Khadija's ease with words. Jamal rewarded both of them with plenty of compliments back. During el-shila's beach picnic he told Sana that she looked like a fresh flower while we were playing frisbee. Then while all of us sat on a blanket to eat, he told Khadija that her egg salad sandwich would taste extra good because it had been made with such elegant hands. Samya received no compliments whatsoever because Jamal was afraid Ma'an would punch him in the face if he did. Jamal always addressed Samya with a decorum suitable for a married woman. The only individual attention I got was "You are so smart, you always have a book with you. What are you reading these days?" I was about to dig out the Sahar Khalifa novel from my purse when Ma'an interrupted. "Oh please don't encourage her, she will start talking about social justice and we will never hear the end of it." The whole shila laughed in unison. And so I smiled, shrugged my shoulders and gave a brief reply: "Just another novel." Now I know if I was a proper feminist I would be happier with being called smart than being told that I had elegant hands. But at age 20, I yearned to be told I was beautiful. Oh! To be admired for the most superficial reason of them all.

So Samya and I were excluded from Jamal's flirtations. At least Samya had Ma'an to shower her with attention. I had nobody. Observing our group dynamic, I was sometimes gripped with a sudden attack of loneliness. *Every woman in the world has an admirer, except me. No man will ever look at me in that way.* I would push these gloomy thoughts out of my mind, feeling lucky to have found a group of friends in this faraway land. There was just one incident that was the confusing exception to this pattern.

El-shila was to meet for dinner at a seafood restaurant, Fish 'n' Stuff, which used to be my favorite restaurant back then. It had scattered potted trees all over that made it look like a jungle. I arrived on time to find Jamal sitting by himself. I was wearing a pencil grey skirt and a pink tailored shirt. Jamal got up to greet me.

"Hello Jamal, I see you are punctual as usual," I said.

Jamal sighed and held his chest as if he was uncomfortable.

"What's wrong?" I asked. "Don't tell me you're upset because the rest are always late. You know! Arab time." I laughed as I sat down.

Jamal came over to sit down next to me, "Not at all," he said. "I think you and I are freaks because we always arrive on time."

"I know! How is it that we are Arabs if we are never late?"

Instead of laughing, Jamal sighed again and looked at me with a painful expression.

"What's wrong?" I asked, again. "Did I offend you?"

"You look so beautiful," he said.

I smiled and blushed with embarrassment.

"Thank you! Soon the rest will arrive and I will become ugly in comparison."

"I'm glad they're late so that I can get a few moments alone with you."

"What do you mean?" I asked, unsure.

"Even if all the women of the world were sitting in this restaurant, you would still be the most beautiful woman in the room," he said.

I didn't say anything. I wasn't sure if he was flirting for lack of candidates, or if he was making fun of me.

"Thaniya." He said my name deliberately. "If I had courage, I would kneel down and kiss your feet right now. You are so beautiful it makes my chest hurt." He touched his chest again and sighed.

I was convinced that he was ridiculing me. I looked down at my hands. Tears pricked my eyes. What I wanted to say was *Look! I know you don't find me attractive. But at least we always shared the easy warmth of friendship.* But that darn tongue tie invaded my mouth. Then I felt angry. Angry at myself for not being able to speak up for myself. Angry at him for hurting me for no reason. I looked up into his eyes, wishing I could punch him in the face. I was taken aback. There wasn't a single hint of humor or malice in his countenance. He looked at me with the warm sincerity of a child. His expression was earnest and open. We sat there in silence and we stared at each other. I was softening. Softening. Softening. Melting. Wobbling. And then the rest of the group arrived and it came to an abrupt stop.

He jumped out of his chair to sit between Sana and Khadija and spent the rest of the evening ignoring me. Jamal showered his two companions with flattery that would make your teeth ache. "Oh Sana you are always so delightful." "Khadija, Khadija, Khadija you dazzle me with your brilliance." They both giggled like silly schoolgirls.

Samya looked concerned. She whispered to Ma'an and me: "Look at him, he's putting on quite a show tonight."

Ma'an whispered back: "I already told him twice, stop fooling around and choose one, before you lose both."

I whispered: "What was his reply?"

"Some nonsense about not knowing how to choose between two worthy candidates," Ma'an whispered back.

"They both seem to be enjoying the selection process," I said.

"I fear one of them will get hurt in the end," said Ma'an.

I spent the rest of the evening making fun of Ma'an for ordering steak. "Who orders steak in a seafood restaurant?" I kept joshing at random intervals. Each time he gave me a different answer.

"One who is able to think for himself," Ma'an projected his voice towards Jamal.

"One who dislikes bottom feeders."

"One who appreciates being on top of the food chain."

My choice of food that night was far worse that Ma'an's. I think I made fun of his food because I was thoroughly disappointed with the lobster ravioli I ordered.

The events of that evening confused me. I dismissed it as a joke that went wrong. I resolved to erase it from my mind.

Samya and I proceeded to speculate about who would win Jamal's heart in the end. We frequently met for lunch at the university. She was the one I saw most frequently. I had the feeling Sana had the top position in the husband competition. She dressed elegantly. Her hair was always styled. She walked with an elegant feminine gait. And she was the only woman in our group who knew how to cook. They do say that the shortest path to a man's heart is his stomach. Homemade brownies, cookies and cake would appear at our gatherings courtesy of the always-delightful Sana. Samya, however, was convinced that Khadija would win Jamal in the end, for she possessed the more stylish flair. It was obvious from her mannerisms that her background was more aristocratic that the rest of us. She spoke about the best chocolates imported from Switzerland, custom-made perfumes blended in Paris and fashions designed by names the rest of us had never heard of.

"Jamal wants a wife he can show off," argued Samya.

I gave Jamal more credit. "Jamal will choose the wife that will make him happy," I said. We sifted through the attributes of each woman with a fine sieve. In the end we agreed that both would make a fine wife and mother.

"What does Ma'an think?" I asked Samya while munching on a cinnamon bun one day.

"He thinks that Jamal is an idiot."

"How so?"

"He thinks that a man should let his heart lead in this matter. There should be no hesitation."

"Oh, that is so romantic. You are lucky to have the attention of a sincere man."

Samaya began to cry. "He proposed marriage to me a third time!"

"And?"

"I don't know? He asked to keep the ring this time, so that it might help me think it over."

Samya slipped her hand into her purse to show me a jewelry box. "Have a look."

"It's beautiful!" I admired the diamond solitaire. "Why are you crying?"

"I don't know how to reject him again. I have already said no twice. I even moved from Toronto to Vancouver just to get away from him. Can you believe that he quit his job in Toronto and took a pay cut just to follow me to Vancouver? He is convinced that we are meant to be together. His heart tells him that I am destined to be his wife. Nothing ever discourages him."

"How do you feel about him?"

"I do like him. I think he is a fine man. I just don't love him. But then again how many times in your life will you meet a man who is this absolutely in love with you? In Toronto we both had many Arab friends. He never gave any other woman attention. It's not like there is a lineup of men knocking on my door. There might never be a marriage proposal from anybody else. I am 26 already. If I am to think practically, I should accept him as my husband. He does have all the qualities that would make for a good match. He has a good job. We get along. We make good friends. One day he will make a good father. He worships the ground I walk on. Maybe it's enough that he loves me. Maybe he can love for both of us."

Samaya began sobbing. She rested her head on her right hand and allowed herself to sink into despair.

"I always thought that one day I would feel love as well," she said, when she had collected herself a bit. "That I would meet somebody whom I couldn't live without. Like in all Um Kalthoum's songs. Somebody you want to gaze into his eyes and say "Enta Oumri" (you are my whole life). I never met anybody like that. Perhaps that thing only happens to others. A select few. I am simply not one of them."

"If it's any consolation, I don't know anybody who I would sing Enta Oumri to either."

"Ma'an does sing Enta Oumri to me when we are alone."

"I hate that song."

"Me too."

"Why is Um Kalthoum considered the best Arabic singer anyway?"

"What? You hate Um Kalthoum as well?"

I nodded emphatically.

"Ya Allah! Thaniya, you are the first person I confess this to!"

"You are the first person I confess my hatred to Um Kalthoum to as well," I said.

"Such a harsh voice."

"Stupid sentimental lyrics."

"But if you dare insinuate a criticism people look at you like you are a freak!"

"Worse, an infidel"

"Arabs would sooner stomach sacrilegious sentiments than an Um Kalthoum diss!"

"O Samya, I feel this sudden relief."

"I am so happy that I met an Arab who hates Um Kalthoum like me," she said, looking much more cheerful.

"Until now I always felt that I was weird."

"And I thought I was broken," she said. "Like everybody else has feelings, and I am heartless to not be moved by that song."

"Samya, I love you."

"Thaniya, I love you too."

"Let's sing Enta Oumri to each other."

"Eeeeew!"

We both burst into laughter. We laughed so hard that we wiped tears off each other's cheeks. A sense of lightness permeated our surroundings. It hung in the air like the scent of jasmine flowers when they are in bloom. In that moment I thought that Samya and I would be friends forever.

We sang Enta Oumri to each other in exaggerated sentimentality, waving our hands forwards and backwards as if channelling Um Kalthoum.

All the days of my life were a waste until the second my eyes fell upon you.

Witnessing you makes me regret the past with all its injury.

Until that day, my heart never knew the taste of happiness nor experienced a single hurt.

You are my whole entire life,

That started with the morning of your light.

Taste with me the love,

Taste

Taste

Thoog

Thooog

Thoooooog

We both pointed towards our mouths as if we were tasting the love. And then we would whistle and cheer at each other as we had seen the audience do in live recordings of Um Kathoum.

"Allah!"

"God is Great!"

"Greatness on top of greatness!"

"My soul hurts."

The ruckus we were creating in the coffee shop was disturbing everybody around us. People gave us disapproving looks. Samya and

I didn't care. Little did they know, they were witnessing a historical moment. Arab liberation of the finest kind.

The "Who will Jamal Marry" saga met a most unexpected ending. Not even in your most long-running soap opera could you have made up what actually happened in real life. I learned a most valuable lesson from it all. That men are like ravioli. You have no idea what a secret surprise you will find in them, not even if you are willing to cut through their middle with a knife. Even when you eat it, you still can't tell what the heck was stuffed inside. I challenge you to guess what is in any ravioli without reading the labeling. Spinach or lobster, it all tastes the same. Since that time, I realized that I am totally clueless about the hearts of men. That I will sooner understand Arab's fascination with Um Kalthoum than understand what goes on in the heart and mind of any male that walks the earth.

The beginning of the end of el-shila came when Jamal decided to throw a surprise birthday party for Sana. It was to be held at his apartment. He agreed to order dinner from a nearby Greek restaurant. I was assigned the job of getting the birthday cake. Ma'an and Samya agreed to bring her to the party at an assigned hour. Khadija was to arrange the music for the party on account of her superior taste. I was the first to arrive at Jamal's place, handing over the black forest cake I had picked up on my way.

"Oh no! I arrived punctually again. I guess I never learn," I said.

Jamal looked nervous, he was fidgeting. This was strange. I had never seen him look fazed.

"Actually, I asked you to come one hour earlier," he said.

"You need help with the party arrangements?"

"No! I wanted to have a chance to talk to you alone," he said.

"Okay," I said, sitting on the chair in his living room. "What is it?" Jamal sat across from me on the couch. He placed his hand on the arm of the couch as if he was bracing himself for impact.

He stuttered. He sweated. He began saying things that he didn't continue with. Then he sighed. Then he spoke some gibberish. Then he covered his face with both his hands and screamed: "Aaaaaaaah!"

I sat there with an open mouth, not saying anything.

Jamal got up suddenly, walked to the kitchen, and got himself a glass of water. He drank the whole thing in one go and then sat down again.

"Thaniya!" He said my name as if he was about to give a military command. I felt tempted to shout back: "Yes! Sir!" but instead I said: "Aha!"

"Will you please marry me?" he asked.

"You shouldn't joke about something like that." I was feeling annoyed.

He hit the arm of the couch with his fist. "I'm not joking! I have never been more serious in my life."

Then he softened his voice. He looked down at his left hand.

"I have given it lots of thought. I believe that you are the best candidate to become my wife. You are smart, ambitious, you come from a good family, you are a moral and ethical person, you have a good personality. We are well matched as a couple."

"But I always thought you had eyes set on either Sana or Khadija," I said.

"Yes! I did give that impression. I considered both of them. But after thinking hard on it for many months, I concluded that you would make the best wife for me." He paused and leaned forward. "I would make the best husband for you as well. I am four years older than you. Did you know that scientific studies have proven four years is the ideal age difference between a man and a woman? I am an engineer. I earn a good living. I will give you full support to help you finish your education, both financially and emotionally. Don't worry. I am not like other Arab men. I won't be threatened by having a wife who is superior in education. I will be proud to be a doctor's husband. If it bothers me in the future, I can always do a PhD in engineering and then both of us will have the title of Doctor. Then we will be equal in terms of status. We can delay having children until you are finished studying. I am not in a rush to start a family. We will get married in Egypt, so that you can meet all my relations. We will live in Vancouver. I have already been looking at apartments. We will buy a condo that is in between the university and my work. It will be convenient for both of us. I have done some calculations. I can comfortably support both of us and pay a mortgage on my current salary. I own a car already. I think one will do for the first few years. I know it is preferable to marry somebody who owns an apartment outright. But you are a modern open-minded woman. So I don't think that the mortgage will bother you. If it does, I can ask my family for financial help. But since I am the eldest, and there are three other siblings to take care of, I would prefer not ask for anything. If we work together we can be self-sufficient. Once you start working we will be practically swimming in money. I would like us to have two children. Preferably a boy and a girl. A career woman like yourself will not have time for a big family. That covers all the important points. I think my offer is sensible and fair."

There was a long silence. Jamal didn't say anything. He studied my face to read my reaction. I looked into his eyes to glean the level of his sincerity. I concluded that he was dead serious. As dead as a boiled lobster. His face was red too.

"Why are you holding a surprise birthday party for Sana if you wanted to propose marriage to me?" I asked. It was the only thing I could get out.

"Would you have come over to a bachelor's apartment on your own?" he asked.

"Of course not!"

"I wanted to have this conversation in private, and this was the only way I could think of that would give me time to talk to you without the others around."

"This is a big surprise," I said. Understatement of the year. "I wasn't expecting this."

"I hope it's a nice surprise," he said. His eyes were imploring me to smile, nod, anything.

"It's a flattering surprise."

Jamal smiled for the first time since I met him that evening. His body relaxed as if he was done with a boxing match.

"I don't expect a reply right away. Take time to think about it."

"I feel confused," I said. "Why me? Why me in particular?"

"It's your shyness," he said.

"What do you mean?"

"The way you are blushing right now. Your whole face is red," he said. I blushed even harder. "A shy woman grabs more attention."

I placed my hand on my right cheek. It was feverish. But it wasn't coyness that had turned my heart into a burning furnace. It was shock.

From that point on, Jamal stopped flirting with Sana and Khadija. They both looked confused by the abrupt change in his behavior. They goaded him, but he politely ignored all their provocations. It must have been a confusing evening for Sana. Jamal had gone to the trouble of organizing a surprise birthday party for her, and then proceeded to ignore her throughout the evening. Surprise birthday party for Sana—surprise marriage proposal for me.

And so I spent the next three weeks considering Jamal's offer. I am no fool. I knew that as an Arab woman living in Vancouver my options were limited. What were the chances that I would meet another eligible Arab bachelor who had all the qualities I was looking for in a husband? Rafid had already been placed on my scrap list. Jamal was good-looking enough. He had a pleasant personality. He was religious, but not too religious. He had a job with a good salary. He was neither too western nor too traditional in his mentality. I did enjoy his company. He was amusing and always made me laugh. We seemed to share similar progressive ideas about family life. For example, he never mentioned the fact that I didn't know how to cook. His proposal clearly considered my career aspirations at the time. On paper, Jamal was the ideal husband choice for me.

I consulted with my parents. My father informed me that he had no objections to Jamal. My mother gave me the best advice on how to consider a marriage proposal. "Close your eyes. Imagine that Jamal is the first person you see in the morning and last person you see in the evening before you go to sleep. If thinking about that gives you a happy feeling then you should marry the man, otherwise you should reject his proposal."

I followed my mother's advice. I tried to imagine seeing Jamal's face every day for the rest of my life. The visual filled me with dread. I enjoyed seeing him once in a while. Seeing him every day felt like a waste of my time. I could muster enjoyment for his company once or twice a week. Yet a daily encounter seemed like an endurance test rather than a pleasure.

My ego enjoyed the boast of winning a race in which I put in the least amount of effort. I suddenly felt beautiful and alluring, when only two weeks earlier I had felt completely undesirable. I walked around with the confidence of a woman that could have whichever man she wanted. Oh to be that woman! Men falling at her feet, competing for her attention. Like the actress Shadia in the movie *Maabodat El Gamahir* (The Worshiped Diva). Shadia plays an irresistible famous singer who is worshiped by her audience and adored by every man who ever encounters her. Yet she falls in love with a poor struggling actor who can't believe his luck when the great diva arrives one day, knocking on his door. If you thought that Hollywood had topped the market for schmaltzy love stories, then you have not been introduced to Egyptian cinema. *Pretty Woman?* you might say. *Sweet Home Alabama?* you might put forwards. *The Notebook,* if you are desperate. These movies are serious social commentary next to the impossibly dreamy romance of *The Empty Pillow, My Father is on Top of the Tree* and *Too Young for Love*.

For a brief two weeks I fantasized that I was living an epic love story. Each time I placed Jamal in my fantasy land the fun movie turned into a serious drama with people crying, children dying, lonely figures walking in the rain and a bitter housewife polishing a stainless steel pot.

I asked Jamal to meet in a coffee shop at the university. I attempted to reject him in the nicest way I could think of. I started by recounting all his positive attributes. All the things I admired about him. "I thought long and hard about your proposal. I hesitated. But in the end I came to the conclusion that I will not marry you."

Jamal told me, "I don't believe you. You're just saying that because you're shy."

I assured him that it wasn't shyness that had made up my mind.

"Look! I know it is hard for you to accept a marriage proposal given your shy nature," he said. "Women like you don't want to seem over eager. That's okay. I will ask you to marry me a few more times until you feel comfortable saying yes."

"I am not being shy, I am simply being honest."

"Is there somebody else?" he asked.

"No."

"Then you're shy." His mind was made up.

"Or maybe I don't want to get married," I said.

He dismissed that with a shake of the head. "That's stupid talk. Let's discuss things again in a few weeks."

I had to meet with him two more times to convince him that I didn't want convincing. I wasn't being shy, coquettish, or playing a game. I wasn't negotiating for better proposal terms. I didn't need extra time to think it over. My decision was final and it wasn't going to change, no matter what he did or said. Period. Turn the page. Start a new chapter. The last morsel of this meal has been eaten. The plates have been licked clean. Time to load the dishwashing machine.

I never saw Jamal again after that. He disappeared into oblivion the way tomato disappears into lentil stew. Sana and Khadija snubbed me when they saw me around the university campus. I can't say that I blame them. The one who put in no effort at all received the grand prize of a marriage proposal, and then she wasn't even grateful enough to accept it. It had to seem grossly arrogant to them. The only people who continued to talk to me were Ma'an and Samya. I was grateful for their friendship.

I tried to call Jamal at his work, but I was told by his co-worker Frank that he had quit his job suddenly. Frank told me that he was worried about him, that Jamal was acting all weird. Wasn't answering his phone. Quit without notice. Essentially disappeared off the face of the earth. I met with Ma'an and Samya to discuss the situation. Ma'an told me that after many failed attempts at calling Jamal he finally went to his apartment and pounded on his door until he opened it. He found him dishevelled and depressed.

"Why is he depressed?" I asked.

"He is in love," yelled Ma'an.

"In love? With who?"

"In love with you! In love with you, Thaniya!" Ma'an yelled even louder, pointing two index fingers at me. "He is applying to emigrate to Australia."

"Why go to Australia when he just finished immigrating to Canada?"

"I don't know," he said. "He's not thinking straight. I wasn't going to try reason with him when he's falling apart."

It had never occurred to me that Jamal was in love with me. I thought he just considered me a suitable wife prospect. The "L word" never entered my mind. Had he uttered the L word it might have persuaded me to decide differently. I might have felt so flattered by that sentiment as to say yes to a lifetime of wifehood. How many times do you meet somebody who loves you? In hindsight I am glad he never discussed his feelings with me. I am glad he didn't persuade me. For when I met Samih later on, I was single, fancy-free and without a speck of obligation to any other man. The best state in which to meet the love of your life.

It was during that evening while we were discussing how to help Jamal in his heartbreak that my eyes wandered towards Samya's left hand. I saw the ring sitting loosely on her finger. I shrieked in both shock and delight as I pulled on her hand. "Does this mean you guys are engaged?" Ma'an blushed with happiness as he turned his head to lovingly look at his fiancé. Samya sighed in resignation, staring at her finger.

"Yes, she finally said yes," Ma'an said. "The wedding is in the summer."

I congratulated them both, wishing them all the happiness in the world.

That was my missed chance at living the Arabic version of *When Harry Met Sally*. I never saw Jamal again.

Spinach

I CAME HOME FROM MY "dark and stormy" walk with Gillian wet and agitated. I toweled off, changed into flannel pyjamas and collapsed on the bed like a sinking rock. Samih had put the girls to bed earlier and read them a bedtime story in my stead. I started exhaling heavily. Once, twice, thrice.

Finally Samih asked: "What's wrong? What's bothering you?"

"I'm worried about Gillian."

"Gillian is losing it and there's nothing you can do about it," he said, pulling up the covers.

"I wish I could grab her by both shoulders to shake her violently into waking up!"

"Would that help?"

I considered. "No. It wouldn't make a difference."

"Exactly. There is nothing you can do for her. Nothing. Just give up."

"Why does God give us delusions?" I asked, after a little while.

"If we were perfectly logical then we would be robots." Samih is always very practical.

"Hmmmmmm."

"On the other hand, if we had no logic whatsoever we would animals in the forest. So here is the compromise. God gave us the ability to dream of building a spaceship that will carry us to Mars. The same impulse that carries us into outer space can see us digging a tunnel to the insane asylum."

"So how do you know if you are digging towards the asylum or building a spaceship?" I asked.

"You don't. Both look the same, initially. It's what keeps life interesting."

I turned to him. "You know Samih, sometimes you say the most profound things."

"Does that surprise you?" he asked.

"It does."

"Just because I don't have the words of Mahmoud Darwish memorized by heart doesn't mean that I don't perceive beauty in ordinary things." Samih put his arms up and interlaced his fingers behind his head.

I traced a little circle on his shoulder.

"Both Gillian and Don want to see the movie before they enter it," he continued. "They want to pre-screen their lives before they live them. A psychic is at worse a charlatan and at best like a movie reviewer that gives you all the spoilers and ruins the movie for you. Don is afraid to show his work to the world before he receives a guarantee that it is great. No such guarantee exists. You are afraid, like both of them, but at least you are taking steps forward."

"How come you never asked to see my poetry?"

"I figured when you were ready, you would show it to me on your own."

"I am afraid you will laugh at me," I said.

"I didn't marry your poetry, I married you,"

"God! Is there anything about me that you appreciate? Just one thing? And please don't say my cooking!"

"Your sincerity."

"What?"

"You are always so, so sincere."

"Sincere." I rolled it off my tongue. "I like that."

"You should have been called Sadiqa (*Sincere one* in Arabic) instead of Thaniya."

"You can call me that, I like that."

"It will be my secret name for you. My private Sadiqa."

"Your slutty little Sadiqa," I said, making bigger circles.

"Ooooo, I like that even more. Come over here and give me a warm kiss to make it official."

When my birth date approached, my mother decided to travel back to the Czech Republic to surround herself with motherly love. On the day of my birth, my grandfather made spinach stew, a heavy wintery dish cooked with pork lard and beans. My mother was seized by a devious hunger which compelled her to eat three healthy helpings. Each serving could have fed a miner. Yet the more she ate the hungrier she felt. No sooner did she put her spoon down, and before she had the chance to wipe her mouth clean, labour pains began shooting through her womb. She screamed for help. My grandfather came running but was suddenly seized by an irresistible urge to make a beeline to the outhouse. My grandmother came running, but her bowels made rumbling noises. The outhouse was occupied and so grandma was forced to take care of business behind a large bush in the backyard. My mother was left screaming in the kitchen until a nearby neighbour heard her cry and called the ambulance.

At the hospital, my mother pushed, breathed, pushed, breathed, pushed, and as the baby was about to come out, her intestines pushed their contents out as well. I emerged into the world along with projectile poo that splattered the walls of the birthing room. My mother swears that the cooked stew came out the other end as fresh, bright green spinach. As if her digestive system had restored life into the leafy vegetable. The spinach leaves attached themselves to the walls and ceiling, floated in the air and landed on the hair and clothing of the nurses and doctors. By the time I came out, the birthing room looked like it had been attacked with a violent green snow blizzard. My mother is convinced my birth was a miracle, signifying that I was to be a lucky child throughout my life, bestowing fortune on anybody close to me.

This dramatic story has been told to me thousands and thousands of times, until I have memorized every nook and cranny of its dimensions. Each time my mother prepares to tell the story of how Thaniya was born, I take a deep breath and in my mind I imagine I am in roasted land, a fictional country where mountains are made up of roasted chickens, the land is covered with lamb, houses are built out of pizza and rivers run with roasted red pepper pesto instead of water. Rocks are hunks of cheese. The sky is the most beautiful thing in roasted land, with roasted marshmallows floating gently across it.

With my Zakiya and Shatha, I made sure not to tell them any details about the day they were born so that they wouldn't be forced to invent their own version of roasted land. To my utter surprise, Zakiya asked me yesterday during dinner why I had never told her the story of how she was born.

"I wished to spare you the anguish," I replied, without thinking.

"But, mom! All my friends have a birth story, except me. I want to know how I arrived into the world."

"Well I was pregnant, I gave birth and you arrived into my life." I wiped my mouth with my napkin.

"No, mom! I want the details. Were you in pain? Did dad drive you to the hospital? Was the doctor nice?"

I needed to nip this in the bud. "Do you know the story grandma tells about the day I was born?"

"Yes, the one about the miracle with spinach, that's a crazy story."

"I heard that story thousands and thousands of times throughout my childhood and adult life," I said.

"Aha."

"Grandma told it to my teachers at school."

"Oh."

"The first time she met your dad, she pulled up a chair, sat right across from him and started with 'Let me tell you the story of how Thaniya was born.'"

"How embarrassing! But dad married you anyway."

"I was certain I would never see him again," I said. "It has been a traumatizing experience, hearing that story, never mind the embarrassment it has caused me. I swore that when I had children, I wouldn't subject them to the same pain."

"It's only traumatizing when told thousands of times," said Zakiya. "If you only tell me my story once or twice, it won't be traumatizing."

"I can't break my promise."

"That's so unfair." She pouted. "You have the miracle spinach lucky child story and I have nothing."

"You mean the green projectile poo covering the walls story?" I said. "You want to have nightmares?"

"It's a funny story!"

I shook my head. "I need to make peace with my birth story before I can tell you yours."

"But mom!!!!!"

"Eat your fish fingers. I made them especially for you."

Soya Sauce

DARKNESS. INSIDE IT I FEEL SAFE. I can hide. I am tired of standing in the light. This turning. A tide. I am forgiven. I can't see myself in the mirror. As a child I was afraid of monsters that appeared against the silver screen of my imagination in the dark. My imagination must be shot. Weariness appears invisible against a black backdrop. A sigh of relief.

My kitchen has a secret that I hesitate to reveal.

Whenever people ask me: "What is the secret that makes the food you prepare taste so good?" I tell them the secret is in the fresh herbs I receive from my in-laws in Palestine. My answer is partially true. My sister in-law handpicks, dries and grinds her own herbs once a year. Then, very generously, she sends me a small portion by mail. Without fail, I open her gift to be greeted by a wafting of smells that are like Technicolor to my olfactory system. I bury my face in the Ziploc-sealed bags and take a hearty inhale: sumac, zaatar, oregano, cumin, saffron, turmeric and dried chilli peppers.

The scent of sun-kissed meadows traversed by ancient feet.

The colors of hills and valleys that have inspired prophets to sacrifice all to save humanity.

A giant poking finger that descends from the sky to indicate: "And now ... this!"

Mmmmmmmm, this is life, this is perfection.

Shatha jokes that zaatar is our family's equivalent of weed because we are all addicted to it. Even when talking about it we all enter into a kind of psychedelic dream.

Leaving poetry and jokes aside, the herbs from Palestine are superior to anything I buy in the supermarket and they certainly give things prepared in my kitchen a unique touch. However, that is not the only secret ingredient in my recipes. I feel shy about telling you, because it is so pedestrian. So uninspiring, so anticlimactic.

You must promise never to tell anybody this.

I am blushing with embarrassment.

Shhhhhhhhhhhhhhhhhhhhhhhhhhhhhhhhhhhhhh!

You're going to be so disappointed.

Okay, I'll just say it. Soya sauce. Yes, that is my secret. I put soya sauce in everything.

I learned about this black gold when I first immigrated to Vancouver. The city has a sizable Chinese community. I fell in love with their cuisine right away. Who am I kidding? I fall in love with all cuisine upon first sampling! And so I tried to teach myself to make a stir-fry, which I failed at miserably. The vegetables came out mushy and my chopped meat emerged from the wok mangled and tough. However, that experiment led me to buy my first bottle of soya sauce. Initially I got the smallest one I could find in the supermarket. I added it to my ground beef one day and enjoyed the tangy, salty result. Next I found myself adding it to rice, eggs and yes, even salad dressing. The small bottle got replaced with a larger one. Then I bought the one-liter kind. Nowadays I get soya sauce in a four-liter aluminum can that I buy in bulk at the speciality Asian store. Yes, that's right, I put soya sauce in all my Arabic recipes. It is as if the mansaf and mejadara have lived an eternity, yearning for a missing long-lost cousin. With my improvisation they all rejoice in singing a harmony of such-salty pitches, that they make braised lamb cubes do an energetic belly dance. The Middle East and Far East meet. They don't just meet, they embrace each other, kiss each other's cheeks and cry hot jumbo tears when remembering all the years spent apart.

Now you might think that Samih would be the sensible one. That he might attempt to dissuade me from this madness. That he would say, "Innovation is the enemy of the kitchen."

Or,

"Why do you soil our authentic Arabic traditions with this corrupting influence?"

Or,

"God curse any man who allows a woman to meddle with his ancestors' spices!"

Or,

"Sheick Abu Fankash reported that Sheick Saheb Mlaheb was reported to have said: All woman hiding a secret ingredient in the kitchen go straight to hell."

But you would be wrong. Samih, instead of being the voice of reason, in this case is a collaborator. Even when I omit the soya sauce, he pours a healthy helping with his own hands.

Poor Shatha and Zakiya are growing up thinking that all Arabic food tastes as perfect as my concoctions. One day they will realize that what they ate at home was an aberration.

Ten years ago I saw a Canadian movie whose name I can't remember, about a recent young Chinese immigrant. When she's asked out on a date by a handsome young Chinese man, she accepts excitedly. At the restaurant, the man orders some French fries for them to share. The woman pours soya sauce on the fried potatoes to improve the taste. The young man seems perturbed by her behavior, considering it a sign of backwardness and provinciality. That scene in the movie sent me sizzling. I felt as if I was seeing a soul sister. *Yes! That is so me.* I said to myself. *I must try soya sauce on french fries!*

Try soya sauce on French fries. It really tastes good. Really, really good. You will wonder why you ever thought ketchup deserved to exist at all.

Sardines

SO MAYBE I NEEDED A Zaev delusion as a destabilizing kick in the ass to get serious about writing poetry. Or maybe I am just digging a private tunnel into the loony bin. I can't tell the difference. Maybe not knowing is the point.

Since Samih and I have made up, he has stopped his ritual of reading the piece of paper in his briefcase when he comes home from work. Yet I have this burning feeling that the outer pocket of his black leather briefcase still contains a secret. Something about my husband that I don't know. I am dying to stick my hand in there to fish it out. I need to know what circles in the inner chambers of his heart.

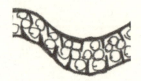

My father is an exceptionally lucky man. Perhaps there is a lucky gene and I inherited it from him. Or perhaps my guardian angel has been trained by his super-efficient guardian angel. Or maybe all of this has no meaning and I am pushing against the outer boundaries of logic to scrape dried sewage out of ancient pipes in search of a fossil that explains the origins of life. I don't understand what I am doing.

My father, Hashim Rasid, was to be executed along with tens of thousands of others who opposed the Ba'athist regime. He was hiding at a friend's house, but somebody must have ratted him out. Two army officers appeared at the door and led him to a jeep. Hashim knew the minute they got to the police station he would be a goner. In a moment of inspiration, he made up a story.

He drew himself up tall and glared at the two lowly army personnel. "Do you know who I am?" he barked. "My name is Ziad Ramih!" And then a whole fictional persona materialized.

"I am a highly decorated army general and a war hero. You have arrested the wrong man."

His arresting officers began to hesitate and looked at each other with doubt.

"The minute we get to the police station, you will be in a mountain of trouble," he said. "I will see to it that you two idiots end up in jail and I will command 50 lashes for each one of you."

They looked at each other in confusion. The seeds of doubt were taking hold.

"This is the most insulting thing that has ever happened to me," my father said, pursing his lips. "But never mind, carry on. You do know your career in the army will be over, though."

The two arresting officers began to shake in fear, drove my father back to his friend's house and apologized profusely for their mistake. By the time they realized they had been fooled and returned to arrest him, he was long gone. This time, Hashim knew to seek refuge in the basement of an abandoned house in the countryside belonging to a co-worker nobody would naturally associate him with.

With the specter of death looming over his head, he imposed imprisonment on himself, never leaving the basement. His rescuer delivered supplies on a monthly basis, and since canned foods were the most practical means of staying alive, it meant that Hashim had no access to fresh meat, fruit or vegetables. It was during that time that my father developed his aversion to sardines. Tiny little fish, packed tightly, swimming in oil. Hashim had to eat sardines on a daily basis in a dark basement for nine months, until he began to wish he would get arrested and executed. The taste, smell, sight— yes, even just the thought of a sardine would send him into apoplexy. Later, when he married my mother, he made his feelings on the subject abundantly clear.

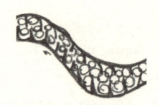

My mother loved sardines, though, and would get the occasional craving. She would wait until my father was at work, then open the can discreetly as if she was committing a crime. Afterwards she would pack the can in a plastic bag and take it out to the garbage. Proceed to scrub clean plates and utensils. Spray air freshener into the four corners of the kitchen.

My father would shoot an accusatory look at my mother as soon as he walked into the house. "Who ate sardines in this house?" he would ask. "I told you to take out the garbage after you eat sardines!"

"I did!" she would say.

"I asked you to clean the dishes immediately after you are finished eating."

"I did!"

"Did you brush your teeth?"

"I did!"

"Did you wash your hands?"

"I did!"

"Then how come I can still smell it? I am certain you skipped one of the steps in the after-sardine procedure."

"I didn't!"

My mother eats sardines with the same trepidation that a Canadian teenager would smoke marijuana in his parents' house.

My father's rescue from sardine hell came in the form of a uniform. A friend of a friend stole a uniform from an army general. This mighty gift arrived in the sardine box one late afternoon along with a plan to smuggle him out of the country. He proudly placed the stolen medals on his chest, adjusted the beret just so and prayed he could channel the fictional Ziad Rameh one more time. He marched into the Baghdad airport with all the haughtiness he could muster. At that time, the airport was manned by the army. All the soldiers jumped out of their seats to salute him upon seeing the high-ranking collection of stars adorning his shoulder pads. He waltzed through the airport, boarded an airplane and swam outside of Iraq like a tiny little fish slides out from between the fingers of a giant.

Slippery.

Tiny fish is slippery.

Fffffffffrlph.

Nobody asked him to show his passport or airplane ticket. No one dared suggest that he should be searched.

The day was November eleventh. Hashim Rasid decided that he would celebrate his birthday on that day from then on because it was the date of his true birth. The sardine-infused basement was like a womb, and his flight from Iraq a rebirth after facing certain death.

Pizza

A MISHMASH OF SENSELESS THINGS. That is youTube. Twelve-year-old boys amusing themselves with pranks. Girls playing dress-up with mother's makeup. Unfortunate challenges. The cinnamon challenge. The milk challenge. Dancing sensations. Extreme sports footage. And then there are the cooking channels. They all look happy. Happy. Happy. Smiling in the kitchen. Look at me! I am happily chopping a broccoli! Big Smile! Watch me drain cooked pasta! At the beginning of each video, the cook announces what he or she is about to do with vibrant enthusiasm as if they were launching into a mosh pit. Then they emerge at the other end oohing and aahing as they taste the end product. The cook admiring her own creation. I never saw such over the top excitement in a kitchen in my whole entire life.

I wish youTube had existed when I started to learn to cook. Today you can learn how to prepare cuisine from anywhere around the world from cheerful, eager-to-please demonstrators. No longer are you constrained by your mother's limitations. You're free to fly on your own. Although I appreciate the value it brings, honestly, I feel like an alien inside this hold-your-hand video repository. I learned to cook the hardest way: trial and error. I discovered all the wrong ways to prepare a dish before landing, by chance, on the correct set of steps.

The way I see it, things gain layers of meaning over time. The way layers of an onion are dry and seasoned on the outside, juicy and fresh towards the center.

I had been married for five months when my mother called me at home to ask me to buy her some age-defying face cream from downtown, since it was on sale. Towards the tail end of the phone call she asked me what we were having for dinner that night.

"I don't know," I answered.

"What do you mean you don't know?" she said, sounding a bit alarmed.

"I'll figure it out in the evening," I said. "I just finished eating breakfast!"

"But what will you feed your husband tonight?"

"I don't know. He's a grownup, he can figure it out for himself!" I spoke slowly, as if explaining something to a child.

"Thaniya," said my mother. "You are a married woman now. You can't act this way!" My mother, when stating a fact of life, likes to speak in a childlike voice. As if the pretense of innocence will give her greater authority.

Without skipping a beat, I rushed on. "Mother! Samih and I have a modern marriage that is different than yours and Dad's. We don't follow tired old gender roles. It is not my job to prepare dinner. It is not his job to bring home the bacon. We don't mind eating delivery pizza straight out of the cardboard box if we have to."

There was silence on the other end. After a few seconds, in a neutral grownup voice, my mother said:

"Oh, okay, sounds like you know what you are doing."

Fast-forward 13 years, guess what are the first words that come out of Samih's mouth the second he enters the house? Hint: it's not "Hello!" Not "How are you?" Not "Honey, I'm home!" Every single day my husband comes home and the first thing he greets me with is: "What's for dinner?" Sometimes he doesn't wait for an answer. He rushes towards the stovetop, picks up pot covers and takes a peek at the contents. Then he proceeds to make a musical sound to express his level of satisfaction with what he discovers.

"Ouweowowowamamamama," means *good.*

"Pikapikapikasloooooooooo," means *excellent.*

"Yeowimamiouchyfabilouse," means *you outdid yourself today*

But when he names the food, it means he is disappointed.

"Oh, its pasta today," he tries to say in a neutral voice, so as to disguise his feelings.

"Oh, it's couscous and roasted chicken today."

"Oh, it's pizza today."

How I miss my youthful ideas of a modern marriage! How wonderful it felt to give my mother that lecture all those years ago. Samih says that this turn of events is all my fault. "When I married you, you didn't know how to cook, but now you are such a fantastic cook that I can't help myself. I come home hungry and one of your amazing creations is waiting for me."

They say that the shortest path to man's heart is his stomach. But what is the shortest path to a woman's heart? I suspect the answer is: "Nobody cares."

Soup

IN IRAQI CUISINE WE BURN rice on purpose to produce a delicacy called hakake. It's not exactly burned, it's a caramelized crispy rice formed at the bottom of the pot, scraped and presented either on its own or placed on top of the plated rice as decoration. A hakake is the crowning achievement of a good home cook, for it requires using all the senses except for sight and taste. A cook must hover over a pot of rice, listening to the crackling sounds erupting from its depth, sniffing for a hint of burning which would indicate cessation and using intuition to determine the right balance of heat, liquid and oil that will produce the golden nuggets at the end, without burning them black. This is a feat of culinary clairvoyance that even Gillian's psychic would marvel at. The end result tastes nutty and rich. Imagine if toffee brittle was savory—it would taste like this.

I have been fasting for six months now, and instead of making me into a better person, it's making me into a more agitated one. At the end of my shift yesterday, while pushing the blood cart in between patients' rooms, my feet were aching and my back was bothering me. Don approached me with an excited but crazed look in his eyes. He told me he had made a revolutionary leap in his artwork that I must see. I suggested that he send me the pictures by email, but he refused.

"Pictures can't do it justice," he said. "You have to see for yourself."

Once again we agreed I would sneak into his basement on a Sunday, behind his wife's back. A burning scorched smell hit me in the face the minute I walked in. Don was sitting on the big brown chair with anticipation in his eyes, looking eager to show me.

"Is your wife baking a cake?" I asked. "You better run up and check on it, I think she is burning it."

Don shook his head and smiled, looking amused: "No, this is the smell of cooking coming from my art studio." He jumped out of his seat and indicated that I should sit in his place. Then he skipped like a teenage girl to grab a painting to show me. It was the same purple one he had shown me before, only this one had burn marks around the outer edge. For a second I was jolted with fear. I imagined that his wife had followed through on her threat and gotten down and dirty in the basement with a blowtorch. Don had a huge grin on his face, though, which made me realize that the burn marks were his own doing.

"How did you do these?"

"I started with matches, then a lighter, then I saw my wife using a torch to make crème brulée and I swiped it. The kitchen torch gives me the greatest control for fine burn flourishes."

Don proceeded to show me the same set of paintings that I had seen before. The black one had his eyes burned out. The green one had his hair singed. The orange one had a uniform pattern of little brown polka dot burnt holes. It certainly looked interesting. I can't say that I liked these paintings. But they were making me feel something. A sort of a complex sentiment that can't be expressed with words. The way rose water in pastries tastes odd, layered. *Am I eating perfume?* You might ask yourself, but still you can't stop yourself from eating it.

"You did make an artistic leap," I told Don after I had a good look at his scorched art. This time I didn't have to lie to tell him what I thought. I encouraged Don to show his work. He insisted that it wasn't ready.

"Something is still missing. It's not right yet," he kept repeating. He informed me that it had been the advice he gave me to hack away at my poetry that led him thinking about how to take away from his paintings.

"So you could say it was your poetry that inspired me," he said. "Not exactly the words but the excessive verbose flourish you tend to resort to that did the trick for me."

"Glad to hear that the badness in my work inspired you to improve yours," I said, a touch hurt.

"Initially I thought about using scissors, then I thought fire would be more unpredictable. "

There are so many things I wish I could burn away from my life.

My first childhood memory is of being force-fed vegetable soup in an airport in Greece, cheered on by a Russian soldier. I think I was about 18 months old. Layal, my mom and myself were travelling to the Czech Republic for summer holidays. The airplane had to land in Greece because of technical problems. The three of us sat in the airport cafeteria waiting to hear the announcement beckoning us back to the airplane. My mother had purchased clear broth with boiled vegetables swimming in it. Little bits of carrot and peas looked like they were stranded in a hot tub waiting to be rescued from a torture session after they had ratted on all their collaborators. My mother had the frazzled animated energy that she got right before she was about to have a meltdown. She spoke in a high-pitched voice and the frozen smile on her face made her look like she was wearing a mask. In that state, she was more terrifying than a chainsaw-wielding clown. I had vomited several times on the airplane, soiling her dress in the process. The tasteless soup was my punishment for the inconvenience caused. I folded my arms across my chest and sealed my lips with the muscular force of a clam. A young soldier sitting at the same table with us noticed the impasse. The Titanic was about to collide with an iceberg. He lowered his gaze towards me, smiling. He opened his mouth and mimed slow eating with an invisible spoon. An exaggerated slurping sound came out with each imaginary spoonful. "Hmmmmmmmmmmmm!" he rubbed his belly to indicate pleasure. Soon my mouth was open and the vegetable soup was being shoved in with rapid movements that gave me little time to chew. I knew I was being tricked, but at least I was being entertained. The Titanic was sinking and most were about to perish, but at least the orchestra was playing cheerful music to ease the voyage.

"Eat what is placed in front of you, it might stop your mother from having a meltdown." This is the secret rule of eating. The one that I won't place on my official ten but only reveal to those I trust. Some things are too true to bear close scrutiny.

The first thing I do after seating myself in an airplane is look for the vomit bag. I pull it out of the pocket of the seat in front of me and arrange it so that it pokes out, to make sure that it is within easy reach. Normally I fast for 24 hours before a flight, consuming nothing but liquid, so that there is nothing sitting in my stomach. Despite the lack of stomach contents, I still almost always manage to vomit on an airplane. Mucusy liquids come out instead. I can't decide which is more disgusting: regular vomit or the mucusy liquid.

If you want to see me at my worst, sit next to me in an airplane during a flight.

Some people suffer from a fear of flying because they have an irrational fear of the airplane plunging out of the sky. Most people confuse my anxiety around plane travel with that. I never correct them. The embarrassing truth is excruciatingly more painful. I wish I had an irrational fear of crashing, burning, or drowning. Acrophobia would be respectable compared with what I have. Claustrophobia would make me look like a bastion of sanity. Do you suffer from an irrational fear of spiders? Consider yourself lucky. I would happily exchange places with you in a minute—my phobia for yours. I have an irrational fear of vomiting on an airplane, which I disguise as fear of flying to make myself seem more normal.

The minute I enter an airplane, I feel like the air collapses around me like melting slabs of concrete. It turns into liquid jelly, similar to clear slop that gets smeared on your belly before an ultrasound. I am swimming in it, breathing it, swallowing it. It fills me with shame.

I will not vomit, I will not vomit, I will not vomit.

Then I take a glance at the vomit bag.

Oh no! I want to vomit!

It takes a mountain of determination to hold it back for two hours or so.

Vomiting gives me relief for 10 or 15 minutes and then the cycle of shame and battle of will power over my body begins again.

I always feel sorry for whoever is sitting next to me, for they have to endure the close proximity of a nervous hurricane devouring itself.

Since September 11th, my anxiety has increased. Not because I am worried about a terrorist attack, but because I think that security personnel are on the lookout for an anxiety-ridden Arab. I fit the bill whole-heartedly. Only I am not hiding a weapon or smuggling goods. I am already remorseful about the crime I am about to commit on the airplane.

The first thing I do when leaving an airplane is to seek shelter where I can. I change my clothes and take a shower. I walk out of every airport feeling thoroughly soiled. Nothing but a meticulous cleansing ritual can restore me to a natural state. Afterwards I feel refreshed and happy, ready to meet any challenge that might come my way. Refreshed. Rejuvenated. I feel reborn. Each airplane trip is Dante's trip to inferno and back.

I wish air travel wasn't such a constant in my life.

Now that I am reflecting on it, I remember something else that happened before I was fed soup in the airport in Greece. I remember that after I soiled my mother's dress on the airplane, she grabbed me by the hand and took me into the washroom to clean both of us up. In the tiny airplane toilet stall, she proceeded to kick me into a ball while accusing me of not only ruining her dress, but destroying her entire life. So I guess my first childhood memory is not of eating vegetable soup. It is of crouching next to an airplane toilet. Holding my head. Cradling my face in my lap. Receiving ample kicks into my side.

That's okay.

Shhhhhhhhhhh!

It's all very fine.

I prefer that image anyway.

At least I wasn't cooperating.

Sausage

ZLIP ZLIPPED INTO MY life the way a drizzle of béchamel sauce overtakes a lasagna. She was like the first friend you meet in a foreign country that makes life less lonely. She left a comment on *The Digital Me* video, telling me she enjoyed it. I clicked on her username to find that she had uploaded 12 videos of poetry. Her format is narration layered over images from nature, such as clouds floating or a slow motion video of a bee pollenating a flower. I was jolted with the joy of finding a comrade in purpose. I left a convivial comment on one of her videos, and we started a correspondence. I don't know her real name, but I do know that she lives in L.A. Zlip told me she believes poetry should be read out loud through the instrument of the human voice, not read silently from a book.

Watching her videos encouraged me to imitate her format. I began videotaping things like trees swaying in the wind, ships passing each other in the ocean, the view outside the window of the Car while Samih drives—anything that would make for a poetic visual accompaniment for my poetry recitation. I continue to get negative comments from people asking me to stop the stupid poetry and get back in the kitchen. And then there are the racist comments. The ones that start with: "You filthy camel rider..." What is so bad about being a camel rider? I don't know. If I knew how to ride camels, it would be something to be proud of. It would be freakin' awesome, like they say. I just ignore them all and wait for Zlip to give me her feedback on each video.

The dirt poor of the Arabs use their fingers to eat, their bums to sit and their native tongue to speak. The higher up you go on the social ladder, the more westernized people become. The higher echelons of society use forks and knives, no different from an English gentleman. However, those who are one stop above the dirt poor, living not too far from the margins yet leagues away from positions of influence, have perfected a unique method of eating that involves a fork and a spoon. Throw away the knife. You hold the spoon in your right hand, the fork in your left. You can use both utensils to place food into your mouth. The spoon handles rice and stew, and you can use the fork to pile morsels of fried vegetable or stray bits of fried beef onto a heap of rice scooped on your spoon right before you put it in your mouth. Alternatively, you can stab a piece of chicken thigh with the fork, use the edge of the spoon to cut off a tidbit and then savor your hard-earned prize. It is an elegant performance to watch somebody handle western implements in a non-western way. The left and right work equally hard, both sides competing to deliver nourishment.

Which leads me to my eighth rule of eating: "How you eat says more about you than what you eat."

So if I were a poet, not the lousy impostor that I am, but a real poet, how would I eat?

I would devise a feeding technology. Little serving plates with bite-sized morsels of food would hover in the air like butterflies. A master of ceremonies or DJ would select a playlist of music before the eating session commenced. Each guest would sit in a reclining position on one of the Afghan pillows scattered throughout the room. Each person would be outfitted with chopsticks, a fork and a spoon. Knives are not necessary, since all the violence has been taken care of behind the closed doors of the kitchen beforehand. The master of ceremonies would choose a choreography for the hovering plates. They would dance in formation or in scattered cryptic patterns. Only when a guest appeared mesmerized by one particular plate would the Master of Ceremonies push a button of his poetic feeding console and have it delivered to its seeker. Commentary on food would be highly encouraged, both verbal feedback and electronic. People could tweet, take selfies with their food or confine themselves to communing with their neighbor. The Master of Ceremonies would be in charge of ensuring that all leave the hall in a state of bliss. This is eating the way sex is meant to be. Excessive foreplay. Most of it taking place in the kingdom of imagination. One day when I have money and time I shall build the futurist feeding hall in which such communal experiences will take place. For now, I shall restrict myself to sketching this poetic future.

My maternal grandmother smelled like sausages. She worked in a meat-processing factory in the Czech Republic and no amount of soap or perfume could rid her flesh of the stink of animal fat rendering. Her job was to fill sausage casing with sausage meat. The smell was at once repulsive yet delicious. It was most abhorrent when I felt hungry. It makes me wonder if all food factory workers smell like what they make. I wonder if out there in the world there are waffle people, frozen pizza people, mustard people, canned tuna people and most stinky of them all—kimchi people.

I wonder what would happen if you invited all the food factory workers from all over the world to a convention. Would they be attracted to each other based on compatible taste? The sausage woman would shack up with a mustard man. Canned sardine studs would have a series of one-night stands with mayonnaise women. The double chocolate waffle people would arrange an orgy with the imitation maple syrup people. They would bring canisters of fake whipping cream to their fiesta for extra sensuality. If I wasn't married already, I would feel tempted to go work in a food factory and then seek out a matching food worker to bang. Just to see if the sex is superior in suitably matched food factory workers. It is a good thing I am married. It stops me from trying out all sorts of craziness. If I were single, I would be in tons of trouble right now.

Thank you for Samih.

Really! I mean it. Thank you.

In her youth, my grandmother was a forced labor worker in Nazi Germany. My grandfather worked in the kitchen. He used to sneak food to the starving Russian slave workers in the factory. Well you can guess what happened next: they fell in love and she became pregnant. The Nazi soldiers wanted to know the name of the father so that he could be executed. When my grandmother wouldn't tell them, they decided that they would let her have the baby and then execute her after the birth. Luckily Germany lost the war on the day my mother was born. My grandparents got married and lived in the Czech Republic. Hurray!

However, all that suffering and starvation affected my grandmother. She was obsessed with food. There was a sandwich in her purse at all times. At home, she surrounded herself with edible goodies. She never ate in a restaurant or in public. For her eating was a private business. She hid to eat. In fact, I never saw my grandmother eat. I saw her cook but never eat. I think her work in the factory fed her somehow. Fulfilled her need to be around food all the time. Until she smelled like a giant juicy sausage. This would be hilarious, if it wasn't so darn tragic. But go ahead. I give you permission to laugh. There is no utility in being serious.

I wonder if injuries travel down generations. What part of my grandmother continues to live through me? I don't want to think about this. It is too disturbing. I put the thoughts away, bury them under a thick sludge of mud. Little bubbles pop up to let me know that what got stuck in the giant mud bath of my unconfirmed truths is fermenting away. One day a giant kimchi tree will sprout and shower me with pickled cabbage and shrimp juice. That day isn't here yet. No need for panic.

Perhaps I should prepare for the kimchi apocalypse. When that happens, all past and present will collide, and I will know nothing about my place in this life. Perhaps I should have as much fun as I can possibly manage until then. Save up joy in reservoirs for when none is present in the future.

Turkey

AND SO I THOUGHT I SHOULD try it out. Microwave a pizza pocket into disjointed bits and see if I can put it back together. Since I never buy ready-made meals, I started my experiment with a trip to the frozen foods section. Maria from work claims that the best way to meet single men is to hang around the single portion frozen food section, pick up an item and then ask the cutest guy in the aisle if it's any good. This is the part of the supermarket I never visit.

As I approached with my trolley, I was clearly out of place, an interloper in an alien zone, exploring a native culture with anthropological interest. In that part of the supermarket all the men were carrying baskets; not another soul was pushing a cart with four wheels. Peeking through the slats of their plastic shopping baskets I glimpsed potato chips, hotdogs and BBQ sauce. My cart held family sized detergent, paper towels, ground beef, dried beans and pine nuts. The only redeeming element in my soon-to-be belongings was a packet of lime Jello. All else screamed *Mother! Mother! Wife! Mother!* Clearly, I had planned this trip poorly. I made mental notes, listing the mistakes I had committed, hoping to perform better on a second try.

Despite my glaring inability to blend in, I resolved to forge ahead and at least get away with my intended bounty. There were about 20 different varieties of folded dough filled with pizza stuff. I attempted to assess which one had the highest potential for explosivity. This proves I am a terrorist—true to my mass-media stereotype, I am obsessed with detonation. Plain tomato sauce and cheese. Herbed tomato sauce and pepperoni. With olives. Vegetarian. Gluten Free. Spinach and feta cheese. There were so many kinds! But which one would be more likely to emulate the big bang? Which one would go BOOM!? I chose the cheapest and plainest of the lot.

Science would have us believe that a cataclysmic blast created everything in the Universe—all matter, both visible and invisible. Inside the grand wisdom of a burst, the Cosmic Terrorist up in the sky thought it would be hilarious to create the bright and shiny sesame seed and then give it a dark, less popular cousin. The black sesame. S/He practiced food racism by giving black sesame all substance and relinquishing fame to the less-worthy white seed. The white sesame gained popularity as a paste, oil and gratuitous decoration over bread buns. But once you go black you will never go back. Black sesame is nuttier, smokier, more flavorful and has a stronger aroma. They taste like something between dark chocolate and coffee and therefore sit between two of my favorite things.

I am willing to bet that whenever you hear the word sesame, you immediately imagine the white variety. Or maybe, if you are of a certain age, you think of Big Bird or Oscar the Grouch. I used to watch the Arabic version of *Sesame Street* as a child, oblivious to the fact that it started its life as an American invention. I was shocked to discover later that my beloved Anees and Bader were originally called Ernie and Bert. It was a disappointment equivalent to a Western child's discovery that Santa Claus isn't real. The Arabic *Sesame Street* was produced in Kuwait, and was massively popular all over the Arab world, the characters in it so iconic that when Iraq invaded Kuwait, the invaders stormed the set and took the Muppets as prisoners of war, never to be returned.

I can imagine Ernie and Bert, sitting in Abu Ghraib, saying:
"Yep!"
"I know!"
"Here we are."
"I think we are done with teaching lessons to children."
"I have nothing to say. What about you?"
"Same here. I am speechless."
"Didn't see this one coming? Did you?"
"Not in a million years."

Thusly, while pondering the lowly sesame seed, I embarked upon my microwave big bang experimentation, determined to explore the creation of the Universe. Like so many other things, that clash just doesn't really make sense.

Holding hands during a stroll on the beach. A barely there kiss on the cheek. A warm caress down the small of my back as I am telling a story at a dinner party. These are the comfortable patterns of married life. Permissible by default, forbidden by exception. I make a deliberate effort to forget these ways when traveling to the Middle East. In my culture all public displays of affection between men and woman are taboo, even between husband and wife. How Samih and I are in public towards each other is different in Canada than in Palestine.

A few years ago we were visiting his family in Nazareth. We had spent the whole morning and afternoon sightseeing in the ancient city and finally made our way to visit Sawsan, Samih's older sister. The hot rays of the sun had bleached our energies away and placed our guard near the lowest end of the cultural awareness meter.

"Welcome, welcome! Come sit down, I have food burning on the stove," Sawsan greeted us while wiping her hand on her apron. She directed us to the living room and ran towards the kitchen. I threw myself on the couch, feeling a rainbow of shades of relief in my loins. My respite was expressed in an audible sigh. It felt good to be sitting in the comfortable domestic heaven of someone else's making. Samih mirrored my actions, slouching his long thin body dangerously close to mine. My head rested gently in a place it enjoyed resting on—a favorite beloved shoulder. Samih leaned over and placed a kiss on my cheek that was as light as a mid-summer's breeze. In that moment, I noticed ten-year-old Tamer stroll into the living room. As the oldest child in Sawsan's family, he walked with a confident bounce that beckoned to be adored. However, in that instant his body language contorted into a position that was at odds with the boy's character. His black eyes widened with the horror of seeing the forbidden. His golden wheat complexion darkened as if getting burned into charcoal. Tamer froze for a millisecond in shock with his mouth wide open. Then, with a swift elegant move worthy of a dancer, he turned around and ran towards the kitchen, seeking the familiar safe sight of his mother. "Mommy! Mommy! I saw uncle Samih kissing auntie Thaniya!" he screamed, with the same urgency a heroine of a slasher movie might have screamed, "The zombie apocalypse is upon us!"

I could hear Sawsan turning off the faucet in her kitchen. "That's okay, dear, uncle Samih lives in Canada and they developed strange habits over there," she said, all sweet motherly milk and honey.

Immediately, I sensed the gravity of my mistake. I burned red with shame. Samih and I sat up straight, stiff as rolling pins on the opposite ends of the couch, muttering apologies as multiple as the variety of shapes of pasta. I knew better than to break social custom in such a flagrant manner. Yet, despite myself, I had acted like an ignorant tourist.

Turkey is the name of a bird and a country in three languages. In Arabic, we call it "habash," which is also the name of an ancient kingdom that dominated the eastern plains of Africa. "Hodo" is what it is called in Hebrew, and the word also refers to the country of India. One day, when I am old and retired, I will dedicate myself to the supreme science of linguistics and study this strange phenomenon. What is it that makes this most peculiar-looking bird make people want to call it after a distant exotic land?

"All my friends have a turkey at Christmas except me," said Zakiya one December.

My answer to that was: "Well! Would you like to have a turkey as well?" That was the first year I prepared a turkey. I read all the recipes I could find, but none seemed satisfying. Instead, I decided to create my own Middle-Eastern version. I marinated the whole bird in olive oil, sumac, garlic, lemon juice, lemon peel, salt and pepper. Then I baked it with the breast facing downward in the oven for two hours. I flipped it upside down and roasted for two more hours. It was the best tasting turkey I have ever eaten. Strange how you can make something for the very first time and it exceeds all expectations. Sometimes intuition can help you strike gold blindly.

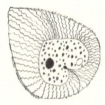

Which leads me to my fifth rule of eating: "Intuition above talent."

The next year, Zakiya complained, "All my friends have Christmas trees in their houses except me."

To which I replied: "Well! Would you like to have a Christmas tree?" Her face lit up at the suggestion. So for a couple of years I erected and decorated a Christmas tree with Shatha and Zakiya. Samih murmured some disapproval, but once I used the "I don't want my children to feel deprived" card, he quickly acquiesced. I even placed gifts underneath the trees. Eventually, both girls got Christmas out of their system and we went back to ignoring the holiday. And even though the turkey I made is the best turkey I have ever tasted, I still prefer eating chicken.

My fourth rule of eating: "Nothing tastes like chicken; even chicken doesn't taste like chicken."

Every time you taste it, it is new. There is a nuanced difference between each individual walnut. My co-worker James, who is a paramedic, eats without discernment. Food gets shoved down his esophagus. There is never any enjoyment or disappointment. James claims he eats in order to stay alive. If God meant for us to live like that He wouldn't have blessed us with taste buds. Each time I see James consuming his lunch I feel an urge to stop and plead with him to take the time to enjoy his food.

In Hebrew people say "Beteavon!" (enjoy your meal) before they are about to eat. In French they say "Bon Appetit!" In Arabic we say "Siha we afiya!" which means "to your health and wellbeing." In English there is no such custom. I think that needs to change. Let's start a new custom. Say "Enjoy your meal!" whenever you are about to see somebody eat. One day I will be able to say "enjoy your meal" to James without feeling like I am preaching.

Did you know that turkey was the first meal eaten on the moon? One day Moonians will call turkey Iraq. But because the first Moonians will be Americans they will call it Airaq instead. I can imagine future moon mothers admonishing their little moon children around the dinner table: "Pipe down and eat your airaq!"

Now that would be hilarious.

Wasabi

ONE DAY I WILL INVENT A NEW religion in which men are required to wear aluminum pots on their heads. From then on, all men will be classified into two categories. Adherent potheads who never leave the house without proudly sporting the unique head gear. Non-adherent potheads who defy conversion and show off their hair in public. From then on, any time a man's name is mentioned it is immediately qualified with the label of either adherent or non-adherent. As if knowing the status of his headdress is the most important thing you can know about a man. His character, education, job or family history pales in importance to what he sticks on his head. Women shall summon their husbands to an outing by slamming an aluminum pot with a spatula. Status in the workplace shall be marked by the size of the pot on a man's head. Non-adherent pot heads will be accused of vagina envy. No matter what any man says or does we, the women folk, will laugh at them. "Oh! you are so cute with that pot on your head, anything you say seems adorable." "You non-adherent potheads are so radical, nothing you say makes any sense." And so it doesn't matter if a man conforms or rebels—he will be equally dismissed.

You play pasta.

I'll play sauce.

Five days ago, Gillian was admitted into the psychiatric ward in Memorial. She was placed in the padded cell under heavy sedation for two days. I heard what happened from her mother who arrived here from Toronto the next day. It all went down during an official visit from the justice minister to Gillian's prison.

The honorable minister had extended his hand to shake hers and got handcuffed instead. "Guilty! Guilty! Guilty!" she yelled maniacally to nobody in particular. Gillian pepper sprayed three of her coworkers before she proceeded to lock the visiting dignitary in solitary confinement. The prisoners, worried they would be blamed for the insurrection, went running to their cells, causing chaos. She then barricaded herself in the prison pantry, slathering mustard all over her uniform.

I was allowed to visit her on the third day. Smudges of dry mustard were still caked in her hair. Since then, I have been visiting every day during lunch break. We sit silently across from each other, she in her hospital gown, me in my standard-issue white lab coat.

Yesterday I held her hand and whispered: "You are going to be fine." She whispered back: "Guilty." My heart turns into minced meat seeing my dear friend in this state. I feel helpless. I am drunk with the pain of it. I didn't see the signs. Didn't anticipate this turn of events. She had seemed so above it all. I can't shake the feeling that I had betrayed my friend. Was there something I could have said? Or done?

Her mother has decided to fly her back to Toronto to keep an eye on her. She is leaving tomorrow, and I might not see her for a long time. What good are my ten rules of eating? They have failed me miserably. At home I read my notebook where I have my precious rules written down. I couldn't find a single thing to comfort me in my state of distress. Not one rule that could have warned me about what was waiting for me around the curve.

It strikes me with flavourless urgency how silly these rules are. I am ashamed of every minute I wasted on creating them. I smeared ketchup all over the pages of the notebook before throwing it in the garbage. That way I won't be tempted to fish it out later. Nostalgia is a red herring.

Gillian, who was a pillar of strength. She who embodied the ideal of feminism, drove over the edge into the canyon. Just like *Thelma and Louise.*

Hummus Again

TWO YEARS AGO I DISCOVERED the poetry of Janet Jenkerson. Wondering around in a second hand bookstore, I was running my index finger across the spines of the books, making a muted thud, thud, thud sound, when right in front of me a book fell onto the floor, with a loud splashing sound. As if it was making a high altitude jump into an Olympic swimming pool. I picked it up and placed it back on the shelf. Splash! The book flung itself at my feet again, the sound vibrating and echoing throughout the store.

That book was such a drama queen! If I were a publisher, I would invent a motion detection device that could be embedded into books, making them jump up and down when a potential buyer walked by.

"Hey you! Buy me, buy me, buy me!" The book would squeak at you.

I picked it up a second time and began to read a poem: *Luxury Depression*. Its lyrics were so clear and unassuming. The meaning wove together threads from the East and West. There was a foreign music to the words. It reminded me of ancient Arabic poetry, only it was written in plain, accessible English. I was enthralled within the first few minutes and purchased this book that had hurled itself at my mercy. I discovered that Janet is married to a Moroccan and lives half her life in Morocco and the other half in England. This is exactly the type of poetry I wish I could write, only ten times magnified in effect.

In a state of euphoria, I sent her an email to express appreciation of her work. This is the first time I have ever sent a fan letter to anybody and it was bursting with fan girl sentiments. To my surprise I received a reply thanking me for my letter. I responded with a list of my favorite books of poetry. Janet shared hers. Back and forth. Back and forth. We became pen pals and Facebook friends. Common ideas splashed between us like droplets in a fountain. I never told her that I wrote my own poetry. I was worried she would ask me to send her a few poems. I was too ashamed to show her the degraded state of my work.

What happened next was completely unexpected. One day she mentioned in passing how much her husband loved chickpeas. I sent her a link to my hummus video. Two weeks later Janet uploaded a picture of her first hummus attempt on Facebook. She commented that hummus was not common in Morocco and she had to buy the tahini sauce from a speciality store in Faz. Her post garnered more than fifty "likes" and many comments of praise from both Moroccan and British friends.

A week later, she posted a new picture of hummus, this time a larger quantity, with a caption that read: "Star of the dinner party." Again there was praise for her hummus. The very next day there was a picture of a large pot of boiling chickpeas. The caption stated: "Hummus is a large hit with Moroccans." Her first batch of hummus was so successful that she was asked to make two more batches by two different friends. She then posted a link to my video with a thank you note. Furious activity followed on Facebook with the default positivity. I was observing all this with horror. "Oh no! What have I done?" A couple of days later, I received an email from Janet:

Dear Thaniya,

You have no idea how much you have changed my life. Ever since I married Omar, I have been ridiculed about my cooking by all the women in his family—his sisters, aunties. All his friends' wives compete with each other in showcasing their culinary skills. With my bland Cornwall cooking, I receive nothing but snorts of laughter. I have tried to learn Moroccan recipes, such as Lamb Tagine and Couscous, but all my efforts have missed the mark. "Nice try!", "Don't worry, you will get it one day," are all the feedback I have received. This has been affecting our social life in Morocco. As you know, people socialize by inviting each other over for dinner. I felt self-conscious about my kitchen skills and therefore hesitant to invite people over for dinner for fear of ridicule. I thought I could never be fully accepted in my new Moroccan home until I perfected the cuisine. Omar kept telling me not to worry about it. He assured me that he loved me no matter my skills in the kitchen. Secretly I was worried that he might wish he had married a Moroccan woman instead. All this changed when I tried your magical hummus recipe. Chickpeas are common in Morocco, but hummus is not. Yet somehow, it is universally loved by all Moroccans who try it. This hummus has magical powers. It is amazing. On the one hand, it is new and therefore people can't compare it with what their wives make at home. On the other hand, it bears the taste of the Middle East and doesn't remind people of my bland English cuisine. I have become the belle of the party. My husband is happy. My popularity is on the rise. I finally have a chance at belonging with my in-laws. People look at me differently since I started making hummus. So please accept my heartfelt thank you and know that you have positively influenced my life.

Love,

J.J.

Oh! God!

What have I done?

I have encountered a world-class poet and turned her into a hummus moron. I was hoping through our correspondence that I would bring myself to her level. That I would be inspired to write better poetry. Instead, I dragged her down into my pit. She is turning into a Hummus Queen and spreading the disease in a country that is better off without it.

This must be what purgatory feels like.

Salmon

I REMEMBER MY FIRST PURE *yum* moment. Like a first kiss. I was attacked by the sudden realization that bodily sensations can be more. That there is more to life than the drudgery of living. That there is a magic, a moment when things click. Ironically, it happened on an airplane. I was around ten, and we were traveling on our yearly summer holiday to Europe. Inside the compartmentalized plastic tray of our airplane dinner, in a little rectangle off to the side, was a shiny orangey sliver of something sitting on a piece of white bread. It looked like a jewel.

It is the benefit and foil of childhood to trust immediate experience, untainted by previous encounters. Today, my grownup self would have thought *Don't trust airplane food! That stuff is mangled beyond recognition, it hardly can be called food*. I lifted the little morsel from its boxed existence and took a bite. Oh pleasure! I soared, transported into a fairy-tale where Muppets are my best friends and when you hail a taxi, a unicorn arrives. I was ejected out of that airplane and floated among the clouds.

When I arrived back at my seat next to my mother, I leaned over, poked her with my finger, and asked: "What is this called?"

"Smoked salmon," came the answer.

Who knew that fish could have such an intense vivid color? Until then I had assumed that all fish came in shades of white. I didn't taste smoked salmon again until I immigrated to Canada. I read somewhere that a salmon always returns to the place where it was spawned. It's a fish that is loyal to its place of origin. A sea creature that has a mysterious mechanism that leads it back home. If only I was so accomplished! On my third day in Canada, I bought a sandwich from the supermarket. It was only later in my room at the student dormitory, the food upon my tongue, that the realization came upon me. I had forgotten. Remembrance came flooding down like boiled kettle water on instant noodles.

This is that same taste!

The thing that I wanted but had forgotten about.

Once again, chance played a funny trick on me. Without meaning to, I had immigrated to the one place on the planet where smoked salmon exists in abundance. Scientists have not been able to decipher how the fish finds its way back. It just always does. My own homing mechanism is broken, though; it leads me further astray rather than back home.

Salmon pinky-orange (#FFA07A) is my favorite color. The seen sound of a gentle secret yearning.

My mother used to read us *Robinson Crusoe* translated into Czech before we went to bed. On days when she was tired or was out with her friends, my father would step in to do the honors. He felt that reading was a private activity, though, and instead of intoning Robinson, he would sit by our bedside and make a story up on the spot. From our beds, Layal and I would interject, participating in making up the story as it went along. The three of us made up a story about a First Nations explorer hero—back then we used the politically incorrect word red Indian—named Jirjir Mas. Jirjir Mas sported a single white feather sticking out of his black headband. His face was painted with streaks of black, white and red whenever he was feeling particularly fierce. Jirjir Mas traveled all over Africa, Europe and China, rescuing the oppressed and championing lost causes. The story always started with my father saying:

Kan ya ma kan, fe qadeem al zama. Hindi ahmar ismuhu Jirjir Mas.

Then we would proceed to lay out a dilemma. For example, a beautiful Japanese princess named ShiShi would be kidnapped by an evil villain. Jirjir Mas would spring into action. He'd scale the side of a building. Jump from rooftop to rooftop. Swim through gigantic water pipes and spring up to rescue ShiShi, using nothing but his bare hands, superior intelligence and wit. The story always ended with the evildoer repenting, vowing to walk the path of goodness, helping fellow human beings along the way.

The genius of JirJir Mas was not in how he rescued those in desperate need of his help, but rather the lengths he went to in order to reform the bad guy. JirJir Mas would take care to spend days talking to somebody. He would point out to them the harm they had inflicted on others. He would demonstrate to them how helping somebody felt better than harming them. He would seduce them with a taste of goodness until they couldn't resist its call. The story always ended with an evildoer thanking Jirjir Mas.

Shukran ya Jirjir Mas.

That was our cue to close our eyes and sink into dreamland feeling reassured that all was well in the world.

A couple of years ago I asked my father: "Don't you think it's weird that an Iraqi family living in Kuwait made up a story about a First Nations hero?"

"Yes, it is very strange," he said.

"Where did it come from?" I asked. "Why did Jirjir Mas inflame our imagination so much?"

He shrugged and shook his head.

Perhaps we subconsciously knew that we would end up in Canada one day.

Perhaps JirJir Mas and smoked salmon are the Universe's way of directing me towards my current abode.

Bread

MY HYPHENATED IDENTITY COMES with three dashes, each one annotated with an asterisk or two. Let me give you a taste. In my kitchen cupboard, the soya sauce resides next to zaatar (a divine herb from Palestine). I have been told that I make the best Russian salad there ever was—this at the same potluck dinner to which I brought my famous hummus. In my stew, the cardamom makes love to pomegranate juice as naturally as it does to mole sauce.

Over-immigration leads to cultural diarrhea.

Acrobatically, I have eaten languages, danced to the rhythm of perspective and cultivated attitudes in a rainbow of colors. Yet no matter how earnest my effort, I could never quite satisfy my lust— the desire to belong. It molests me ceaselessly. When I am here, I want to be there. When I am there, I am missing here. But the delicate aromas of the poetic East don't mix with the bright glare of the seductive West. This kind of gluttony can only be soothed with a seven-layer dip of beans, guacamole, salsa and who knows what else is in that thing. Perhaps cheese? No. I will replace sour cream with mashed sesame seeds. That orange layer, whatever it is, with diced tofu, roasted bell peppers and add extra virgin olive oil. Mmmmmmm! It tastes good. Even better than ...

I must discover the recipe where forever the twain shall meet. It is my quest. One day it will be my gift to the world. MY LEGACY.

How I envy all of you who speak just one language. You intuit a flavor I shall never taste. You eat bread and cheese and innocently say: "It's bread and cheese." In Iraq, we called it *Iranian bread* because it was immigrants wearing tattered thread from Iran who made it. In Israel, the same bread, same taste, is called *Iraqi bread* because it's made by Jewish immigrants from Iraq. In Vancouver, the Iranian baker calls the same exact bread, the same smell even, *barbari bread* because in Iran it was immigrants from Khorsan who brought it. Do you realize how terrifying bread is to me?

Khobos, pan, chleb, lachem, eish, nri, nan, pain. Repetition, in all the languages of the world, soothes me.

One morning after a weary sleep, I woke up declaring to the Universe: "I give up!" Twenty years of this tasteless, useless quest: be good, be authentic, find a place to belong, to have my life mean something. All have led only to spoilage. I accept my lot: rotten. Gillian has vanquished herself in a mustard storm. Zaev taunts my imagination with his razor sharp looks. Healing alludes me. I can neither satisfy this lust, nor make it go away. Defeat!

The ocean doesn't care if fish believe in water or disbelieve. All get caressed by currents just the same.

All the landscapes belong to me. The Alps. Euphrates. The heartbeat you skipped. All mine. I don't need to learn your cuisine. Shhhhhhhhhhh! Listen with a whisper.

Mix flour and water.

Apply heat.

Sugar

WHEN IT COMES TO DESSERTS, I excel at making a
catastrophe. I think the reason for my sweets-making impediment is
my inability to follow a recipe. Something inside cringes when I read
instructions. A secret desire to rebel overpowers me. It is a type of
mental illness. A disease. I call it *the measuring disease*. It's a
profound and deep-seated inability to measure things in a precise
manner. I should have become an architect! I would have invented a
new wave of building structures, everything sagging in the middle
and flopping to one side or the other. It would be all the rage. In
most cooking I rely on my intuition. I sprinkle, heap, crumble with
my hands and allow my intuitive sense to guide me. When it comes
to cakes and cookies, my instincts fail me, yet my logic refuses to
take over. Deflated cakes, shrivelled biscuits and puddings that run

like the river Euphrates have failed to teach me the merit of measuring things. Perhaps a hopeful part of me thinks that one day my sensual side will simply evolve into candyland. Even when by mistake I baked a perfectly serviceable cake, I couldn't replicate the success since I failed to note down what I had done. It is a total cluster fiasco.

Sugar remains unused in my pantry for months. It mocks me. Stares at me. I ignore it.

Forget it!

Come on! How can you call yourself a cook if you are afraid to use a main ingredient in your cupboard?

I am not falling for you again.

But you love experimenting!

You always fail me.

I am as cute and adorable as an Easter bunny, I am never at fault.

Okay, I always fail at you. It's not you, it's me. Happy now?

No, how can I be happy when I see a mother unable to make a birthday cake for her daughter?

Ouch! The guilt trip. I buy better birthday cakes at the bakery.

All the other mothers participate in the school bake sale.

I just write a check to the school instead. Achieves the fundraising goal more efficiently.

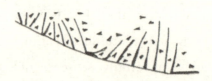

Leigh made that beautiful peach raspberry pie two days ago. It looked gorgeous. With little crisp edges, and melted baked fruit mush which you could see through a latticed crust. You can't look at that pie and not believe that all is good in the world. You can't look at Leigh the same after experiencing that pie. The prophet Mohammed himself said, "A true believer has a sweet tooth naturally." Sugar says I believe in happy endings. I have hope. Don't you want to believe?

I find myself grabbing the canister of sugar. I whisk eggs. Mix flour, sugar, oil and milk. I sprinkle vanilla extract. The batter gets poured into a baking pan. I sigh a lot. I hold my breath. The mouth of my oven opens to spit out yet another mangled scruffy sponge-looking disaster. It is baked onto the pan, so I can't flip it onto a plate. I scrape off bits of burned black crust in attempt to salvage some edible heart inside. Oh darn you, sugar! You have fooled me again.

There is one type of cookie I have mastered. Ironically, it contains no sugar at all. It is the only cookie in the world with no need of the devil's powder. Iraqi kleicha is a type of cookie that is stuffed with date paste mixed with butter, rose water and cardamom. A date contains 80% sugar. It is called nature's candy. Dates used to be Iraq's main export before the discovery of oil. Iraq was called the land of blackness, because right before the date harvest, a pilot flying over southern Iraq would look down and see a carpet of black. You could say that dates are the old black gold. Today all those palm trees have been burned. I buy fine quality dates grown from

California. I always cry when I make kleicha. You would think I was creating onion paste instead.

Beets

MY MOTHER CALLS TOMATO soup borscht. I grew up thinking that soup made out of canned tomatoes is some folkloric specialty of Russia. Inspired by the cold winters of Siberia! Laced with the gossip of babushkas gathered around the back of the barn to forget that they are enduring yet another life trial. Eating it made me feel I could get away without having to read any Dostoevsky. To get to the heart of the Russian soul, I could either eat my mother's sludgy tomato soup or read *Crime and Punishment*. Since I was already forced to endure the former, there was no need to suffer the later. I was forgiven. I slurped each bland spoonful with a sense of respect. I didn't enjoy the experience, but I endured, the way great countries with great histories repel invading armies. The way Petersburg bore Napoleon's siege. My spoon would click against the bowl. *For every famer who watched his crops set ablaze.* Long hearty slurp. *Every soldier fallen dead in a muddy ditch.* My spoon would come down with the militaristic intention of a sword to slice into the fresh hot liquid.

Click.

Slurp.

Swoop.

Fill.

Repeat until the task is done. All the soup was shoveled down my esophagus in an efficient manner.

I was sleeping in Samih's embrace early one evening in Lazzazza feeling full of contentment after a day of harvesting tomatoes in the field. My back hurt as if my spine had been replaced with a ton of bricks. My neck felt as if it had been mistaken for a pincushion for a week. I was happy, for I was being a productive member of society as evidenced by the 40 crates of tomatoes I had managed to fill in one day.

Jenin rushed into our bedroom with an alarmed expression on her face. "Um Asi has just been rushed to the hospital!" Um Asi was our neighbour. Apparently, her youngest son, Mohammed, had been misbehaving. The nature of this misbehavior was never specified. Mohammed's uncle, who lived across the hallway from Abo Asi and Um Asi, decided to discipline him by delivering a strike across the face so powerful that the four year old claimed to have felt his teeth shaking in his mouth. Um Asi felt angry at this turn of events and rushed to confront her brother in-law. Things got heated. Um Asi used vulgar language and received a punch to the face as a reward for her efforts. Later that night an ambulance was called to the house. Um Asi was bleeding, and later miscarried the baby she was carrying in her womb.

The next morning, Samih drove me the hospital so that I could visit Um Asi. I walked into her room while Samih gestured he would wait in a visitors lounge down the hall. Um Asi was sitting on a sterilized hospital bed surrounded by 20 women. Most of them were blood relations—sisters, cousins and in-laws. Everybody was yelling over one another. Nobody was stopping to hear the other person speak. Um Asi was waving her hands sideways and upwards like she was a music conductor. With a voice strained with anguish, I could hear her yelling:

"I will report him to the police."

"He will go to jail for what he did to me."

"I will ruin his house."

"He will regret this for the rest of his life."

"I want revenge."

"I am seeing red."

"He will pay for what he did to my unborn baby."

All the other women were yelling at Um Asi while gesticulating wildly as if they were violently kneading bread. Their fingers where flicking imaginary flour dust on the outwards reach, and gathering invisible threads on the way back. Each one screamed her admonitions at Um Asi:

"You used bad language, what did you expect the man to do?"

"You already have nine children; why do you need a tenth? You are just showing off right now."

"Think about the family!"

"Think about the man's children. Think about his wife."

"What will people say?"

"Palestinians don't report each other to the Israeli police. Do you want to be a traitor?"

"Think about your reputation."

"Just shut up and endure."

"Don't be an idiot."

"You will lose everything!"

"Think about Abu Asi, how will he face his family after you send his brother to jail?"

I stood in the room saying nothing, holding on to a bedpost as if it was a life raft. After twenty minutes the argument died out. All the women looked exhausted with the hysteria. The animated hand motions were reduced to calm stirs. The occasional sigh erupted into the room and floated away with the breeze.

Um Asi looked me in the eye with a piercing gaze: "Thaniya! What do you think? What should I do?" I met her eyes. Opened my mouth. I took a deep breath, filling my lungs with oxygen, hoping to have the courage to eject the right words. Before I had the chance to utter a single syllable, all the women around Um Asi started up again, this time staring and yelling at me. They were moving their hands forwards and backwards, targeting me with their magical influence.

"Shut up! And don't you dare get her going!"

"You think you are intelligent because you have a university degree, but really you are the biggest idiot in this room!"

"You are a foreigner, not one of us, you have no say in matters you don't understand."

"You have your husband wrapped around your finger, not everybody is lucky like you."

"Measure your words carefully and know that god is watching you."

"Nobody wants to hear your woman liberation mumbo jumbo right now."

"Yeeeeeeeeeeee! Keep your stupid ideas to yourself please."

The mob worked itself into a frenzy. The yelling got louder and higher in pitch. I tried to remember how Gillian faced prison inmates. What did she say? Something about making them eat out of the palm of her hand? Before I had the chance to conjure up magic of my own, I felt hands grabbing me by the forearms and shoulders. I was getting pushed outside the room and into the hallway. The door was slammed behind me. I was standing outside blinking my eyes with surprise, like one of my poems stunned by a sudden shearing. Samih ran down the hallway.

"Why are you standing here by yourself?" he asked. "What's going on?"

"I was kicked out." My manner was matter of fact. I didn't know yet how I felt about what had just happened.

"What did you say?" Samih softened his voice. His eyes looked kind.

"Nothing. I said nothing at all." I shrugged my shoulders.

"Emotions are running high today," he said. "Everybody will calm down in a day or two."

Samih drove me home, where I grabbed six tomatoes from the crates piled up in the backyard and went straight into the kitchen to make borscht. I was in need of some time with Russian soldiers defending the motherland against a foreign invader. I chopped, minced and sautéed until red-hot liquid was produced. Yassir, the village doctor and Samih's best friend from childhood, came for a visit. I served him a fresh bowl. "Here, have some borscht. It's my mother's recipe."

"Is this a joke?" laughed Yassir as he slurped the first spoonful.

"What do you mean?" I asked, surprised.

"I was educated in Russia, lived there for eight years. Borscht is not made out of tomatoes, it is made out of red beets." Yassir looked amused by my ignorance.

I burst into tears. I was inconsolable. Yassir looked apologetic. Samih's facial muscles contorted into uncomfortable-looking knots.

"I am so sorry," said Yassir. "I don't understand why this has got you so upset."

"I need *Crime and Punishment*." I was heaving out the words like a broken locomotive trying to get up steam.

"What?"

"I need to read *Crime and Punishment* by Dostoevsky! I never read any of his work," I said, with tears rolling down my cheeks.

"It is a great novel. I would be happy to lend you my Arabic translation of *Crime and Punishment*. In my opinion Dostoevsky is a far greater writer than Shakespeare."

"Nobody is greater than Shakespeare," I said, hiccupping.

"You might change your mind once you read *Crime and Punishment*."

"Have you read *Hamlet*?"

"What?"

"*Hamlet*, by Shakespeare." I was starting to feel better.

"No."

"I will lend you my Arabic translation of *Hamlet* and we will see who will change his mind."

Imagine my surprise when I discovered that to the rest of the world borscht didn't contain even a hint of tomato. That my mother had appropriated the name and affixed it to her red watery concoction. Like my soya sauce rice pilaf, my mother had created her own cuisine. It wasn't even the right hue of red. The dense screaming color of beets bears no resemblance to the coquettish vanity of tomatoes.

Is all mothering an act of deceit?

I told you before that I hadn't anticipated anything before immigrating to the West. But that statement isn't entirely true. I suppose I was being a bit dramatic when I said it.

I wish to issue a correction at this point. I had the idea that I would be moving to a country where women were equal. *I am so ready for women's equality,* I enthusiastically told myself on the airplane on my first trip to Canada. I would have to endure leaving all that was familiar, all that I loved, but at least I would gain residency inside my equality with the other gender. This sweetened the trade, the way a spoonful of sugar helps the medicine go down.

The first inkling of my disappointment came when I realized that none of my teachers at the university were women, and in fact the whole university had only a smattering of female faculty members. The West has advertised itself to the rest of the world as a bastion of women's liberation. Sadly, like my mother's borscht, it is just a beautiful propaganda, empty of substance.

One week ago Emily was admitted to the hospital. She had been beaten so severely by her husband that she required emergency surgery to fix a burst spleen. Dr. Nikmailean spent three hours in the operating room and two hours in the recovery room to ensure all went well. You know a patient is in dire straits when Don Nikmailean is speaking to her in a soft voice. I was touched by Don's care for Emily. I approached her to collect a blood sample. She was lying in bed, staring motionless at the ceiling. She had bandages on the left side of her face, her right arm, right leg and the surgical incision. She had so many bruises, she could have been mistaken for an alien, what with all the blue covering her.

She took one look at me and hissed, "Get out!"

I introduced myself and reached to grab the requisition form. "Get out!" Emily said again, still barely audible, but visibly straining her jaw as she spoke.

"Okay," I said, and left her room, not wishing to agitate her any further. Emily was flat on her back in her bed, all alone. There were no family relations yelling at her from every which way. She had been visited by a potpourri of social workers, and a number of female police officers had come to her room for a chat. Through it all, Emily insisted that she fell down the stairs by accident. Her husband is nowhere to be seen, but he is innocent. So innocent that he is ashamed to show his face. On the second day, I tried again to get a blood sample from Emily. She was stretched out on her right side, facing away from the door. As soon as she heard my cart wheels rustling behind her she yelled: "Get the fuck out of my room!"

I said nothing and backed away. Poor Emily. She has nobody to yell at and nobody is yelling at her. I can understand how screaming at me is an outlet for bottled-up emotions. At least Um Asi had a gang of women, all of them enduring while holding hands side by side. Nobody was making magical hand gestures at Emily. On the third day I tried again. I walked into her room like a mouse, attempting to make as little noise as possible. I found her curled in a fetal position on her left side. Her right hand was covering her face. I said nothing and waited for her to acknowledge me. She slipped her hand on the pillow, blinked at me, said "Ouch," then said: "What do you want?"

"Dr. Nikmailean has ordered CBC."

"You mean like the radio station?"

"No, it stands for complete blood count. It's a blood test used to evaluate your overall health and detects a wide range of disorders. This will help the doctor evaluate your health and decide on a course of treatment."

"What do you need from me?" she asked.

"I need to take a blood sample that I can send to the test lab downstairs."

"Will it hurt?"

"Not at all." I smiled, a paragon of reassurance. "You will feel a needle prick. Like a mosquito bite."

"Okay, get it over with."

I put my gloves on, got my needle ready, held her right arm to massage the spot I was about to prick.

Emily took a deep breath and asked, "Thaniya, are you married?"

"Yes," I said.

"Do you love him?"

"With all my heart." Prick, the needle went in.

"Does he hit you?" She looked right at my face, avoiding the sight of her blood rushing into the vial.

"No."

"He will."

I finished taking the blood sample in silence and placed the tubes in their designated place in my cart. I took off my gloves and threw them in the garbage. Then I stood by the bed next to her legs, holding on as if it was a life raft. I took a deep breath in, gulping down oxygen to energize a courage that wasn't necessary. I wanted to tell Emily that she was wrong. But it felt wrong to take advantage of her vulnerable state. She was all alone. What does Emily know about carrying the weight of a whole nation's colonization rolled up in your kitchen apron? Instead I rolled my hand forwards and backwards. Flicked my fingers towards her with invisible magical dust. On the way back towards my chest, I rolled invisible threads that were connected to my heart. Then I grabbed a thread that was connected to her heart, I pulled at it. I tugged. I saw that it was attached to the umbilical cord of her husband. I gestured with my right index figure and middle figure to make the sign of scissors. Then I mimed cutting the string. In my mind I thought: *Emily Gilbert! I set you free. I untie the tie that has placed you here.* Emily blinked at me with a sheepish innocence as I walked away from her room.

The truth that I never confessed to anybody, not even to myself, really, at least until now, is that I was relieved I was kicked out of Um Asi's room that day those many years ago. I am grateful I never had a chance to tell Um Asi what I thought she should do. The humbling reality is that I am a coward.

It sucks to be a woman in the East. It sucks to be woman in the West. It sucks in different ways, but it sucks nevertheless.

Honey and Vinegar

WE DO THIS THING. A family thingy. All four of us lie in bed, scrunched up against each other to watch a movie. Samih has gotten a set of DVDs about Planet Earth. He popped *Amazon Forest* into his laptop and placed it in the middle of the bed. Zakiya and Shatha huddled in the middle. I plunked myself on the right edge of the bed. Samih grabbed the other side. Eighteen minutes into the movie we were attacked by footage of a python eating a whole wild hog. The python was opening its mouth unnaturally wide to swallow the whole dead carcass in one mouthful.

"Wow! Look how lucky the python is. It gets to eat with its mouth open," said Zakiya.

"It doesn't have a mother that keeps harassing her to keep her mouth closed while it eats," said Shatha.

"I wish I was that python!" said Samih. "To eat without silly rules."

"It's my fault that I try to teach you basic etiquette?" I was feeling irritated.

"Each time I eat, I hear your voice in my head chastising me," said Satha.

"Me too," said Zakiya.

"Me three," said Samih.

I waved my left arm into the air as I got up from the bed. "So find a stinky Amazonian python to cook dinner for you from now on! I am on a cooking strike." I dashed out of bedroom, down the stairs and into the living room. I could hear all three calling after me.

"Mom! We're only kidding!"

"Come on Thaniya! Don't be so serious."

"It's just a joke!"

But I was fuming.

My eyes fell on Samih's leather briefcase sitting innocently by the front door. Holding that secret. I finally succumbed to the temptation. *Throw ethics into the wind,* I told myself. *I don't give a toss.* I tiptoed towards the briefcase. Kneeled in front of it. Slowly I pried the front flap away with my fingers, making sure the Velcro divulged its secret silently. Inside was a folded piece of paper. With trembling hands, I slid the paper out. My heart was beating against my ribcage like a crazed prisoner demanding to be let out. I took three deep breaths to calm myself before I unfolded the paper. There it was. A love letter I had written to my husband ten years ago. My words. My handwriting. Floral sugary sentiments. Unabashed.

Girlish. You might think a teenager had written it. My eyes welled up.

Holy Shit!

I can't believe he kept my love letters!

I can't believe he carries one of them in his briefcase all around the world everywhere he travels.

I owned a nuclear weapon all along and didn't know it.

Weapon of mass destruction: found.

So here it is. I come to the end of my story. I don't know why I told you all this. Actually, I lie, I do know why I told you all this. Ignorance would be charming. Self-awareness is a bitch. I am too embarrassed to confess my expectations. Their magnitude would repulse you. I told you a silly story and in return I anticipated a mountain of treasure. Drained and pathetic is my state at this point. Nothing can soothe the sour taste of disappointment I am about to experience. The logical side of me realizes that it is my own expectations that are about to be my downfall. It is all my fault. You were always you. My senses cheated me. But tell that to my heart. It makes no sense. It makes perfect sense.

I was complaining to Zlip, via email, of the hummus problem. How I made this one popular hummus video and now people just want me to make happy recipe videos. Zlip replied, "Why don't you make poetry videos with footage of yourself cooking in the kitchen? It would certainly be unique. Poetry cooking videos."

Reading Zlip's message, an electrical buzz traveled from my eyes, down my spine, and back up through my stomach, zapping my brain. This is brilliant! Everything is clear. I can visualize it. Smell it. Taste it. I know exactly what to do.

I will tell Zakiya and Shatha the story of their births in private and never repeat it to anybody. Not even to you. Some things are sacred.

I will stop fasting, starting right now. It is playing weird games with my mind and it never worked, anyway.

I need to quit my job as a bloodsucker and find something non-medical to do. Maybe I'll be a real estate agent.

And I will make poetry cooking videos.

Boom!

A crack opened up in my life, splitting it into two movable soft parts. I have been so busy attempting to mend the split that I failed to notice it was the opening that allowed nourishment in.

سمع الله لمن حمده

Get the Recipes

To receive recipes related to this novel, subscribe to the Spoonful Recipes mailing list here:

http://ihath.com/MailingList/?p=subscribe&id=5

One Last Thing

If you enjoyed reading this book I'd be very grateful if you'd post a short review on Amazon. Your support really does make a difference. I read all the reviews so I can get your feedback and make future novels even better.

Other Books By Elen Ghulam

Graffiti Hack

A novel

Don't Shoot! .... I have another story to tell you

A memoir

Acknowledgements

To Mary Knapp Parlange I owe a debt of gratitude. She painstakingly edited this novel providing valuable feedback along the way. Many thanks to my friend Dr. Huda Ali Almahdi who gave me permission to incorporate her personal story about a family watching a video of an anaconda devouring a wild boar into my novel. The idea for this novel came to me after a trip to Italy. I am grateful to our many Italian friends who hosted my family and I, passionately sharing many eating experiences. Thank you to the Fraccarollo family (Luigi, Laura, Tobia, Chiara and Lucia), Matteo Saletti and Marco Repetti. To my family: Malik, Alexandra, Marwan, Ibrahim, Rawan, Yarra and Yusuf—for your love and patience.

Made in United States
North Haven, CT
04 August 2022

22274111R00203